DEAD SPIRITS

A Dakota Mystery

M.K. COKER

Copyright © 2022 M.K. Coker. All Rights Reserved.
Cover Art by Streetlight Graphics.

ISBN: 9798362965006

This is a work of fiction. All characters, places, organizations, and events are the product of the author's imagination or are used fictitiously.

The Dakota Mystery Series:
Dead White
Dead Dreams
Dead Wrong
Dead Quiet
Dead News
Dead Hot
Dead Poor
Dead Head
Dead Tunes
Dead Ball
Dead Spirits

DEDICATION AND EPIGRAPH

In memory of Oscar Howe, Yanktonai Dakota, who combined old and new into phenomenal art and touched the hearts of many, myself included.

In memory of Tim Giago, Oglala Lakota, who owned and published the first independently owned Native newspaper and helped educate wasicus about Indian Country.

In memory of Zitkala-Sa, Yankton Dakota, whose essays echoed my joy of growing up on the plains along the bluffs of the Missouri River.

When the spirit swells my breast I love to roam leisurely among the green hills; or sometimes, sitting on the brink of the murmuring Missouri, I marvel at the great blue overhead. With half-closed eyes I watch the huge cloud shadows in their noiseless play upon the high bluffs opposite me, while into my ear ripple the sweet, soft cadences of the river's song. Folded hands lie in my lap, for the time forgot. My heart and I lie small upon the earth like a grain of throbbing sand. Drifting clouds and tinkling waters, together with the warmth of a genial summer day, bespeak with eloquence the loving Mystery round about us.

—Zitkala-Sa (Gertrude Simmons Bonnin), *The Great Spirit*

CHAPTER 1

As dawn broke over distant river bluffs, a red-winged blackbird arrowed toward the grassy mound that lay like the smoothed-over remains of a sleeping buffalo on the flatlands of Dakota prairie and farmland. Approaching the summit, the bird fluttered in flight, as if ruffled by restless spirits, winging away to the west. It landed on a fence post and cocked its head in question. Then it startled back into flight as a lone figure trudged up the trail winding along the western side of the mound.

Walking in the footsteps of the famed Corps of Discovery, Ann Grigsby-Clark huffed and puffed. Though she'd gotten an early start, she felt her fair skin radiate back the heat of what was predicted to be a sweltering August day. Just as it had been when her however-many-times-great-uncle, William Clark, had made his way up the same mound in 1804.

But she had the advantage of a short hike on a well-maintained trail and plenty of water, even basic restrooms. Instead of an arduous nine-mile hike from the Missouri River, hers was less than a mile from the small parking lot. Nor did she face marauding Indians, though from his journal, William Clark had reported that all the surrounding tribes, including the mighty Sioux, were afraid to approach the mound. They'd told him it was a hill of "little deveals" or evil spirits who shot arrows at anyone who approached.

Had William Clark and his fellow Army officer, Meriweather Lewis, been afraid as they walked up the mound with their ten men? Or had they thought they'd been told a tall tale to keep them from trespassing on prime hunting grounds? Whatever the case, they'd been compelled to make the trek, perhaps by that inexplicable drive of exploration, that thirst to be first, to bring back knowledge of the mysterious far-off lands that were now theirs.

Ann stopped to sit on a big boulder beside the path. Looking back south from where she'd come, she watched the landscape glimmer into being—fields and more fields with little islands of tree-shored farms. The sun glinted off roofs and a white dome in the university town of Vermillion, which she'd just left. The parkland directly below her was an untidy patchwork of prairie grasses, shorter seed-topped brome and a swath of tall big bluestem, and native flowers like purple asters and yellow coneflowers. A small almost-dry creek ran through the lowlands, and to one side, a series of canvas tents ended in a raw scar of upturned prairie. A flyer at the trailhead told her that it was part of an archaeological dig, something she associated with the pyramids of Egypt or the Mayan temples of South America, not the Great Plains.

Just what exactly did they think they'd find, a few arrowheads from the little devils who supposedly lived here? She laughed to herself. That seemed pretty far-fetched.

But what would it have looked like, back then, in 1804?

She'd visited the W.H. Over Museum in Vermillion the previous day and seen a painting of what an artist had imagined that momentous day had been like. The expedition members were making their way up the mound, holding rifles. At the top, William Clark was in the lead, pointing westward, where prairie grass and herds of buffalo stretched as far as the eye could see. The western frontier. What a thrill it must have been. The lure of the unknown, of adventure, of breaking new ground. The journey must have been perilous, among Indian tribes—some friendly, others anything but. Somehow, though, the Corps of Discovery had made it all the way to the West Coast and back. Trying to spread peace among warring tribes and opening trade routes for the newly acquired lands from the Louisiana Purchase. The Americans' belief in Manifest Destiny, she'd told her students, even gave God's stamp on the push to acquire the land between "sea and shining sea."

The weather-worn boulder under her still held the heat of the previous day, and she rose to her feet again, thinking that it was a good reminder to get off her duff. That was what her trip was, after years of trying to cram young minds with history, so as not to repeat it, though repeat it, she had. Over and over. To mostly unwilling ears and minds.

She passed a stand of Indian paintbrush, its bright orange a bit of color amid the waving brome. The trail circled around, and a surprisingly small but steep summit awaited her—though *summit* was stretching the term—with several steps cut into the side. Feeling a bit let down, she put one foot in front of the other, pushing her creaking knees to make it up the large steps. At the top, a gust of wind seemed strong enough to push her right back down and crack her head on the hard gravel.

Wouldn't that make an interesting headline: *Retired Virginia History Teacher Is History after Visiting Ancestral Site.*

Hands still on knees, she steadied herself before standing erect. And gasped. Instead of the lonely summit she'd expected, she found someone lying on the small, flat top, arms crossed and staring up into the bluing sky.

"Pardon me," she said, thinking she'd stumbled over someone's special moment, at the same time resenting that he'd interrupted hers. But it was a Saturday, so perhaps not unexpected. Sometimes she forgot the days of the week now that she was retired. "I didn't realize anyone was up here."

When he didn't answer, she took a step back then had to catch herself. Was he, or she—Ann saw the snake of a ponytail—sleeping? On first glance, she thought it was a teenager. Maybe a drunk college student on a lark. Or a nature lover had fallen asleep while looking up at the stars. The rising sun brushed the still face, turning it almost red... and as she hesitated, she saw the streaks of red, like war paint, that ran down it.

Then as her eyes adjusted, she screamed. The wind whipped the sound away into an empty landscape. She stumbled back, almost off the summit. Gravel fell down the terraced steps and hit the wooden trim, sounding like the din of distant drums. With her hands over her mouth, she tried to wrap her head around what she was seeing on this sacred ground her forebearer had walked.

Rather than the Corps of Discovery, she'd discovered a corpse.

CHAPTER 2

SO MUCH FOR A HONEYMOON.
Sheriff Karen Okerlund Mehaffey glanced in her rearview mirror to see her newly minted husband pull up behind her in the small parking lot on the southernmost reaches of Eda County. Instead of winging their way to the Caribbean, they were grounded. They'd almost escaped into the wild blue yonder.

But when the call came as they'd loaded up their luggage to head to the airport in Sioux Falls, they'd looked at each other, acknowledged silently that their vacation was history, and stowed their bags. Muttering imprecations under her breath, she'd headed for the Sub, the ancient Suburban SUV that was her official vehicle. With a sigh and a snort, Division of Criminal Investigation Agent Dirk Larson had loaded himself into the white crime scene van. Despite being a Chicagoan by birth, he'd inherited some of the close-mouthed Dakotan traits of his maternal line.

Though the rough edge of his mother's tongue—and hand—had likely had more to do with his hoarding of precious words, never to be given out on a whim. Whereas her younger half-uncle and part-time detective came by it naturally.

Marek Okerlund, his dark corn-syrup hair shining reddish in the unfettered sun, towered six inches over her and Larson's six-one as they walked over to him at the trailhead at Spirit Mound. Before Karen herself, who hadn't inherited the close-mouthed bit any more than she had the pale blue Okerlund eyes of her uncle and father, could say a word, a biker roared up in arm-baring black leather on a black Harley-Davidson. He glanced down at his GPS then at the mound. He also snorted rather than spoke.

But his plates were from Nevada. Then he opened his mouth, and his candidacy as an honorary laconic Dakotan was dispelled.

"*That's* supposed to be historic?" He looked like he wanted to punch it. Or, given his next words, pop it. "It's no bigger than a damn pimple. I drove thirty miles out of my way from the interstate. You people don't know what a mountain is." He snorted again, though much of it was lost in the exhaust expelled as he revved his engine. "So frigging flat that it's gone to your head. Anything breaks the horizon, it's historic." Then he seemed to register their official presence and perked up. "Say, something going on?"

Marek, his subsonic voice rumbling over the quieted engine, said, "Nothing much."

The biker's face fell. Clearly, he didn't speak Dakotan. *Nothing much* usually meant something. You just didn't want to tempt the fates into making it more.

"Figures. Waste of gas, waste of time, just a waste. People warned me it was nothing but a wasteland after the Black Hills. Should've known better than to take a side trip. Got bored with the frigging fields. If that's historic, I'm the king of Siam."

And the king of Siam was gone in a huff of smoke and foul air.

As a child, Karen had agreed with the biker's view of the mound. Back then, the mound had been owned by a cattle farmer. An elementary school trip to visit the historic Lewis and Clark site had been a huge disappointment. Expecting to see the little people with arrows or at least feel some thrill, all she'd seen were bored cows chewing their cud and shitting cow pies in a muddy paddock that went halfway up the mound.

The only excitement of the trip had been when their teacher's car got sideswiped on the way back to town and Karen's father, the previous sheriff, had rushed to their rescue. Her bestie, Laura, had opined from the back seat that the little spirits had caused the accident. Karen and her father thought it had more to do with a drunk driver, who was soon after snoring off spirits of the alcoholic variety in the county jail.

But times had changed here on the mound. Despite the rising heat, Karen could appreciate the clouds, lonely and scattered, that skidded over the bright-blue canvas as a background to the oddly shaped mound with its two humps, one much more prominent than the other. It didn't look particularly natural, but signs she'd passed as they walked the treeless trail assured her it was. The bedrock was chalk—fossilized shells from an ancient sea—that had been partially eroded by glacial ice, which, when it had melted, left a deposit of glacial till.

She wiped sweat from her upper lip. Marek and Larson were doing the hard work, loaded with crime scene equipment as she led them up the trail. Given the heat, maybe they'd expire right here, leaving two more humps on the mound and more to the legend.

Lewis and Clark. Okerlund and Larson. One more attraction to snare unsuspecting tourists who could snort and disparage. At least it didn't have the tackiness of tourist-trap Wall Drug in the Black Hills. East River Dakotans were far more understated and, as the biker had noted, under-hilled.

Up ahead, Karen saw three figures on the mound, one spare and one rotund, and another figure in the middle—both literally and figuratively. The first two were easy to identify, the odd couple of the dayshift. The imminently upright and correct Kurt Bechtold, her oldest and longest-serving deputy, and her friend Laura's husband, Walter Russell. Karen imagined that even from the distance, she could see his windsock of a mustache float out in the wind while the sun glanced off his bald pate.

The last figure must be the woman who'd found the body. She was turned into the wind, which kept her at least somewhat cooler and, probably more importantly, looking away from the body. Even as Karen watched, Kurt escorted the woman down the summit, likely to the bench at the turn of the trail. Time and a quarter mile later, that was proven true. Karen had a quick word with the woman, who clung to a water bottle as if it were a life jacket, to reassure her that they would get to her soon.

"Timing sucks wide," Walrus said as Karen stepped onto the flat top. "You were supposed to be on the way to sun and fun right now."

"Happens," Larson muttered as he set up a tripod. "Job."

"Still shitty."

"Tish?" Marek asked, taking in the sight. No one approached the body, and it was getting crowded on the flat-topped summit.

Norman Tisher was the county coroner and a full-time mortician. In the rural areas of the Dakotas, multiple jobs went with the territory, for financial and civic gain.

Walrus said, "Funeral in Fink. He should be here any time now."

Karen took a look at the two-way Highway 19 that passed by the mound and saw Tish's black-shelled pickup zooming down from the north. Right on cue. A squad car followed more sedately, its driver obviously disinclined to arrest the coroner. Good call.

Karen turned back. Kurt, holding a roll of crime scene tape, seemed at a loss as to how to attach it anywhere. The summit held nothing but beaten-down grass and the body. He tucked the roll under his arm and stood at attention. "Bjorklund and Two Fingers are on their way."

If word of the body got out, her two swing-shift deputies would be needed for crowd control, along with any other "jobs as assigned," per their lengthy job descriptions. Like helping move the body. Getting a gurney up here wouldn't be easy, not on the gravel trail. Body bag? Well, that was Tish's problem.

But she couldn't do anything until he was here. Fortunately, the tall toothpick of a figure moved with astonishing speed up the trail and was there within minutes—funereal black suit and all, despite the growing heat. And on the coroner's heels was the enigmatic Two Fingers, a man apart, not just for his Native American visage but some natural distance that seemed part of who he was. At least when he was dealing with her.

As if to prove that difference, as Tish hurried to the body, Two Fingers approached Walrus and Marek. "You met the little spirit people yet?"

Walrus gave a snort that undulated down his belly. "The ones with deadly arrows? Crap. You Indians just didn't want people coming up here, that's all."

"Not crap. I've seen them." Two Fingers looked almost as serious as Kurt, who was ignoring them, standing on hand for the coroner.

Walrus's brows drew down. "What do you mean, you've seen them?"

"Not only seen them. I've gotten the arrows in my hide. When I was a boy and my mother brought me here, I ran all the way down the trail to escape them. My mother had to put me in the tub and treat my wounds." He put his hand in his pocket. "If you're going to stay up here, you'll need some protection."

"Oh, come on," Walrus said. "You peddling medicine bags now? Pay not enough?"

"It's never enough," Two Fingers returned without a shred of humor, a sentiment that got nods all around, including from Karen. She wasn't in control of their salaries, alas; the county commissioners were. They were also the ones who refused to get her a new vehicle.

"Of course, we call the little devils something else these days," Two Fingers went on, showing no particular discomfort in the heat. "You'll be wanting protection when the wind dies, as the weather channel predicted." Two Fingers pulled a bright-orange cylinder out of his pocket and held it out to Marek.

Walrus gave a huff that served as laughter as Marek took the cylinder. "I appreciate this, Deputy." Her detective proceeded to spray, making a small hill even smaller as they tried to back away.

Two Fingers flashed his rare smile. "Just keeping you from getting sick or even dying. Never know."

Marek handed back the mosquito repellent. "West Nile is here."

Walrus snorted "It's all talk. I've been bitten by mosquitoes for years, and I'm just fine."

Deputy Two Fingers gave the long, undulating mass of humanity a long look. "A matter of opinion."

But the ever-present wind did seem to be dying. As if to prove it, within minutes, Walrus swatted at his head and got a smear of red over his already-reddened pate. After another swat over his eye, he held out his hand. "Geez, give it over. I'm not dying of West Nile, but I ain't itching to itch for the next week."

Two Fingers's lips twitched before he handed it over. "Told you. Little devils."

Tish stepped back into their cluster, took the spray, and doused himself as delicately as a woman headed to the opera before handing it to Karen. "Eau de DEET."

"Cause of death?" Walrus asked.

"Blunt trauma to the back of the head, it looks like. But as ever…"

"The medical examiner will determine," the assembled purveyors of the law answered in chorus.

Tish nodded sagely and gestured a blessing. "I'll send the boys out ASAP to transport the body to Sioux Falls." He paused, looking back. "Poor kid."

That had all of them concentrating harder on what they'd all been studiously ignoring. Some from squeamishness or respect, she guessed. Some from trying not to start the job before the job allowed. Or all of the above.

Karen took the first step forward, followed by Marek, her silent shadow. Though the body was the size of a budding teenager, not much over five foot, Karen took him to be in his twenties, even thirty at the outside, but very slight. His reddish-brown hair, liberally doused with blood, was several shades lighter than Marek's and was tied into a ponytail with a beaded thong. With the dip in the wind, flies started to congregate. Even a couple of monarch butterflies flitted in a dance over his head before rising into the sky and flying away.

Larson knelt and put a gloved hand into the pockets of the khaki shorts that ended just shy of the knobbly knees. He shook his head and rose to his feet.

"Nothing?"

"No wallet, no keys, no phone." Larson's bullet-gray eyes narrowed. "His arms are crossed over something."

Kneeling down, Karen took a look. "Piece of a poster board. I think it says something, but I'll let the medical examiner handle that."

"Any of you seen him before?" Larson asked.

Kurt shook his head, and Walrus spoke for both. "Nope. Maybe he's from Vermillion. A student?" His eyes narrowed on the face, apparently seeing what she had. "Grad student or even prof?"

"Maybe he's part of the dig," Two Fingers began as he stepped forward for a better look. "I know someone who..." Then he stilled, his face going completely blank, a still life.

After an awkward pause, Karen went to him, let him absorb whatever he was seeing, and waited. It wasn't easy.

Impatience had been her besetting sin for all her life. And time was of the essence. They needed an ID.

Finally, Two Fingers took a breath, and life returned. To her deputy, at least.

"Who was he?" she asked.

His eyes rose slowly. "My blood brother."

CHAPTER 3

MAREK TRIED TO PROCESS THE deputy's words. Normally, Marek only had to try so hard with the written word, not the spoken, given his dyslexia. So far as he knew, Two Fingers had only two blood siblings. Both were sisters who lived on the Flandreau Reservation up northwest of Sioux Falls. "Your... father's... son?"

Two Fingers's dark, unfathomable eyes, which had always seemed a bit haunted to Marek, perhaps because of his traumatic conception as the product of rape, blinked. Then Two Fingers shook his head. "I have no idea if there are any." Nor did he care, going by his tone. "No, we did the blood oath thing when we were kids."

"White style or Indian style?"

Walrus's question got a faint smile. "So far as I know, there's only one style. Get out your pocketknife, make a cut on your finger, and press fingers together so you share blood. I think we were about eight. Brothers for life."

And one life had ended far too soon.

"You were very close?" Karen asked.

He shook his head. "Not for some time after high school. But more lately."

"Flandreau Indian School?" Marek asked.

"No, public high school. Hunter wasn't enrolled in a tribe, and I didn't meet the blood quantum."

His biological father, long dead, was white. Marek took

another look at the man on the ground. The ponytail. The beading on the thong. Otherwise, he looked about as white as Marek himself, who hadn't a drop of Native blood. Unlike his daughter. "Did your friend meet the blood quantum?"

Two Fingers nodded. "I believe so, despite being white-passing, but there were a lot of things messed up when he was a kid. He talked some about pursuing enrollment when the rules changed, but if he did, he never told me. His biological mother didn't enroll him back when that was a requirement. He was taken away from her and fostered. After some back-and-forth with the tribe, who had no authority as he wasn't enrolled according to their own rules, he was eventually adopted by a white family in Flandreau."

The carefully neutral words hid the pain of what had become a scandal in the country at large. Many Native American children in South Dakota had been pulled out of their homes for simple poverty, cutting them off from family, culture, and identity.

As if reading that thought, Two Fingers relaxed slightly. "This was a bad situation. *Really* bad. No one knew he existed. No birth certificate. His mother had left Lower Brule and was living on the streets of Rapid City. She was an addict and often neglected him. He was so malnourished when he was found at age about two that it stunted his growth permanently."

Larson stepped up. "Name?"

The abrupt question didn't seem to bother Two Fingers. "Digges. Hunter Digges. No, wait. I think he might have changed his last name. But I don't know for sure. He was just Hunter to me." The haunted look returned. "His parents will know. Trent and Peggy Digges."

Karen pulled out her phone. "They still live in Flandreau?"

Nodding, Two Fingers pulled out his own phone then gave her the number. "They went through a lot with him. This might break them."

Marek heard a lot of complicated emotions in those simple words.

"Drugs?" Walrus asked. "Alcohol?"

"Actually, no. Especially as that's what killed his mother. That wasn't his way. Not unless it was peyote, and that made him sick as a dog. He was... suicidal... for a time. And searching." His eyes fell to the trampled ground. "The Diggeses weren't bad parents. Just not Indian. They stuck by him through thick and thin. A lot of thin after high school. But things were better. A lot better."

No easy path to justice, then. Marek looked out at the dirt-scar and scattered tents, all empty. "Hunter was involved in the dig?"

"Yes, he was a grad student at the University of South Dakota, hoping to eventually get his doctorate in anthropology with an emphasis in archaeology, but it was a slow process. He was a social studies teacher at Flandreau for the last couple years." Before Marek could ask, Two Fingers added, "Indian School." His lips twisted. "Neither of us could go there, but he could teach there."

"Like you could be a policeman at the Rez?" Walrus asked. "You almost took that job, when we thought Karen lost the election."

Two Fingers's face turned inscrutable. "I chose not to."

Closed book there.

Karen put hands to hips as she glanced at the body. She looked almost hopeful. "Does this change jurisdiction, that he's Native? FBI?"

Marek, being the ace detective he was, figured out the hopeful. If she could hand it off, she and Larson might be able to salvage their honeymoon.

Two Fingers glanced to the north. "If he was killed on the Rez, yes, you'd have to turn over the case to The Seasons." That would be the resident agents Sommervold and Wintersgill in Sioux Falls. It was obvious to all of them that Hunter Digges, or whatever his name was, hadn't been killed where he lay.

Walrus scratched his head. "Why's the FBI involved? You've got tribal police, right?"

Two Fingers nodded. "We do. For a number of years, there was even an almost unheard-of joint police force between the City of Flandreau and the reservation, but that disbanded a couple years ago." Again, closed book. "But felonies were taken out of our hands way back with the Major Crimes Act."

"What, like back in the seventies or something? Why would they do that?"

"The eighties. The *eighteen hundred* eighties."

Walrus's jaw dropped. "Geez, are you kidding me? Why?"

"Congress didn't like Native American notions of justice." Two Fingers's dark gaze winged west. "Particularly those of the Sioux."

Marek tilted his head. He might know little about the tribes in South Dakota. But he knew one thing. "I thought you didn't use the name Sioux anymore. Doesn't it mean 'enemies'?"

"It's from the Ojibwe, one of our traditional enemies, as pronounced by the French. Nadouessioux, meaning 'little snakes.'" That got a sharp smile. "The Sioux name is still useful for talking about the Lakota, Nakota, and Dakota. We are all part of the Great Sioux Nation on official records. Most people only know about the Lakota, who are mostly West River now on the big reservations like Rosebud and Pine Ridge. And most think of the Sioux from movies. You know, the stereotypical warrior on horseback, living in tipis, roaming the plains, either noble savages or just savages, depending on your take."

Walrus asked, "So which are you?"

"Savage? You tell me." Then he shrugged. "Dakota and Nakota. From the Flandreau and Yankton reservations."

Karen tapped a toe. "Major Crimes Act?"

"Yes, well, short version is, Brule Lakota Chief Crow Dog shot and killed another Lakota, the uncle of Crazy Horse, Chief Spotted Tail. Some say it's because Spotted Tail was seen as a traitor, appointed to his position of chief by the US government—who called him a great peace chief—rather than by the tribe. He signed treaties that didn't benefit them. He also refused to go to war when the government illegally took the Black Hills contra to the treaty."

Anyone with an ear in South Dakota knew about the Black Hills, taken in the gold rush and never returned. The Supreme Court had finally agreed, over a century later, that the government was in violation of the treaty and the tribe was due compensation. The tribe wanted the land back, not the money. So far as Marek knew, the money still sat in a trust fund, accumulating interest, though he had heard something about the Lakota buying a chunk of Black Hills land recently. Whether they'd used the money to do so, he didn't know.

Two Fingers swatted at a mosquito buzzing his ear. "There was also some bad blood over the tribal police as well. And there may have also been a woman involved. Only Crow Dog knew the truth. According to Lakota tradition, Crow Dog made restitution of six hundred dollars, eight horses, and a blanket to Spotted Tail's family. But the government, outraged that their notion of justice wasn't met for someone who they considered an ally, arrested Crow Dog, tried him, and sentenced him to death by hanging."

For some reason, Marek thought that the method of death as much as the actual sentence had outraged their deputy. He wasn't sure why. Maybe hanging was taboo.

Two Fingers continued, "Crow Dog appealed his case to the Supreme Court, who unanimously ruled that the government did not have the jurisdiction to try an Indian for murder against another Indian on Indian land. A matter of tribal sovereignty."

Karen tapped her toe again. "So why is it an FBI matter?"

"Because Congress was so enraged by that ruling that it passed the Major Crimes Act, taking justice out of tribal hands for felonies. Effectively making the tribes rely on the whims of federal agents to bring justice to the reservations."

That included rape, especially rape by a white man against an Indian. The FBI got in hot water in the media over the last decade for ignoring those cases. It was the push to get DNA rape kits processed that had identified Two Fingers's mother's attacker. The Seasons had been very helpful in that quest, which couldn't be said of their predecessors.

Ever forthright and clueless, Walrus asked, "Would your mother have taken horses and money for what happened to her?"

The dark eyes turned on him.

Walrus cleared his throat. "Sorry. Just curious. I don't understand how *stuff* would make up for murder or rape."

Her phone still in her hand, Karen stopped it there. "This isn't a social studies class. And until and if we find out that our victim was killed on Indian land, he's ours. We need to get moving. Two Fingers, other than his parents, did Hunter have a partner, a girlfriend, anyone else we should contact?"

His eyes dropped again to the trodden grass. "He dated another teacher at the Indian school a few times, but that didn't work out."

"No hard feelings?"

"Hurt feelings, but not hard. Life wasn't easy for Hunter. Ever. From start..." His gaze went to and lingered on his friend. "To finish."

Karen stepped away to make the call. Normally, they would go in person to make the notification, but with the way news traveled so fast these days, she wanted them to know from her before they heard it elsewhere. She was a bit surprised that it hadn't already hit Nails Nelson, their county's only newshound, a legless Vietnam vet who ran a low-power FM station. Fortunately, he always contacted Karen, not Marek, when he wanted the scoop.

When Karen stepped back, her sweat-glistened face was pinched. "That was hard. They kept saying that he'd turned things around, like that should prevent him from getting killed. We'll drive up after we're done here." Her fjord-blue eyes lit on Two Fingers. "You'll go with us. At their request. They want you to make sure Hunter doesn't fall into the cracks."

Though it was a backhanded insult, Karen didn't look offended. Perhaps she'd heard as much as Marek had about the lack of equal justice between whites and Natives.

"You can also smooth things over with the police chief there," she went on then turned before she saw Two Fingers flinch. Something there. "Marek, let's go talk to our wit."

After one last glance at Two Fingers, who'd gone to kneel beside his friend, Marek followed Karen, nearly stumbling on one of the steps. He reached out and caught Karen's shoulder before he went down.

She stopped, glanced back, and smiled. "Little people trip you up?"

"I don't need any other explanation for my clumsiness," he said, and the woman on the bench smiled at him tentatively. Kurt must have given her his hat, as he was the only one who wore one of the old brimmed ones rather than a ball cap.

"I almost fell, too, after..." Rather than finish, she took a deep sip of water from the bottle in her hands. She heaved a big sigh. "This was supposed to be such a great day."

"Ms. Clark," Karen began.

"Grigsby-Clark. My husband was the Grigsby. We flipped a coin to see whose name went first and he won—or lost, if you go by tradition. My mother was horrified that I didn't take his name and drop the Clark entirely. She wondered what on earth the children would do when they married, but I never had any children, so it wasn't an issue. Well, except *not* having children *was* an issue. Fortunately, my brother had a whole passel of them. Seven, if you can believe it.

Sorry, I'm babbling. I don't know what I can possibly tell you. I'm from Lynchburg, Virginia, and I've never been to South Dakota before in my life. First time west of the Mississippi. I just retired this summer."

Marek put in his oar. "You can tell us when you came, if you saw anyone, if you noticed anything unusual."

The woman blinked up at him in surprise, as if a molehill had become a mountain, but she did answer. "Well, it was the break of dawn when I arrived. Literally. Whatever time that was. I didn't see any other vehicles. I mean, passing, I did, on the highway there, but not so as I noticed anyone, and he was already... well, dead. No one pulled out when I pulled in."

Marek pursed his lips. Surely Digges had a vehicle. Did someone bring him here in theirs, or was his car stolen?

"And I didn't see anyone. At all. At the time, I was relieved, since this was something of a pilgrimage for me. A very personal one." At Marek's quirked brow, she smiled faintly. "While some are skeptical, saying it must be one of those misguided family traditions just like those Cherokee princess stories, I did the documentation myself, and the link's solid. I'm a great-great-something-or-other niece of William Clark." She opened her mouth again, as if to explain who that was, and looked a bit surprised when she registered their comprehension. "I'm used to teaching teenagers. They don't know, or care, about the Corps of Discovery."

Karen pointed to the southwest. "Lewis and Clark Lake is down there by Yankton. Made from damming up the Missouri River at Gavin's Point. We all grew up with Lewis and Clark as part of our history." Karen glanced back. "For good or ill."

"Ill? How could the settlement of our country be..." The woman flushed. "Oh, the Indians. Native Americans, I mean." Her nose wrinkled. "Or is it Indigenous people, now? I can't keep up. I mean, I'd be happy to use whatever, as long as they agreed on it."

Karen hooked her thumbs into her belt. "Do you think

you could get our people to agree on Caucasian, European, or White?"

"Anglo," Marek offered. Actually, he'd heard some of his Native coworkers in Albuquerque say that they preferred to be called by their tribe. But what would one call Two Fingers, who came from several? As for the Scandinavian and Slavic settlers he came from, Marek added, "Or perhaps Immigrant People?"

The teacher laughed ruefully. "I guess I never thought of it like that. I don't want to offend anyone, but these days, everything's an offense. Anyway, this mound is part of my heritage, my family's heritage, and I hate to see it desecrated. Who would do such a thing?"

Looking more than a little jaded, as they'd had more than their share of homicides lately in Eda, Karen answered. "You're a history teacher, right? I think history has a great deal to say about human nature."

Again, the woman acknowledged the hit. "It's never been personal before. Just history." She glanced blankly toward the west. "I don't know what to do. Do I have to stay here? I'm already off schedule. I've planned this trip for years and years as my retirement present to myself. My husband was going to come with me, but then he got pancreatic cancer, and that was that." She sighed. "I'm sorry. That poor boy up there is dead, and all I can think is that my trip is ruined. I wish I could wave a magic wand and save him *and* my trip, but I can't." She braced her shoulders as she looked up. "Do you need me to stay? I will."

One rotten thing about good people who found themselves caught up in bad things was that they had to weigh their own good against the common good. When Karen looked at Marek, he shook his head.

Message received. Karen told her, "We need to take your official statement at the courthouse. One of my deputies will take care of that. Afterwards, so long as we have your contact information and you are willing to return if needed, you are free to continue your trip."

Perhaps only Marek heard the envy in his half-niece's voice. Instead of turquoise skies and waters bisected by white sands, she got grass and gravel, searing heat, and a dead body.

The woman's shoulders relaxed. "Thank you." She rubbed her eyes and looked out at the 360-degree panorama. "It's such a grand sight from here. You can see for miles, not like where I'm from. But I'm probably going to have nightmares about this for a long time." She smiled weakly. "Looks like the evil spirits finally caught up with the Clarks."

CHAPTER 4

As Karen parked on the street where the Diggeses lived in a pretty yellow ranch home, she made sure that Two Fingers was still on her tail. She got the feeling that he would use any excuse to peel off and hotfoot it back to Reunion, despite the hour's drive.

She didn't really blame him. If her friend Laura had been the body on the top of that mound, Karen would do anything to avoid sitting down with her parents, whose home had been almost as much hers as Laura's. Had Two Fingers been that close to the Diggeses, or was it that he was no longer as close, just as she and Laura hadn't been until recently. Guilt?

Karen got out of the Sub, with Marek just behind her, and they waited for Two Fingers to make his way to them, looking like he was on the way to the gallows.

The brightly painted blue door of the ranch house flew open, and a thin-boned bird of a woman flew at Two Fingers. Whether in self-defense or in genuine affection, he caught her and hugged her, her flyaway blond hair a flag against his dark.

A man in a dress shirt, tie loosened, trailed out, looking lost. As he hesitated between them and his wife, Karen stepped forward. She wondered if Trent Digges was related to Alan Digges, a greedy asshole who'd tangled with the powerful Baytons of Sioux Falls and was even now cooling his Italian loafers in jail. She hoped not, but every family had their black sheep.

"Mr. Digges, I am Sheriff Karen Okerlund Mehaffey."

He stared at her hand for several seconds before taking it gently, his fingers shaking lightly in hers. "Trent Digges. You spoke to my wife. I was presiding over a special city council meeting. She called me. Hysterical. I didn't believe her at first. Are you sure? He was doing so well."

That seemed to be the consensus. But something in Hunter's life had gone terribly wrong. "Yes, I am sure. Though he had no ID on him, my deputy identified him."

"Your deputy? Oh, yes." He said a name that sounded like *ee-yawn*.

Karen had seen Two Fingers's first name on office paperwork, though when she'd asked what he preferred to be called, it was by his last name. "Ian? I thought it was Inyan."

Coming up together, both Two Fingers and Peggy Digges winced.

"Long story," Two Fingers said with a tone that said it wasn't forthcoming.

Karen let it go. For now. Initially, she'd resisted asking if Inyan was a family name because something about her deputy made her unwilling to probe deeply. He had depths not even a sonar-equipped submersible could plumb.

She faced the Diggeses to say the most hated words in her lexicon. "I'm sorry for your loss." She gestured toward Marek. "My detective, Marek Okerlund. I know it's hard, but we have some questions for you. The sooner we have information that might help us, the sooner we can find justice for your son."

"Justice?" His mother's face just crumpled. "Justice won't bring our son back. I just got him back, the last couple years, and now he's gone. He was our only."

Her husband hugged her to his side, looking helpless.

But he took a deep breath and nodded toward the open door. "Why don't we go in?"

Before any of them could take a step, a sleek silver bullet of a 'Vette raced down the street and stopped practically on the bumper of Two Fingers's squad car. Had Tish commandeered a ride? But no, it was a Native woman in her forties, Karen guessed, with a great deal of animation and energy in her high-cheek-boned face. She jumped out of the 'Vette, leaving the door wide open, and ran to Peggy Digges. With both relief and resignation on his face, Two Fingers went to close the car door.

The two women did a dance without words, a keening wail from one punctuated by hiccupping sobs from the other, and Karen closed her eyes. She didn't do well with such naked emotions. Marek was better, but, as she opened her eyes, even he looked taken aback, unsure how to proceed.

Finally, Trent Digges broke the impasse by simply walking into the house, tripping on the steps.

Karen caught his arm as she followed him. "Watch the step."

"I'm not usually so clumsy," he mumbled. "You'd never know I played basketball. Just high school, though. And yes, I know you. Of you, I mean. Followed your career, first as a player. Much later as Inyan's boss. You've been in the press a lot."

Once again, it was Inyan with a silent *n*. "More than I want."

Trent gave a wry smile as he sat down on a linen-colored sectional sofa littered with wildly colored throw pillows and blankets. "Those of us in public service could often use less press."

"Tell me about it." She glanced around. Paintings, sculptures, and ceramics littered walls, tables, and every nook and cranny. "Quite an art gallery."

His lips twitched up. "Peggy can't draw a stick man to save her soul. But she knows art. And artists. She runs a gallery in town. We have an ever-changing gallery of art here as well. I never quite know what I'll see when I open the door."

"But we'll never again see Hunter slouching on that couch. Oh, Trent." Peggy Digges, one hand in Two Fingers's and the other in the Native woman's, pulled the two down beside her on the other side of the L-shaped sectional. "What are we going to do? I don't know what to do." Her dazed eyes lit on Karen. "What should I do?"

Karen sat gingerly and spoke gently. "You can answer our questions."

"Inyan—" the Native woman began, clearly upset, but he shook his head, and she subsided. Barely. She crossed bared arms that showed a feather tattooed on one and an electric guitar on the other.

"What do you want to know?" Trent opened helpless hands, palms up. "If you want to know who would kill him, I have no idea. Now, if he'd killed himself..."

"Hunter was beyond that," his wife insisted, though her husband looked a little less certain. "He *was*. He'd found... I don't know, his center. His way. Whatever you call it, he was steady. Excited, even, for the future."

In this, at least, Karen could reassure her. "Suicide is not on the table."

Trent looked torn at that news. "It would be easier, in some ways, if it was. Knowing however awful, it was his own choice. This..." He shook his head in clear bafflement. "Hunter didn't have enemies."

"Trent," the Native woman said, clearly in disagreement, but gently. "Not enemies, perhaps, but he was bullied. Even at his age."

Peggy wiped at her face. "The story of his life."

Marek had kept silent, perhaps waiting for some of the emotion to dissipate. He was looking consideringly at the Native woman. "Are you Two Fingers's mother?"

Surprised, Karen looked at her deputy, whose darker skin couldn't hide the reddening of the tips of his ears.

The woman was equally taken aback but recovered with a flashing smile that was familiar to Karen, only far rarer on her deputy's face. "Why, yes, I am. Much to my exasperation, on occasion. My son does the stoic Indian too well. And he's far too proper to have a rocker as a mom." Her jab had Two Fingers closing his eyes. "But I love him nonetheless. It takes a while for sons to come around." Then, realizing what she'd said, she hugged Peggy closer. "It breaks my heart that you've lost yours. It's not right."

"No, it's not. Not after all we've been through together, Winona."

"I feel I've lost another son as well." A single tear ran down Winona's face. "Hunter was in and out of my and Unci's home so much that it seemed like it. I haven't told Unci yet. It will kill her. He visited her sometimes, you know, listening to her stories of the Santee. He really had a good heart."

Karen frowned at the unfamiliar name. "Un-chee?"

Winona glanced at Karen. "Unci means 'grandmother.' Mine. She raised me, and I lived with her for a number of years after... that is, before I married."

After she'd been raped and been left pregnant. Without justice, until recently. If justice could be an answer, at least. Winona Two Fingers, or whatever her last name was now, was very unexpected. Somehow, Karen thought Two Fingers's mother would be a soft-spoken, retiring sort, with an even more haunted look in her eyes than her son's.

And while they were red-rimmed at the moment, Winona's eyes were steady and bright. "I see you know something of my story. But today isn't about me."

No, it wasn't. And time was ticking. "I'd like to know of any conflicts, past or present, that might have led to this."

Wryly, Trent Digges spoke up. "If you're looking for conflict, we had plenty since he was a teenager. He decided that we were the source of all his problems, that if he'd been raised with his own people, he'd have been what he was meant to be."

Peggy nodded while Winona remained a support, but silent. "Maybe he was right. I don't know. It wasn't talked as much about, back then, and I know the tribe fought the adoption, but it was their own rules that meant he wasn't enrolled. All I know is that when I first saw him, a little bag of bones with big sad hazel eyes, I fell in love. I wanted to do everything I could to give him a good life. We spent a lot of time going to doctors, dentists, and psychologists in those early years. Living in Flandreau, I thought we could give him enough access to his heritage that he would feel a part of it."

Trent leaned forward. "Flandreau is almost unique in the country, the way it developed, with settlers on both sides, Natives and whites."

When Karen glanced at Winona, she nodded. "True enough. After the Dakota War, a small number of Santee Dakota that had been moved to Nebraska from Minnesota, our ancestral home, took up homesteads in Flandreau. They were—what's the word? Assimilated? Christianized." As one of the two dangling earrings she wore had a cross, the other a lightning bolt, apparently her hostility didn't extend to the actual religion.

Karen wasn't sure what the Dakota War was, but homesteading had been in the mid-to-late nineteenth century. The government had wanted to fill in the vast empty spaces with settlers like her own Scandinavian ancestors in Eda County.

Trent waved toward the north. "There was a Presbyterian church jointly attended by both that still stands. And together, they had a school. Eventually, in 1892, Congress appropriated money for the Flandreau Indian School." He sighed. "And yes, I know, Hunter regaled us for years with the horrors of boarding schools. It became compulsory that same year of 1892. The staff cut the students' hair, cut their religion, cut their language, cut them off from their culture and family."

Winona, surprisingly, seemed to be less hostile. "All boarding schools, even white ones, had a lot of abuse. But Flandreau was better supported by the people. I went there, as did Unci. She met my grandfather there. His parents had also attended. Practically a family tradition." Her hand went out to her son then fell. "Until now."

Peggy hugged her friend closer. "But going to the public high school meant that Inyan and Hunter became friends. I will be forever grateful for that." Her reddened eyes transferred to Two Fingers. "I know it wasn't always easy. You saved him twice, at least. From himself. You were a good friend."

"Not always." His eyes were on his booted feet. "Not so much after he ran away."

Karen leaned forward. "Ran away?"

Trent leaned his head back on the sofa. "Yes, Hunter ran off to Standing Rock, the reservation that straddles the border of North Dakota, where his mother was enrolled. She was long dead. He tried to get enrolled there himself but found he couldn't, at least not under the rules the tribe had then." His gaze flicked to Two Fingers then back. "He found a relative, and they let him stay in an abandoned car that had been boarded up against the elements. He tried to fit in with the others, but as he looked more white than Native and didn't know how to behave their way, many rejected him, which left him angry and hurt. After somehow surviving the winter there, he finally hitched his way back to Flandreau, told us we'd ruined his life, and then tried to jump in front of a train. Inyan stopped him. Not once, but twice."

Two Fingers stirred. "I was right beside him. He knew I'd save him."

"No, I don't think he did know. He found out otherwise. Maybe he needed the reminder the second time. He also learned that on the reservation, with its grinding poverty, he was just one more mouth to feed. Eventually, he got his GED, and we agreed to send him to college. He spent a year there then suddenly left before finals, crossed the country on trains, doing God knows what to stay alive. Once in a long while, Inyan would get a text and tell us. We thought for sure we'd lost him, one way or other. Then one day, long after we'd resigned ourselves to him turning up dead or in prison, he showed up, his hair down to his butt, and an old man's eyes under a battered Twins baseball hat. He wanted to try college again. He wanted to learn his history, that of his people, and he didn't qualify for assistance because of not being enrolled. He was twenty-three at the time."

A silence descended. Peggy broke it. "Trent and I had quite a discussion."

"Fight, really," Trent said ruefully. "Peggy felt he deserved a second chance. I thought we'd done everything we could for him, that he needed to find his own way, just as he'd always claimed he'd wanted. He was of age. More than. And he could've gone to Dartmouth tuition-free like Inyan did. But Peggy said that if I wouldn't help him, she would on her own, even if she had to sell the gallery. So I gave in. And he made the most of his second chance. He finished his undergrad in anthropology in record time then said he could handle the finances from there. He got the job teaching at the Flandreau Indian School and pulled his own weight."

Which wasn't much, in reality. In truth, it sounded like he'd fought well above his weight, given everything. Karen said, "Hunter beat the odds."

"He did. And we were very proud of him." Trent rubbed at his reddened eyes. "Things were still a bit awkward for a while after he returned. One night, we had a very long talk. He said there was a lot of hurt out there in the world for a lot of people. But for his people, there was a hurt so deep that we would never really understand. And we don't. We try. But we don't. But he…"

As Trent choked up, Peggy finished. "He thanked us. He

still thinks the tribe should have taken him, not us, but that's not what happened. And he..." She glanced again at Two Fingers. "I'm sorry. I don't think he told you, but he was finally able to get enrolled at Standing Rock. That gave him some peace, I think. To finally be accepted. He also changed his name from Digges to Redwing-Digges. We said he didn't have to keep Digges, given how he felt, but he said he was from both of us, his mother, and from who knows what kind of a father, probably white, because of how he looked. And he said Digges was kind of appropriate, too, because he wanted to be an archaeologist. An Indigenous archaeologist. There aren't many of those, especially here."

Karen nodded at that. Marek had called USD on the drive up. "The field school is off for the day, apparently, which is why no one was there at the dig. Did Hunter have any plans? Do you know?"

His parents looked blank. But Winona nodded. "Unci said he was going to participate in the *wacipi*."

Marek tilted his head. "Wa-chee-pee?"

"The powwow. It's held once a year and will last several days."

Peggy blinked at her friend. "He's never participated before. As a dancer, I mean. Two left feet, he always said. I took him every year as a kid. The Grand Entry is really a sight to behold." Peggy pointed to a large wood-framed painting in a place of prominence on the far wall. "That's an impressionistic rendering."

Karen saw a number of barely recognizable Native people dancing—she got an impression of movement, even of joy.

"The artist is Santee Sioux. JoAnne Bird. Another who attended Flandreau Indian School. Hunter and I both loved the beauty of the dancing, the regalia, the beat of the drums. So much bright color, so much energy. Even if Hunter tripped over himself, he'd dip and dance, when he was just a mite."

Her face fell, as if she were once again realizing that he'd never do so again.

CHAPTER 5

In a room full of bright colors, the dark art of death was jarring.

Plus, Marek was having a hard time concentrating on the investigation, as the whole discussion had brought up something he hadn't thought of. His daughter, Becca, had Indian blood. Tewa. They'd only recently met some of her extended family at Nambé Pueblo in New Mexico. But Val had never talked about her Native heritage, only about her Hispanic. Should he be doing something about that? Was Becca eligible to be enrolled? He did the math in his head. She would only be something like an eighth, if that. But that didn't matter as much as the culture.

Maybe he'd ask Two Fingers. But not now.

Instead, he asked the Diggeses, "Can you give us access to your son's home?"

Peggy's free hand fluttered to her mouth. "Oh, I don't know. That's so private."

Her husband closed his eyes. "The dead have no privacy. Legally, anyway. I don't think he left a will, but you never know. Hunter didn't tell us everything." He opened his eyes and looked at Two Fingers, who dropped his. "But I want to know who did this. Who *could* do this. How... how did he die?"

Karen told them what she knew and what the medical examiner had yet to determine, ending with the often-unknowable reassurance, "It would have been quick. He didn't suffer."

As if suspecting the lie, Trent Digges held Karen's gaze for a long moment. He looked away first. Given the blow to the back of the head, Karen was likely telling the actual truth.

"That's something, at least. But from the back? He might never have known who did it."

That might have been true also, but Marek was more doubtful. "Do you have a key to Hunter's place?"

"Ah, no. Actually, Anita does. A... friend... of Hunter's." Peggy looked like she had a different word in mind but didn't enlighten them on what that was. Marek guessed it was the woman Hunter had dated. "She waters the plants, feeds the cat... Oh my, the cat. Whatever are we going to do with Sphinx? Hunter loved that cat."

And Peggy burst into tears. Her husband got up, Winona got to her feet, and they switched places. Winona, however, didn't sit down as she hovered over them. "I'll take care of this for you. I have Anita Asplund's number. She's sent some of her students my way."

"Thank you," Trent said with obvious relief. "We owe you—"

"There is no owe. Not between us." Winona gave her son a long look. "Come on, my wayward son. I'll hitch a ride with you." She tucked her arm into his, as his hands were in his front pockets, and propelled him down the driveway.

Marek didn't know what to say to the Diggeses, but he tried. "I'm sorry. We will do whatever we can to find out what happened. But I know it doesn't bring him back."

To his surprise, Peggy smiled at him, if very shakily. "I believe you mean that. And I believe you know it personally. Not just your work."

He said softly, "My wife and unborn child. Drunk driver."

"Oh, no. How awful. Why is there so much hurt in this world?"

"That's a mystery I've never solved," Marek returned. "We'll let you know if we learn anything. If you have any questions..."

"Hunter. His..." Trent couldn't finish.

But Marek knew what he meant. His body. "The medical examiner in Sioux Falls will be in touch." After the autopsy, but he wouldn't say that out loud. "You can go ahead and start making arrangements, if you want, but it will be a few days, most likely."

After Marek slid into the Sub, Karen headed north. It turned out that Hunter lived in staff housing at Flandreau Indian School. The drive was short, but it took longer to get through the gate. They arrived in front of Hunter's place at the same time as a small, older Toyota sedan in sedate silver.

Marek raised his brows as the woman uncurled from the car. She was a hair—a very white-blonde hair—shorter than Karen. "That must be Anita."

Her eyes were shocking red in comparison to her hair and face, but she'd made some attempt at cleaning up her obvious crying jag. She looked from Winona to Two Fingers, then at Karen and, finally, Marek. She seemed bewildered by their presence.

"You've heard, then?" Winona asked the young woman in a more confrontational tone than Marek had yet heard from her. "I didn't tell you. Who did?"

Karen seemed equally puzzled—and suspicious. "Not even the local newshound has tagged me yet."

"Hound? There is a dog?" Now the young woman looked alarmed as well as miserable. "Did a dog get to Sphinx? I promise, I did not let him out."

While she spoke almost impeccable English, she obviously hadn't figured out all the idioms. No one had mentioned that the sometime girlfriend was from overseas. Scandinavian of some sort, to go by accent and looks.

"You know about Hunter." Marek made it a statement,

though he was far from convinced. But if she did know, how?

"Of course I know about Hunter." When that got hard looks, she held out her hands, as if to fend them off. "I work with him. I am his friend. I do not understand. Winona asked me to come with the key, that she was at the Diggeses', and so I am here. Who are you?"

Karen stepped forward. "First, let me ask, why were you crying?"

The young woman stiffened. "That is... personal. Private."

Marek took a stab. "Is Hunter involved?"

Surprise parted her unpainted lips. Her gaze went to his badge. "No." Then she started to sob. "Yes. Yes, yes, yes. I did not mean for it to happen. I did everything right. Will I be deported?"

When Karen took a step forward with her hands on her cuffs, Marek stopped her. "Deported for what?"

"For... for... I don't know. I could lose my job. Americans do not like noncitizens having babies that become citizens."

That rocked back Karen. "You're pregnant?"

Anita nodded like a bobble-head doll.

"By Hunter, I take it." Winona's tone, rather than gentler, became even more biting. "Friends with benefits?"

"Benefits?" Anita wiped at her tears. "I have health insurance." Then another tear leaked. "But it is not the same as in Sweden. If I lose my job... Everything is wrong. And I don't want to keep Hunter from what he wants."

Current tense, not past. She believed him to still be alive.

"And what did he want?" Winona challenged her.

"To get his doctorate and be an archaeologist and teach and travel all over. To bring knowledge back to his tribe. It is the same for me. After one more year of teaching and researching, I am to return to Sweden to finish my degree in musicology and eventually to teach in university and spend the summers recording ethnic music all over the world."

"He loved you," Winona accused.

Anita's face fell at that. "I told Hunter that we could just be friends. I was not going to stay in America. I did not want to hurt him. I did not know he loved me. I am very... fond... of him. But now... now I am pregnant. I did not want this. I *do* not want this."

Winona looked like an avenging angel. "So you'll get rid of the dirty little Indian baby and go back to your whitewashed life."

"Dirty?" Anita clutched at her stomach. "How can it be dirty?"

Winona made a strangled sound and turned on her heel. She stalked away, as if to prevent herself from strangling the young woman.

Now Anita looked insulted. "Why is she so angry? She is not pregnant. *I* am."

Two Fingers, completely silent during the exchange, answered after a beat of silence. "You just hit one of her major flash points."

Looking between the two women, one quickly disappearing into a wooded area, Karen looked torn, and Marek thought he knew why. She'd faced a similar dilemma, what with being committed to the Army and finding out she was unexpectedly pregnant. "When did you find out?"

Anita hiccupped. "I am on contraception. I thought I just was sick. But I was sick every morning for a week. I went to the store and got a test. I took it before Winona called. I was happy she called. We are both interested in ethnomusicology." Her unhappy gaze followed the rapidly disappearing woman. "We were friends. Before I hurt Hunter."

Marek decided it was time to break the news. "You asked who we were." He introduced himself and Karen. She apparently already knew Two Fingers. "We represent Eda County, which is where the dig Hunter was on is located. I'm sorry, but Hunter is dead."

"Dead? How could that be?" She looked truly horrified, her hands flying to her mouth. "Was it... an accident? He drives too fast. But no, 'It is the speed limit,' he says. I do not drive that fast. It is faster than anywhere in my country. He calls me a slowpoke."

"It wasn't an accident," Karen said shortly. "Do you know if he had any enemies?"

"Enemies?" She made it sound like a foreign word. And perhaps it was to her.

Marek clarified. "Someone who would want to kill him."

Her red-rimmed eyes popped wide. "Kill him? He was a good person. The superintendent, he had some differences of opinion with, but not to kill. The kids, they tease him, because he is so short, but they also like him. Most of them. A few boys are not so nice."

Her tone conveyed that they also weren't so nice to her.

Then her hands went back to her mouth. "Oh, his parents. They were so nice to me."

Before she descended into tears again, Marek intervened. "We need the key to his place. The Diggeses gave us permission."

"Oh. Yes. I have it." As if relieved that, finally, there was something she could do, she slung a small beaded purse on a long leather thong in front of her from the back and rummaged around. She took out a key and went to the door. Her lips crumpled as she opened it, and a cat... meowed? It sounded more like a mini-foghorn. "Oh, Sphinx. What will happen to him? I cannot take him. I mean, I am happy to take care of him. Here. But I cannot have pets. I will leave in another year."

Karen told her, "It will sort itself out. I would keep feeding him for as long—" She hissed as a gigantic sand-colored cat with a torn left ear shot out and over her foot.

"Get him!" Anita cried.

Two Fingers came to the rescue, scooping up the pudge of a cat before he could make his escape. He did not, however, seem upset. He head-butted Two Fingers, who walked through the open door and deposited the cat on top of a cat tree, where Sphinx settled and stared unblinkingly at the intruders.

Marek noted that Karen gave the cat a wide berth. His lips twitched.

Anita stood in the living room, clutching her hands, looking helpless. At least there were no new tears.

Until Winona stalked back in. That drew twin but silent tears down the pale face.

Winona held up her hands. "First, I'm sorry. I embarrassed my son and myself. The Dakota do not wear their emotions on their sleeves—if I had any." She looked down at her bared arms. "For the Dakota, the more emotions, the more silence."

So Marek and many of Karen's fellow Dakotans followed that Indian path as well? Interesting.

Winona grimaced. "Obviously, I rebelled. Silence covers too many wrongs. But I have reason to be angry, and I'm still mad—at you." She pointed at Anita. "You tripped every single one of my triggers on top of what happened to Hunter."

Anita didn't say a word, just let more tears fall.

Winona took a deep breath then released it. "My mother was a student teacher at the Indian School. Young, naive, idealistic. From the Twin Cities. White, upper-class, come to save us Indians from ourselves." She let out a breath. "She had a fling with a student. My father was a strikingly handsome boy, and I'm the result. I'll give her that she stuck it out initially. Until her upper-crust mother got wind of the secret life her daughter had been leading, diddling with an Indian, playing house with an Indian, and that was that. My mother dumped me on my seventeen-year-old father, who couldn't handle me or her rejection and killed himself. So I ended up with Unci. She was fifty years old and thought her childrearing days were over. They weren't, by a long shot. First for me. Then, I regret to say, for my son, when he was young. I'm not proud of that. I've made mistakes. I had to do some growing up. And none of it was my choice. I'm so tired of whites stealing from us. Lives, land, children, music, whatever."

Anita's tears stopped. "I am saving your music, not stealing it!"

"Don't push my buttons, Anita. It's not what you do. It's those who will use what you gather. It's like taking hymns meant for worship and selling them for profit." Then she seemed to lose some of her edge. "Look, I've been where you are, pregnant and wondering what to do next. Have you talked to your parents?"

Her lips trembled. "My parents were killed in a car accident when I was twenty-one. That's why I came to America, to get away, to keep busy. I have only an uncle who is a professor of biology and unmarried."

"I forget how many wounds this world inflicts." Winona blew out a breath. "I'm going to take you over to the Diggeses. We can discuss this like adults."

Winona put her arm around the much taller Anita. But she looked at Two Fingers. "I promise I won't kill her on the way. You do what you do for Hunter. He deserves your best."

Her son stood as stiff and still as a toy soldier. "He'll get it."

"I know, son. I know." She placed her free hand over his heart. "And I know your heart is breaking like mine."

And Marek finally saw the haunted look in her dark eyes, naked and stark, that made mother and son a matched pair.

CHAPTER 6

Karen had expected Hunter Redwing-Digges's two-bedroom home to be a typical bachelor pad—strewn with takeout and a beer-stained comfy couch along with whatever mismatched furniture could be scrounged from family, friends, and the local dump. Instead, it was filled with art—perhaps not a surprise—mostly of Native origin.

A pictorial of his short life was lined up along one wall: as a boy at the wacipi, dipping and dancing as his mother had described—one obviously out in West River on a lonely plain with what must be his Standing Rock family; one of a dirty but beaming Hunter holding a geometric-decorated pot at some dig; another at his graduation from USD with beaming parents on either side; and finally, one that must have been of several teachers at the school seated while Hunter stood in the middle.

The natural wood and light-gray furniture in Hunter's home was spare, modern, and neat. The place was nearly immaculate, except for the cat's overturned and empty food and water bowls in the kitchen. Sphinx deigned to allow Two Fingers the privilege of filling them. Karen had no doubt she would have been raked from head to toe if she tried.

She didn't really dislike cats. Cats seemed to dislike her. Or at least pretend they did. But this one was like a brooding ancient spirit in a cat's body. As if reading her mind, the cat's head swiveled her way, and unblinking yellow eyes had her turning away.

Unlike the cat, she had a job to do. She pulled on her latex gloves and moved into the first of the two bedrooms with Marek. The bed was actually made, though since he had Anita coming in to take care of the cat and he was gone, perhaps that was why. Or maybe he was just a neat freak. While Karen knew she had the reputation for being a ship-shape boss because of her time in the Army, she often didn't bother to make her bed. That, she abruptly realized, might have to change now that she was married.

She and Larson still hadn't figured out just how their two-household marriage was going to work. Sort of like friends with benefits. Her daughter was already making noises about moving out, if not out of the house, out of the master bedroom on the first floor.

But Karen liked her second-story room under the eaves, where she could look out across the street and from the other window, off the bluff. The master bedroom looked out either toward town or back at the neglected orchard where her grandmother had fallen and died. Not a happy sight.

Karen looked down at the nightstand, where a small ceramic bowl held ashes of some sort. Did Hunter smoke? If so, it didn't look like standard cigarettes. She pulled out the nightstand drawer and found matches and a large Ziploc bag filled with some kind of plant material. Not marijuana, though she knew the tribe sold medical marijuana, the only kind allowed in South Dakota at the moment. She held it up. "Any idea what this is?"

"Sage?" Marek hazarded.

She opened it and sniffed. "Don't think so. Or not just. I think I smell cedar, for one."

From the doorway, Two Fingers said, "Probably a mix of cedar, tobacco, sage, and sweetgrass. Though he may have a different mix, depending on his tradition and need. It's for smudging."

Karen blinked at him. "What, like New Agers waving sage sticks around a room to remove the bad vibes?"

Two Fingers gave her a bland look. "Where do you think they stole the idea from? It's far more than that to us. It's a lifestyle, a part of who we are, and how we deal with the world. And we don't usually use those trendy tourist sticks, which are starting to deplete our Indigenous supply." He looked troubled. "In my experience, outside of ceremonial gatherings and the like, Hunter only smudged when he was upset."

Did Two Fingers smudge? And if so, when and why? Barely, she kept her questions to herself. She had slightly more control over her tongue than Walrus. There was so much she didn't know about Two Fingers or his life. He was a good deputy, a good man, and certainly the most educated of her roster, barring Deputy Seoul Durr, who was currently en route to Reunion from visiting her parents in Iowa. Why, she wondered, hadn't Two Fingers taken the job here in Flandreau to be closer to his family, his people? She imagined it had to be his ideal job.

Was it because of Seoul? Karen had gotten the impression recently that there was something going on between her two deputies, but she had nothing to confirm it.

Marek picked up the smudge bowl. "It's still fragrant. Any idea when he was last here?"

Two Fingers shook his head. "I saw him last Saturday at my place when he took a break from the dig. One of their regular Saturday free days. Hunter said they did that to give everybody a break. In some digs, Hunter said, they were more remote, so they never got away from each other for weeks, even months, on end."

"Sounds like a recipe for murder." Karen moved over to the other bedroom—and decided that this was where, other than sleeping, Hunter Redwing-Digges lived. It was comfortably messy, with a large desk as the centerpiece. Strewn across it were papers scribbled with what looked like a combination of simplistic drawings—not quite stick figures—and Indian and English words. Bookcases lined the walls with titles like *Black Elk Speaks, The Soul of the Indian, Archaeology of the North American Great Plains,* and *Battlefields and Burial Grounds: The Indian Struggle to Protect Ancestral Graves in the United States.*

Marek asked, "Do you know what differences Hunter had with his superintendent?"

The dark eyes tracked from one of the drawings on the desk to Marek. "One of them, at least. He wanted to use ground-penetrating radar to search for unmarked graves."

Karen frowned as she tried to understand the various papers on the desk. "Where? In your tribal cemetery?" Did they even have cemeteries? She had no idea. Somehow, she had this idea that they put bodies on scaffolds. But maybe that was West River. Or from wildly inaccurate old westerns.

"Near the school."

Karen considered a legal pad with a torn-off corner. It looked like a grocery list. "Why would the school have a cemetery?"

Surprisingly, Marek answered. "Because a lot of Native children died at boarding schools. No one knows how many because most were buried in unmarked graves. The records are sketchy, at best." He shrugged at an equally surprised Two Fingers. "It was on NPR recently."

And what her dyslexic detective heard on the radio, he remembered. Karen frowned. "So why would the superintendent have a problem with that?"

Two Fingers shook his head. "Ask Dana Todacheeny Ellis. She lives at the school. She can answer all your questions about any conflicts with or within the school."

Karen nodded and went back to her search. But other than Hunter's work, both at the school and at the dig, she didn't see anything that added up to murder.

Stretching, she turned to look at the far wall. A big

blowup poster-sized piece of art was tacked to it, with lots of little pictures in a circle. Art?

Except he'd been writing on it. Or someone had. In fact, now that she got closer, she recognized the basic style as similar to those he'd drawn on the papers on his desk. "What's this?"

Two Fingers looked up from a book that had been sitting on the corner of the desk: *Traditional Narratives of the Arikara Indians*. "Winter count. A history of a *tiospaye*." Before she could ask, he explained, though with a pained expression, as if it were not a good translation. "A community. Small or large. Extended kin, in some cases. Every winter, they'd pick the most significant event of the past year and create a picture for it. Hunter found that one tucked away at a museum a few years ago, and he's been working on deciphering it. He wants... wanted... to do his dissertation on it, though his dissertation prof wasn't buying it. At least not initially."

Karen blew out a breath. She had nothing to go on, and that irritated her. So she continued to look at the winter count. "It's pretty."

Two Fingers's dark eyes lidded. "It's history. Just whose, Hunter didn't know. Probably Sioux. Lakota maybe. We've lost a lot."

Marek came over to look at the winter count tacked on the wall. "I wonder if I'd have done better in school where everything was a picture. What's this one with all the stars?"

Karen looked closer. "He's written 'Stars Fell.' And '1833.'"

"That's pretty standard across all winter counts, from what Hunter told me," Two Fingers said. "It also dates it to the Leonid meteor shower of 1833, so they can match it up. Kind of the Rosetta stone of winter counts, which is why I remembered it."

The Year the Stars Fell sounded a lot more meaningful than 1833. What would she, or her family or community, have picked for the last year? It had been a hell of a year for her personally, but the community? How could they pick just one?

Maybe a drawing of an election box. Her loss, and subsequent recount as a win, had rocked the community in ways that would have left lasting impacts if it had gone the other way. The man elected on first blush, incidentally the stepson of Two Fingers's rapist father, would have corrupted everything he touched.

Karen's phone rang. Pulling it out, she gritted her teeth. And there was the man who'd almost lost her the election: Rusty "Nails" Nelson of the radio station YRUN. Though to be fair, he'd just been caught up in a game of media one-upmanship with a big-name outlet from the Twin Cities.

He'd even apologized. On air. And directly to her. Multiple times.

She'd grudgingly forgiven him, but not forgotten, and she tended to be far more Dakotan with him than previously. She gave him the silent treatment.

He waited a beat then launched. "Sheriff Mehaffey, I hear you're in Flandreau. And that you left a body at Spirit Mound in the care of our county coroner. Care to comment?"

As she heard the click, she knew she was being recorded. Out went the stars. In went her communications training. "Early this morning, a tourist found the body of a man at the top of Spirit Mound. The medical examiner will make the final determination as to cause. We have identified him and just notified his family." She stared at one of the figures on the winter count with obvious wounds. They would never heal. Not completely. Human nature was human nature, whatever the culture. "His name was Hunter Redwing-Digges. He was a social studies teacher at Flandreau Indian School and working toward his doctorate at USD with the goal of becoming an archaeologist."

A pause. "Was he an Indian?"

What a complicated question. "He was an enrolled member at Standing Rock."

"Does this have to do with the protest at the dig?"

A protest meant poster boards. She suddenly itched to get to the autopsy. Was it going to be that easy? Maybe she'd get to the Caribbean after all. "It's too early in the process to narrow our focus. We are investigating all angles."

The click told her that she was now off record. Without prompting, Nails offered, "From what I hear, it was a group of students from USD. Nothing violent."

That's what they all said. Though it was the first time she'd heard of the protest, which meant the violence part was true. Up until now, at least. Time to go to school.

But first, a visit to the one here in Flandreau.

CHAPTER 7

They found Dana Todacheeny Ellis standing like a squat brown boulder in the midst of a swirling mass of teens in the middle of the commons area of the school campus. It didn't take a detective to figure that they were about to head off to the wacipi.

Marek couldn't make out a common theme in their brightly colored outfits. Some had bone jewelry, some had shawls, and some had metal sewn onto skirts. A few of the boys wore black T-shirts with Native Lives Matter or NDN Country on the back with an American flag. Shoes were sandals, moccasins, Nikes, or anything in between. Perhaps some were going to participate and others simply watch or mingle.

It wasn't a large group, but it was boisterous.

As Two Fingers passed, a whiplash of a boy in black muttered, "*Iyeska*. Go back to the *wasicus*, where you belong."

Marek had no idea what the first word meant, but it was obviously an insult. As for *wasicu*, even Marek knew that one. White.

A willowy girl in one of the more elaborate dresses whirled, her skirts billowing under her ribboned shawl, and she smacked the boy on the arm. Hard. "Shut up, Dano. My brother's more Indian than you are. He was raised right."

So this was one of Two Fingers's half-sisters. She was a

striking—in more ways than one—young woman with hair not that different than Marek's own, dark but with the deep-red tint and brilliant in the sun. And her skin was several shades lighter than her brother's, despite presumably having more Native blood. And she'd obviously inherited her mother's retiring personality. Not.

"Jaydyn, that's enough. Physical violence will not be tolerated. Daniel, I will be talking to you after the wacipi. Privately." The superintendent's tone said, *Again.*

Another girl, younger than Jaydyn, simply went to Two Fingers and hugged him. Like Two Fingers, her hair was black, her gaze almost so, but her face lacked his high cheekbones. Like her sister, she was also lighter skinned.

Interesting that Two Fingers's sisters both looked whiter than he did. Obviously, blood quantum did not equate with genetics.

"Sticks and stones, Shania," her brother told her. "Ignore him. He acts like he has no family."

The boy hissed and took a step forward. The squat superintendent, with surprising speed and strength, grabbed his arm. "Daniel, stop proving his point. He is your elder and has done nothing to earn your disrespect."

"I just told the truth. Iyeska means, 'They speak the white.' Mr. Wannabe told us that."

"As you are also speaking 'the white,' that makes you Iyeska as well. And that's Mr. Redwing-Digges to you. An enrolled member, I'll remind you. He also told you that term is demeaning and, as you well know, is used to mean mixed blood. Many of us have some European ancestry, whether Hispanic or white."

"Not me. I'm a one-hundred-percent certified purebred." He patted his back pocket, where he presumably carried some kind of ID card.

"Card-carrying bigot," someone in the crowd called out.

The superintendent clapped her hands. To Marek's surprise, everyone quieted. "This is a sacred day. Do not shame the community." She beckoned toward a tall, extremely white man with an Adam's apple that bobbed in response to her summons. "Please take the students to the bus for the wacipi. I will follow."

With trepidation, the man began herding teens down a sidewalk that led to a school bus. They went about as well as cats were wont to do. Not well.

After saying something to her in their own language, Two Fingers released his sister. Shania gave him a shy smile and went to join her classmates.

Karen asked, "Isn't school out for the summer?"

"For many of our students, yes. Especially those from Flandreau. Some are simply joining us today if their family is unavailable to take them or if they want to go with their friends. But we have some full-year students. This *is* a boarding school."

Marek looked down at her. "So it's not just Flandreau kids?"

"No, Flandreau Indian School is one of four off-reservation boarding schools still in operation across the country. We have over forty tribes represented."

Marek smiled faintly. "Including Navajo, like yourself?"

Her lips parted, then she nodded. "Diné. How did you know?"

"Your maiden name. It means Bitter Water Clan, right?"

Her rounded face beamed up at him. "You know something of my people."

"Not much. I just spent many years in Albuquerque. I was just surprised to hear the name Todacheeny, since I thought this was a Flandreau Reservation school."

"It's not on the reservation, which is just north of here. Flandreau Reservation is absolutely tiny, not much more than two thousand acres, compared to over twenty-seven thousand square *miles* of my homeland."

A Native man with a buzz cut walked up to them. Marek noted that he had no visible signs of his affiliation, simply a white polo shirt and khaki shorts. "To compare apples and oranges, or acres and miles, Flandreau is 2,356 acres and... 3.68 square miles. A drop in the bucket."

"Armon Ladeaux, our math teacher."

He nodded at the introduction, and his gaze lingered on the three of them, notably on their county badges. "I was just coming to inform Superintendent Ellis of the sad news."

"Sad news?" She turned her eyes from her math teacher to the three of them. "Has one of our students gotten in trouble in your county?"

"It's not one of your students." Karen stepped forward into the awkward gap. "It's one of your teachers. Hunter Redwing-Digges."

The superintendent gasped. "Hunter? He wouldn't hurt a fly."

"He couldn't hurt a fly—it would win. Flyweight." Ladeaux put his hands to his temples before dropping them. "Sorry. That was inappropriate under the circumstances. Dana, he's dead. He was killed. Chief Goodthunder just called the office."

The superintendent's face fell. "Killed? A car accident? Or on the dig?"

A short pause. "Murdered, that's what the chief said."

Marek knew bad news traveled fast, but that was at light speed. Then again, when a city council member's son was killed, that gave it some juice.

Karen stuck her thumbs in her belt. "The medical examiner has not yet ruled on the cause of death. Until then, we can only investigate it as a suspicious death."

Ladeaux snorted. "Doublespeak."

The superintendent finally seemed to find her tongue. "Who on earth would kill such a harmless man as Hunter? It makes no sense."

"You had your run-ins with him," Ladeaux said. "As did I."

"They were understandable differences. We all want the best for our people."

Ladeaux shook his head. "Looking forward is the only way, not looking back. Anyway, I was in the office to call Anita. She was supposed to be out here helping with the kids."

Karen said, "She's with the Diggeses."

"Oh, I see. I didn't realize they were still... friendly." Shaking herself mentally and physically, the superintendent said, "Armon, I'm sorry, but I'll need you to help out Durwood. He won't be able to keep the kids in line himself."

"On that, we agree." He strode down the sidewalk.

"Let's go to my office. I need to get out of the sun and sit."

The superintendent led them to her office, where Marek was stopped in the entry by a picture of a very large, multistory stone building. Likely made of quartzite, and like many built in the late nineteenth century, it was of the same Richardsonian Romanesque style as the Eda County courthouse.

Noting his interest, the superintendent said, "That was the original school building from 1892."

Marek tried to think how a people close to the earth, to nature, would take to being cooped up there. "Imposing."

She smiled a bit wryly, as if reading his thoughts, then sobered as they all sat. "This is such terribly distressing news. Hunter had a way with the kids, despite the occasional teasing, and I think it was because he'd been through so much. Almost every imaginable situation—adoption, rejection, enrollment, homelessness, poverty, attempted suicide—he'd been through it all. And being the child of an addict, he could speak to that as well. He wasn't even thirty yet."

Karen said, "I take it that Daniel was one of the boys who gave him a hard time."

The superintendent sighed. "Daniel is the son of a tribal councilman and casino operator out west. A man far too busy and important to spend time with a boy of a failed marriage, hence year-round boarding school. Despite his blood quantum, you were right, Deputy Two Fingers. He acts like he doesn't have family. Because he doesn't. His mother left him for a wealthy German industrialist when he was six. You know, the kind enamored of all things American Indian. Not to be outdone, his father married an Italian woman with supposed ties to the nobility, and they have five apparently gorgeous children, none of whom were sent to boarding school. About all Daniel has to hold on to is his blood quantum to differentiate him from his siblings. What he hasn't learned, what we try to teach him, is that being Native is about responsibility. To his people. However, as I am part Hispanic, he doesn't listen to me. Not to mention, I am a woman."

Two Fingers shifted uncomfortably in his swivel chair. "Then I am sorry for him."

Marek asked, "What about the teachers and staff? What were the conflicts there, Superintendent?"

"Please, just Dana." She sat back and considered. "I can tell you that Hunter and I were at odds about looking for unmarked graves here at the school." Seeing their nods of understanding, she relaxed. "As this is a still-operating school, I am sworn to protect my students from such an undertaking. It would no doubt be traumatic for them. I am actually very much in favor of finding our lost children and bringing them home. Like at the infamous Carlisle Indian School in Pennsylvania. General Richard Pratt, who participated in the Indian wars, established the school to 'Kill the Indian... save the man.' It was cultural genocide. Everything that made us who we were was crushed mercilessly."

Dana stopped abruptly. "You think that's extreme. But let me ask you, what if we had been the winners, you the losers? Forced off the lands you owned because it belonged to Mother Earth, not any individual person. Instead of farming, you were given bows and arrows and horses, not plows and oxen, and forced to roam the plains to hunt bison, to learn to make tipis instead of cabins and survive the winters. Forced to wear your hair long, beaten and abused whenever you spoke English, or worse, when you prayed to your god or tried to quote your bible. Rather than learn arithmetic or writing and reading, you were forced to learn by ear, by oral tradition, with only a few mnemonic devices to help you. And you were only a child, confused, scared, and away from all your family, all you ever knew. Just what would you call that?"

"Cultural genocide." Karen tilted her head. "I'd never thought about it that way."

Nor had Marek. He'd had no easy time of school, given his dyslexia. But take him away from his parents, especially his ever-supportive father, and he might have become the mean drunk his grandfather Marek had been. Add stripping everything that made him who he was? Yeah, that was murder.

Dana folded her hands on her desk. "I learned long ago that, to have any hope of understanding another culture, you have to have a reference to do so. If you try to tell non-Natives just how horrific it all was, they just say, well, they themselves got beaten in school for talking back to the teacher or were forced to learn things, like algebra, that they would never use. Or Shakespeare when they couldn't understand every other word. But it was far, far more than that. There was, sadly, also much abuse of both boys and girls sexually. And yes, that also happened in white boarding schools. A large number of Native students died and were buried at these schools, often without their families' knowledge or notification. Some just disappeared."

Dana looked at Two Fingers. "My nation, the Diné, were not as impacted as yours. The Sioux Nations, all of them, even those not involved, were punished severely for the Dakota War."

There it was again. Marek let his curiosity lead. "Dakota War?"

"Sometimes in your world, it's called the Sioux Uprising." When that got no traction with him or Karen, the superintendent looked a bit surprised—and sad. "Well, I suppose Minnesota students might be more familiar than South Dakota ones, but I'm still surprised you aren't aware of it. Of course, many whites here in East River still think we go daily in feathers and loincloths and ride horses to and from school."

Karen said, "We don't often come in contact with Natives in Eda except through TV. Other than Two Fingers, I don't know that I've known any other Natives outside of a few at USD that I had in classes. And one basketball player I helped mentor from here, Hannah Redbird."

Marek had known some Indians in Albuquerque, but he had to agree—he didn't remember any growing up in Reunion or Valeska. They'd had their own intertribal warfare between the Slavs, Scandinavians, and Germans, each in their own towns.

"You'd be surprised," Dana said. "Many who are white-passing simply don't discuss it. Or you thought they were part Asian or something. But I'll leave the history lesson to those better qualified. Unfortunately, that would have been Hunter, but there are many others. Probably your deputy here. But you are looking for reasons anyone would kill Hunter. I can't imagine anyone here at the school doing any such thing."

Surprisingly, it was Two Fingers who asked, "Ladeaux?"

Dana gave him a wry look. "Hunter and Armon had a very fundamental philosophical difference about how to educate our people. I quickly learned not to pair them for any joint duties, or they'd end up arguing in front of the students. Both are very passionate about the matter. That makes them good teachers but bad colleagues."

Marek didn't have to guess the philosophical difference that ran so deep. "Old versus new."

Surprisingly, Two Fingers chimed in. "For Hunter, it was more like back to the future. You need to know who you are, where you come from, to have a solid foundation. Otherwise, it's too easy to fail once you hit the white world. Different expectations, different rules. You need both. Ladeaux wants us to beat whites at their own game."

For the first time, Marek wondered if Two Fingers had had difficulty, moving off the reservation and Flandreau and living in Reunion. As if hearing that thought, the deputy turned his head. "It was difficult. Sometimes still is."

"I wish you'd told me." Karen blew out a breath. "I guess I just thought, different traditions, no sweat."

That got a laugh out of the superintendent. "More like, for your deputy here, more sweat."

Seeing Karen's confusion, Two Fingers said, "*Inipi*. Sweat lodge."

"You've done that?" Karen asked.

"I have." But he offered nothing more.

Dana leaned forward conspiratorially. "It's like many male rituals. Hush-hush." She straightened. "And no, I am not making fun of you, Inyan. I am aware perhaps more than you are comfortable with of what you went through after Afghanistan. Winona makes for an unusual friend but a loyal and true one."

Marek decided to head things off there before Two Fingers got up and walked out. "We know that Hunter and Anita Asplund were a couple for a while."

Dana sighed. "Yes, not something I encourage, but it happens. Anita is actually a very good teacher and tries to get the kids interested in various kinds of Native music. She doesn't want it lost. But it's probably like trying to interest teens in... I don't know... hymns? Well, unless it's drums. They dig that. But they'd rather listen to the latest rock hit. Of course, if it's Native rock, like Winona's, then all the better."

Marek would have to look that up. It sounded like an interesting combination. But right now, he had a murder to solve. "Anita broke off the relationship with Hunter but remained, at least in her view, a friend. Was there another man?"

Again, Dana sighed. "Only in his own mind. Armon. Anita did not play that game. She genuinely cares—cared—for Hunter. Yes, I think she is overly intrigued with Natives. It's not an unusual thing for Europeans, I understand. Witness Daniel's parents. The thing is, the more Native children are born to white parents, the more we lose."

Her sad gaze fell on Two Fingers. He did not react.

Marek wasn't entirely sure if she meant his mother, his white grandmother, or perhaps—as she apparently knew quite a bit about him—Seoul Durr. And that would mean no hope of his children ever being enrolled.

Marek had never had to consider his wife based on an arbitrary blood quantum. That Val had been Hispanic had, perhaps, intrigued him, but it wasn't what had drawn him to her. She had believed in him, encouraged him, and helped him believe in himself.

Had Winona chosen her husband based on blood quantum, he wondered. Or limited her choices only to those with the right amount? Obviously, her husband was over a quarter Indian, or her daughters would not be attending the school.

Karen started as her phone vibrated. She took it out and read the text. "Dr. White is ready for us."

That made Two Fingers flinch.

Which made Karen flinch. "Not you, Two Fingers. Sheesh. What do you take me for? Marek and I will cover the autopsy. You drive back to Reunion and help out at Spirit Mound. Now that the news is out, we'll have gawkers. And we have a large area to search there."

For the kill site. If it was there. Maybe it was somewhere else entirely. Even here in Flandreau. Though why someone would drive down to Spirit Mound then hike almost a mile from the parking lot with a body—even a light one—on their back was hard to understand.

Maybe it was a cultural thing.

CHAPTER 8

As they drove down Interstate 29 to Sioux Falls, Karen wondered just how many missteps she might have made with Two Fingers. He'd never brought up anything to her, but given his culture, maybe he really couldn't. She knew he faced prejudice—she'd seen it a few times firsthand, like the time she'd backed him up in arresting one of her stumbling-drunk Forsgren relatives. He'd lashed out at Two Fingers about Indians pissing away their free government money on drink. At least he'd had to pay for his. There'd been worse.

But another difficulty had to be just living outside of his community, his comfort zone, and all the things he'd once taken for granted about how life was. She'd gotten a very slight taste of it today. "Did you feel out of place at the Indian school?"

Marek turned from his contemplation of the heat mirages on the highway. Or at least that was what it looked like. At least the Sub's air conditioner was working again. For the moment.

He shrugged. "Not so much. I worked with a lot of Hispanics and some Indians. I was the one who stuck out, so I kind of got used to it."

Karen had met Manny, Marek's former partner at Albuquerque PD. She liked him. He talked a mile a minute. Very much unlike Marek or, for that matter, Two Fingers.

But she'd felt comfortable in Albuquerque, with the blend of cultures—Anglo, Hispanic, and Indian. She stood out because of her height, but so had Marek.

Still, cities were melting pots. Small towns in East River, South Dakota, not so much, where Norwegians and Swedes still kept their own traditions. But eventually, it did all meld together. She was both, as was Marek. She was German, too, and Marek wasn't, but he was also Slav. His daughter Becca added Hispanic and Tewa. Though that was still fairly rare to see. Karen's father's adopted grandson was also Hispanic. And she wondered just how much of little Joey's maternal heritage, which was Guatemalan, he would ever learn while growing up in Reunion.

Then again, had she ever really thought much about her own heritage, other than when it came to food? Beer and brats, lefse, and pickled herring.

Did it make a person, a community, stronger for all the different flavors? She didn't know. It was probably easier to all be one tradition, but better? Was her marriage—one of small-town South Dakota and Chicago projects—better for being so different?

Having kids wasn't on the agenda, if that was even possible, which she doubted. He had his two, and she had her one. Thinking of Eyre, Karen wondered again if life would have been better or worse for her daughter if Karen had given Eyre to her own parents to raise while Karen went off to the Army. Instead, she'd given her daughter up for adoption—unknowingly to her college basketball coach and his wife, who'd since divorced.

Karen's father had said numerous times since finding out about Eyre that it *would* have been better. For a girl such as Eyre, always searching for her identity and her heritage, it might well have been. But that wasn't what had happened.

As much as her father might deny it, though, the loss of his wife while Karen was still in the Army would have greatly impacted his ability to raise her. A busy sheriff for a large county simply couldn't have given Eyre as much as her adopted mother had. Yes, Karen could have come home to take over when her Army commitment was done—and maybe she would have. But again, that didn't happen.

"Do you ever think about Becca's Tewa heritage?" she asked Marek.

"I didn't. Much. Until now. Maybe I should contact her relatives. See if we can go down there again before school starts so Becca doesn't lose touch."

She heard ambivalence. "It's the culture thing, isn't it? She wasn't raised Tewa. Heck, you didn't even know she *was* Tewa until recently. How much can she really pick up in a few visits?"

"I could send her for the summer. When she's older." He paused. "If she wants. Maybe she'll want to go to New York instead."

Marek's artist mother-in-law had let him know in no uncertain terms that a rural backwater was no place to be raising a precocious artist. "Adrienne bugging you again?"

"In her slanted way. If I can get away, I'll take her for a visit. But I'm not sending her."

"Afraid you won't get her back?"

He smiled faintly. "Adrienne would send her back within a week. A month at most. Art comes first for Adrienne and always has."

"True." Karen pulled into the hospital parking lot. "It's all so complicated. I mean, I mostly ignore my German heritage. The Brethren, that is." Her mother had fled the Amish-like community in Eder when justice was ignored. "Different values, different rules. No way would I want to join the Brethren to regain that heritage. I mean, yeah, I'm happy to have Mary Hannah stay with me while she goes to school, and to see my uncle on occasion, but that's it." She thought of her adopted cousin and Marek's, who also had ties to Eder and was now Marek's significant other. "Does Nikki ever visit Eder?"

They walked down the steps to the basement morgue. "She's gone a couple times with Eyre and Mary Hannah. She thinks of it as a living history museum. She likes some of the women and admires their fraktur skills. But mostly, she feels sorry for them, trapped in the past."

Karen pulled open the door to the morgue. "It's a strong pull, your own culture, where you know all the rules without having to think about them. My mother kept them, you know. Not the rules, but the bonnet and dress. In a chest. I think my father was never sure she wouldn't disappear one day."

And she had. By death. Too early. But not as early as Hunter Redwing-Digges, who lay under the white sheet. "Hello, Dr. White."

Other than a red bowtie, the pathologist was dressed all in white, emphasizing the coffee color of his face and hands. "Hello, Eda County. You always bring me such intriguing victims."

That made her blink. "Intriguing? Looked like blunt force trauma to me."

"Ah, yes. Let's get that done. Then we can look at the intriguing part."

He uncovered the pathetically small remains. Without clothes, Hunter's body was even frailer than she'd imagined.

The pathologist looked at Marek. "Detective? While I can handle his weight, it would be helpful if you assist me in turning him over."

Marek stepped forward and did so. Effortlessly.

"I will say," Dr. White said before beginning, "that your victim's death was caused by no small weapon. And given the amount of dirt embedded into the hair and skin of what remains of the back of his head, whatever it was, it was filthy. I'd hazard a large rock, except that there do not appear to be any rough edges. It was something heavy and relatively smooth."

Karen thought about that. "There are some huge boulders

at Spirit Mound and lots of gravel on the trail but nothing around that size. Maybe the kill site really is somewhere else."

Karen waited, her eyes trained just above what was going on, so that she could say she saw it all but peripherally. When it was done, she let out a breath. "Cause of death?"

"Subdural hemorrhage caused by blunt trauma to the cranium. Basically, his skull was shattered. Someone was very, very angry with your victim."

"And came at him from behind," Marek mused. "He wasn't expecting it."

Karen pursed her lips. "Or was running away."

"About to, perhaps." But Marek sounded doubtful. "Running behind someone with a heavy weapon would mean they were in really good shape."

"Or had a lot of adrenaline or were high on some substance," Dr. White offered. "As for Mr. Redwing-Digges, I've sent a vial off for a tox screen. However, I have seen nothing here to suggest he was into drugs. I do, however, see evidence of childhood malnutrition, something I haven't seen since I did a mission trip to the old Congo."

Karen shared a look with Marek before answering. "He was badly neglected early in his life."

Dr. White's dark head tilted. "I spoke to his father. Trent Digges wants to claim the body as soon as possible. He sounded sincerely grieving. In fact, he had a hard time getting his words out."

"Hunter Redwing-Digges was adopted by the Diggeses when he was a toddler."

"Ah, I see. He was Native American, then? I saw the name, but he does not have any of the classic Indigenous American features, and people are wont to adopt names that take their fancy. But it may explain the intriguing part of your victim."

The pathologist turned to pick up something on the counter. "This, however, may help you pin your killer. He left a calling card, if you will. I don't often—in fact never—have occasion to consult the Lakota language."

Karen stared at his back. "Excuse me?"

He turned and held up a poster board toward them. WAMANUS A.

"I believe it's pronounced *wah-mah-nues ah*. I looked it up. Though I didn't really have to. Not for the meaning, that is." He turned the poster around, and it said, THIEF.

Bilingual killer.

CHAPTER 9

By the time Karen and Marek got back to Spirit Mound after grabbing takeout in Sioux Falls, TV crews had set up in the parking lot where Kurt was keeping them penned. Or he had been. With a remarkable amount of energy given the heat and humidity of the long day, the newshounds quickly surrounded the Sub, baying their questions.

"Back off," Karen told them as she got out, and remarkably, they did. Then again, Dakotans were generally a ruly bunch. It didn't hurt to have Marek as her giant shadow—even more so as the sun's shadows slanted. The reporters raised their microphones at the ready, as if to ward off the darkness that enveloped them. "I will give you a statement shortly, but I need to talk to my men first."

And one woman. Her youngest and newest deputy at twenty-two had returned to the fold. The five-foot-nothing Seoul Durr, German-Korean to her little toes, was looking, not at Karen, but at Two Fingers. Rather oddly. As if she were trying to figure out the answer to some puzzle there.

Karen went to Larson—her *husband*, she reminded herself—first. Knowing the camera crews were recording, she didn't get personal. Nor did he seem to expect it. Should he? Should she? She shook her head. "You haven't found the kill site."

His bullet-gray eyes glared straight into her fjord-blue ones. "Don't assume."

Marriage hadn't lowered his crime scene standards. "You did?"

"Near one of the tents. No, don't look. Just found it."

And he wanted to keep it under wraps until the news crews left for greener pastures. Though this might be as green as it got in August in the Dakotas.

Well, that let out the possibility of a Flandreau kill site. She'd spent much of the day on the wrong path. "So we're stuck here. My case."

"'Fraid so."

"Weapon?" Marek asked. "Dr. White said it was like a rock but fairly smooth. Dirty."

Larson pursed his lips but shook his head.

Karen moved over to Walrus. "Have any protesters shown up?"

His bushy brows rose. "Protesting what? Death by little devils?"

"The dig," she said shortly. "Guess not."

He leaned closer. "You got a lead?"

"Maybe." Don't assume, she told herself. "When are they supposed to begin the dig again?"

"Tomorrow at daybreak. They drive the students up from Vermillion, where they're staying at one of the dorms. A baker's dozen of them. Want me to head them off?"

Karen thought about that. She watched as Larson went to stand nonchalantly just under the canopy of the farthest tent as if to keep the sun at bay. He was shorthanded today, as his sidekicks Jessica and Blue were pulling overtime on a double-homicide in Mitchell. Still, once she gave her statement, Larson could probably finish processing the site before sundown.

She made her decision. "We have a better bet at getting them all together and interviewing them onsite than trying to track down a bunch of students on a Saturday night. The head digger or whatever will know. And let me know when you've got some names for the protesters."

Walrus nodded amiably and got out his phone. "Hey, Doll, got an update."

"Doll?" Karen asked ominously.

He lowered his phone. "That's her last name. And what everyone calls her." Then he turned away stiffly, as though offended Karen would think he was being an asshole. He was often clueless, but not that much. She'd apologize later.

Right now, she had to face the hounds. Punishment enough. Wishing she had her podium instead of being surrounded by a host of bayonetted microphones, she cleared her throat. The sun was starting to hit her and she squinted, wishing she'd picked a different spot. She probably looked redder than any Indian. When had *red* as a racial term dropped from the language, she wondered. That was one she hadn't heard in a long time, other than the Washington Redskins, who had finally gotten around to changing their name to the Commanders.

Karen ran the case through for the media, with the bare facts, minus the poster board. "The medical examiner in Sioux Falls, whose office we have just returned from, has confirmed it was homicide. We are pursuing all avenues." Blah, blah, blah. She hated the empty phrases, but the media needed words to fill the airwaves.

Her Uncle Sig's son Blake stepped forward. She'd been ignoring him—and wished that she'd never supported his desire to become a reporter. When it came to the job, they were on opposite sides, as it were. Technically, she used the news outlets, and they used her. Tit for tat. But lots of times, she got tattooed with not-so-friendly fire.

"I heard that your Native American deputy was a good friend of the victim and ID'd him."

Blake's cameraman—or woman—panned toward Two Fingers standing straight and still at the trailhead to prevent anyone from compromising the scene.

"Yes, Deputy Two Fingers identified Mr. Redwing-Digges. They were classmates and friends at Flandreau High School. Public, not Indian," she added, as she could almost see the next question form. "As I was there when he first saw the body, I can assure you that he is as eager as the rest of us to find the killer. But I'm sure that you will respect his privacy during this time."

As if. But that might prevent them from trying to get a quote from him tonight. At least not while she was here. Blake had gotten into hot water on her last case, letting out sensitive information from the investigation. She hoped he'd learned his lesson.

"Is this a hate crime?" the grizzled reporter from Sioux Falls asked.

"Certainly someone hated Mr. Redwing-Digges enough to kill him, but if it was because of his Native ancestry, I couldn't say. Not at this time."

Blake barged back in. "What about the Native American Studies students at USD who were protesting the dig? Have you interviewed them yet?"

Way to tip said protesters that they were under the gun. Fortunately, she had put on her sunglasses, so he couldn't see her killing gaze. That wouldn't look good on camera. Killing reporters, not to mention relatives, wasn't a good career move. "We will be interviewing any and all persons who may have been at the dig or at Spirit Mound on Friday, including the archaeologists and, yes, any protesters."

At least the segment wouldn't air until ten o'clock. She hoped Walrus got some names for her before they had a chance to cover or flee. "Anyone who has any information related to this homicide can call the Eda County Sheriff's Office."

Blake had one last question. "Is it true that a descendant of William Clark of the famed Lewis and Clark Expedition found the body? Is she a suspect?"

That brought some excited buzz from the others. She

didn't blame them. That would make for national headlines. She dashed Blake's hopes. He really was too good for this market—and for her own good. She couldn't wait until someone else picked him up after he graduated. Like, say, Chicago, Los Angeles, or Boston. Anywhere but her turf. "Not a descendant, no. A however-many-times great-niece. And she has been cleared and moved on. Which I need to do."

Karen walked away, even if she did get hit by a couple microphones that weren't withdrawn fast enough. Counting coup by striking the enemy?

Walrus was waiting for her beyond the crime scene tape that Kurt had finally been able to string up using construction cones nabbed off a stalled highway project.

"First, I apologize about the Doll thing," she told him. "I know you better than that. But you calling a grown woman 'doll' took me off guard."

"Yeah, me too," he said easily. "But that's what she said. Dr. Abigail Doll is her full name, but she said she gave in to the inevitable a long time ago. Just never call her Dolly."

"Good to know." Karen glanced back at the parking lot and saw the TV crews were loading up. But Blake, dammit, was still hanging around. "Any names?"

"Yeah, I got an earful about one in particular. Not a student. His name is Tonto—I am *not* kidding. You know, the Lone Ranger's Indian sidekick from that old western. Geez. Last name is Hawks. He travels around the country, protesting whatever the latest outrage is."

Not a crime. But what kind of Native mother would call her kid Tonto? Off-rez, perhaps, as a joke. But why keep it? Perhaps he, too, had given in to the inevitable. "Does Doll have any idea where I might find him?"

Sadly, Walrus shook his bald head. "Tonto only appears with the protesters, so maybe he's staying with one of them. She's heard rumblings that several wanted nothing to do with him. She wasn't all that down on the students, actually. Said they were sincere if, in her view, misguided."

"Any names?"

"Sorry. She did say Hunter knew several of the protesters and one in particular, a grad student. But since she's not from USD, she doesn't know them."

That was a bit odd. "She's the field director?"

"Co-director. She's from the University of Colorado at Boulder. The USD prof on the dig is Dr. Alden Hardy. She said not to call him anything but Dr. Hardy. Even she doesn't call him Alden. He's giving a talk later tonight in Vermillion to discuss some of the finds. She'll be there to lend support."

So much for that angle. "What about the Native American Studies profs?"

"Apparently, major turnover there with the latest director of the program leaving. But Doll didn't know specifics. Only that they've sort of made do with a mishmash of one-course adjuncts. Apparently, Tonto Hawks has applied to run the program."

Karen rubbed her temples. Not going well at all. "Someone has to know these students. The archaeology students probably know them."

"Not necessarily. This is a field school, Doll said. People come from all over the country, sometimes the globe, to learn how to do a dig."

"Great. So what you're telling me is that I'm not likely to run any of them down tonight. That I should wait until morning."

"Daybreak," he said cheerfully.

"That would be about six in the morning." She smiled back just as cheerfully. "We'll want all hands on deck for interviews. That means you and Kurt, too. Incident meeting at five."

His face fell. "Geez."

Karen glanced surreptitiously at the parking lot. Darn.

Blake had apparently convinced his crew that something was afoot, and they were still waiting to see what it was.

Well, he wasn't going to see anything. She'd wait him out. But she couldn't do it standing still. That was too much for the limits of her impatience. She decided to stretch her legs.

Karen glanced at the sky, where the panorama changed, day by day, hour by hour, minute by minute. To a native Dakotan, the sky was where the action was, not the land. A veritable herd of small clouds—she didn't know the name—arrowed up off the mound. The brome grass bent and twisted in patches, as if the wind were playing hide-and-seek.

She was glad that this place was now public property, where she could roam at will. Unlike when Karen and her best friend, Laura Connor, had been run off what they'd assumed was the same back in Reunion. Like tonight, it had been a beautiful summer evening in August, not long before the school year began. Laura had been away that summer, working at Wall Drug, and they'd gone hand in hand on a walk together along the bluff.

A good mile later, they'd edged Elmer Forsgren's buzzcut lawn and made their way through the wild grass down the bluff to sit together on a big boulder—one of the glacial erratics that hadn't been moved to plow. Talking, talking, barely stemming a babel of summer discoveries, they'd eventually run out of words. Pulling a piece of grass, stripping it down to the edible green and chewing it, they'd watched the clouds above. Then they'd watched the sun mine diamonds out of the river below, shimmering and dancing. Not unlike a natural version of the Grand Entry, Karen thought now.

Then they'd talked some more: the future, their dreams, all shimmering and bright.

When they'd talked themselves out, Karen and Laura started to return to Okerlund Road, again carefully skirting the lawn, when Elmer Forsgren had stalked over and read them the riot act. *Personal property. Rights. Respect. Asking permission.* They'd honestly not known, or even suspected, that it was personal property. That was the lawn, the fields, in their minds. The bluffs? Kids ran wild over them during the summer and on toboggans in the winter. At least at her place and Marek's.

They'd never wandered that way again. And she'd felt just aninkling of what it was like to lose what had once belonged to all, to one. *Mine, mine, mine.* That's what she'd heard from Elmer Forsgren. Just who was more free? The Indians who'd roamed free or them, with their individual plots of land they guarded so jealously?

Whatever the case, their joyous reunion had been destroyed that afternoon. Her father had pointed out that at least Elmer had held off blasting them until they'd finished their jawing. Others of their Forsgren relations wouldn't have let them so much as sit down before they'd have tanned those behinds. Even at sixteen.

Well, no one was going to blast her here. Or tan her hide. Karen glanced over at the parking lot and saw Blake being dragged into the TV van by his associates. His frustrated face was plastered to the window as the van left. Life as an intern.

As soon as the van was no longer in visual distance, she rushed back down the trail and over to Larson. "Where?"

His brow furrowed deeper than a spring planting. "Suit up first."

Right. Once they were all looking like astronauts on a grassy moon in their white hazmat suits, he loaded them up with equipment, and they all headed to the last tent.

"Ghost Society," Two Fingers muttered as they went.

Walrus's eyes brightened. "Is that a spin-off of *Ghostbusters*? Haven't heard of it before."

Dark eyes rolled over to Walrus. "Arikara spiritual society. They painted themselves white."

Walrus's face fell. "What are Arikara? Some kind of New Age cult?"

That got a long sigh. "We're standing on what was once their land. That or Mandan."

Walrus looked dubious. "I thought it was Sioux." Then he corrected himself. "Lakota."

Her affable deputy was learning. As was Karen. But all these different names were hard to keep track of.

"That was later." Two Fingers brushed against a milkweed and sent cottony seeds into the wind. "Nakota more likely than Lakota. Yankton and Yanktonai." Karen recalled that Two Fingers was all of the above: Nakota, Arikara, Mandan, and Dakota thrown in. If anyone had a claim here, it was him. "Depends how far back you go. Hunter could have told you the entire history of this region. I just know bits and pieces."

Once they had the lights set up, Larson moved to just outside the back of the tent. Karen followed in his footsteps, with Marek close behind.

Larson got down on his haunches. "Move that light."

Marek moved it, and Karen could see what Larson had. The broken blades of bluestem, the dark spots on some coneflowers. And there, following Larson's finger, she saw the dark matted grass where Hunter's head must have fallen after being struck. Flies zipped around, feasting.

"Looks like he was there for a while. I mean, he wasn't immediately moved."

Larson nodded at Marek. "No blood drops going from here."

After Larson took swipes of the blood and pictures of the scene, including some blood drops that had hit the inside ceiling of the canvas tent, he said, "There doesn't appear to be any trace evidence. No footprints." The grass was far too dense for that. "No sign of the weapon."

Walrus said, "I'd dump it in the creek."

"What creek?" Larson asked.

"You crossed it on the trail up to the mound. If you blink, you'll miss it." Walrus beckoned, and they followed.

Karen would have stumbled right into it. Or nearly. It was a very narrow creek—only a few feet wide—and with the August heat, mostly dry. But after spreading out and traveling up and down its length, they found nothing that fit Dr. White's description. Just some trash and lots of mosquitoes. Despite Two Fingers's magic cylinder, they all ended up bitten.

Walrus slapped at another mosquito. "Geez, I'm going to die of West Nile after all. That many of the little bloodsuckers, one has to have relatives in Egypt." As they hit the trail, a bunch of grasshoppers jumped and groused at them. "What now, a plague of locusts? We done here? I'd like to get a little sleep between applications of calamine before our confab tomorrow."

Karen looked at Larson. He nodded. "We're done."

"Your house or mine?" she asked Larson as she headed back to the Sub. "Or to our own?"

"Yours. So I can roll over and go back to sleep in your bed and dream of you while you go to work in the dark."

"Ah, newlyweds." Walrus wiped away an imaginary tear. "Ain't the lovey-dovey sweet?"

CHAPTER 10

Lovey-Dovey Larson hadn't even woken when Karen stumbled out of her bed at four the next morning to the jarring beeps of her alarm clock. What kind did he use if hers didn't even merit a flinch? Five-bell alarm?

That mystery, regrettably, took backseat to a homicide. She should be waking with him naturally to the late-morning light of a glittering Caribbean sun with a beach in reach and a mai tai in hand.

Instead, she showered, dressed, and got into the Sub without so much as a twitch from her beloved. Off to work with her, as there was no fun to be had with him.

By the time she'd brewed a boatload of Sisters Blend free-trade premium coffee, normally something she reserved for the truly needy, she was on a caffeine high.

"Good morning," she said cheerfully to Walrus as he zombie-stepped his way into the office. "Up and at 'em, Sunshine."

She put a mug in his hand before he could punch her.

Fortunately, Kurt came in on his heels, looking neat and pressed, alert and ready for work—and, thank God, carrying a tray. From the smell, whatever it was, was freshly baked. His spinster sister either had been up battling her phobias by battering up delicacies, or she'd taken pity on him—and them. Eva Bechtold was a godsend to the Eda County Sheriff's Office. If she had the money, Karen would put Eva on the payroll, but she didn't think that would get past Harold Dahl, the parsimonious county commissioner. He would, however, partake freely if given the chance.

Which he wouldn't get, especially on a Sunday morning. He might work weekends, but he attended church faithfully—or at least to the tune of his mother, the city mayor.

"What've you got?" a rejuvenated Walrus asked. "Smells like pastries."

Kurt lifted the covering cloth. An array of golden-brown puffy creations lay there. The door opened as Walrus muttered, "I thought it'd be cinnamon rolls or something. Those look kinda plain." But he reached out anyway.

"Fry bread."

Karen looked up at Two Fingers, who'd just arrived. "Fry bread?"

Kurt nodded. "Eva thought it appropriate. Traditional Indian food. She had never tried making them before."

Walrus took a gigantic bite, chewed, and nodded. "Got some sugar in there to make it sweet. Not bad. So they're traditional, huh?"

Two Fingers snatched up one and blew on it before he took a bite, nodding at her when she handed over a mug. "Sort of. It goes back to when rationing started."

Marek came in, yawning, and accepted coffee with a grateful nod.

Walrus swallowed. "You mean, like during the World Wars?"

"No, back when Indians were herded onto reservations in the 1860s and given rations of flour, sugar, salt, and lard to replace their traditional diets. Hunter said it started with the Navajo and Apache in New Mexico then spread from there."

Marek's ears apparently woke up at the mention of his former home. "What?"

Two Fingers gestured. "Fry bread."

"Like sopapillas, then." Marek snatched a fry bread and

blew on it. "Val said that the Pueblos had to get creative to survive on those rations instead of their usual beans, corn, and squash."

"Of course," Two Fingers went on, "they're loaded with all the things that cause diabetes and obesity."

"But you'll die happy," Walrus said, snagging another.

Kurt frowned at Two Fingers, looked at the offending fry bread, and went stiffly to his desk. Apparently, he wasn't sure what to do when his gift had been linked to gastronomic genocide.

Two Fingers dropped his eyes. "Please thank your sister for her thoughtfulness. I only meant that it's not healthy as a staple. But it's often fried up for gatherings. Every tribe has its own way of making it, its own recipes. Some use it for tacos, some just plain. I don't eat it every day, but I like it on special occasions. No different than cinnamon rolls."

Apparently satisfied, Kurt took the mug Karen held out—and a fry bread, though he stared at it for a long moment before taking a bite.

Having not heard any of the history or the carb and fat content, Travis "Bork" Bjorklund came in and pounced on the new offering. His response was predictable: "Mmm."

He was followed by a sleepy-eyed Adam Van Eck, who mimed instant alertness when handed his mug, which read Mug Shot.

The last to enter, rather surprisingly, was the only one to which Sisters Blend actually applied. Normally, Seoul was eager to get to an incident meeting. She hadn't slept, but that was because she was on the night shift along with Adam. But usually, she was bright-eyed and bushy-tailed, no matter the hour she was summoned.

Oh, to be in her twenties again, Karen thought. Or not, as she saw Seoul give Two Fingers a frowning sidelong glance. Trouble in paradise? Assuming they'd ever gone there.

"Okay, people, listen up." Karen caught them up on the autopsy results and the poster board. "Comments?"

Bork crossed his arms. "Seems a pretty stupid thing to leave if you're the killer."

"Some people with a cause want that cause known," Kurt replied.

"Mmm. But what's to protest on a dig? They're trying to figure out more about Native history, right?" Bork's receding hairline receded some more as his brows rose. "I mean, it's all going to be preserved in some museum somewhere, right? Anyone can see the stuff. None of it does anyone any good in the ground."

Two Fingers looked tired again, as if having to explain things that were obvious to him was taking its toll. "It's not just stuff, though some of that stuff is sacred to us. Sometimes, it's remains."

Walrus shrugged. "Bones. What's the big deal?"

Two Fingers cocked his head at the rotund deputy. "There's an abandoned cemetery near Aleford. Any of your ancestors buried there?"

"Yeah, used to be a church. A couple generations of my family are buried there."

Karen winced, thinking of her Okerlund and Forsgren ancestors buried in various locations in the county, some maintained, some abandoned.

Two Fingers waited a beat for Walrus to clue in. "And you'd be okay if some archaeologists wanted to dig it all up, move the bones and stuff to a museum, put them on display?"

Walrus shuddered. "Geez, no. But that's recent. We're talking ancient."

"You're English, right? Have any ancestors buried in New England?"

"Geez, yeah, my mom dragged us off to some cemeteries on a vacation to Boston once. And yeah, that'd give me the shudders, too. But there are records and stuff for all that time frame. But I'm talking like digging up King Richard in the parking lot a while back in England or those mummies in Egypt."

Two Fingers shook his head. "A lot of these digs are more like your New England people than mummies."

Karen pursed her lips, recalling her discussion with Dana Todacheeny Ellis in Flandreau. "If Natives are against digging up remains, then why are they so eager to dig up children at boarding schools?"

That required a rundown of boarding school abuses and the connection to Hunter, who wanted to search for remains at Flandreau Indian School.

Walrus shook his head in bewilderment. "They're dead. You just told us why we shouldn't dig them up. Why disturb them? *That* seems disrespectful."

Two Fingers was quiet a minute then said, "The military spends considerable time and expense finding casualties of war who died in other countries then bringing them home."

And the ceremony, the pageantry, of repatriation, when one was buried in Arlington Cemetery, was a sight to behold. Karen had seen it happen.

Walrus nodded. "Sure. I get that. But this *is* home. It's the US of A. I mean, you're a vet. I know a lot of Indians are vets."

"You forget, tribal reservations are sovereign nations." He grimaced. "In some things, at least. That's our home."

And they wanted to bring their dead back home. That actually made sense. But that wasn't getting them any closer to a killer.

Karen glanced at her watch. Half an hour gone. "Okay, people. We need to get to Spirit Mound. Marek and I will take the field directors. Walrus and Seoul, take the archaeology students. Two Fingers and Bork, take the protesters. Get timelines nailed down. We need to find out what happened to Hunter's car. I've got a BOLO out." The be-on-the-lookout was one of the things she'd taken care of while the coffee was brewing. "We also need crowd control. That's on Kurt and Adam."

Seoul, who'd been uncharacteristically silent, startled as Karen took a step toward the doors. "What?"

Karen looked hard at the young deputy. She seemed off her feed. She hadn't even touched her mug, and she didn't have any fry bread on her desk. "Are you sick, Deputy?"

"What? No. Sorry. It's just..." She glanced at Two Fingers. "I got some news at home."

Uh oh. At home. Seoul had just returned from there. To talk to her mother? Was Seoul pregnant? That was just what Karen needed. Drama on the roster.

As everyone was staring at her, Seoul reddened—as much as her burnished skin could under her liver-colored hair. "It's not about me. It's my mom."

That had Karen's sympathy. "Is she sick? Do you need time off?" Karen wasn't sure how she would manage it, but as she'd been robbed of being there for her own mom—by her mother's unilateral decision—Karen wanted to give Seoul the opportunity she'd never had.

"No, nothing like that. She took a DNA test a while back to see if she could find her biological father. You know, right, that my mom is Korean?"

"Yeah, and your dad met her and married her in Seoul. Hence, you."

"Well, Mom's father was a GI. One who promised to come back and marry Halmeoni—that's *grandma* in Korean—after he got out, bring her to America. Blah, blah, blah. He was being shipped out when they learned she was pregnant. Halmeoni waited for years before realizing he'd lied to her. Now she doesn't talk about him. At all. The only thing she'd tell Mom about him was that he claimed to be Santa. By then, she knew she'd been had." Seoul rolled her eyes. "We figured he was Scandinavian or something. Somewhere north and cold."

Karen smiled. "Welcome to the club."

Seoul's eyes fell. "Um, well, not exactly."

Walrus was staring at her with an open mouth, his second or perhaps third fry bread unbitten in one sausage-fingered hand. "So your mom fell for a GI, too? How'd that go over with your grandma?"

That brought a wry smile. "Halmeoni was not a happy camper. At least she wasn't until my parents got properly married in Seoul and *then* had me ten months later. Mom wanted to bring Halmeoni to America with them after his deployment, but after staying with them in Onawa for a while, she decided to go back. She was too old, she said, to change, to learn the language, to leave her big city and her friends for rural Iowa, and she hated the cold."

Karen had a sinking feeling that this wasn't going to end well. She and Eyre had managed to come to some level of relationship, but biology didn't always guarantee anything. "Did she find him, her biological father? Did he want nothing to do with her or deny it?"

"No, she hasn't found him. Yet. But she got her ethnicity results from the DNA test. Half Korean, we expected." She let out a big breath. "Half Native American, we didn't."

Two Fingers's head snapped around from where he'd been looking at something on his computer. "What?"

"Yeah. Big surprise. We had no idea." Her hands sifted through liver-colored strands. "I mean, Halmeoni must have known that he wasn't white, but she never said a word. Mom's got a close match on the DNA site and sent a message, but no answer yet."

Marek asked, "How close?"

"Not father. Not sibling. But close."

Two Fingers said, under his breath, "Santee." Then in a louder voice, he asked, "What was his name? The match."

"Oh. Get this. It's a really cool name. Goodthunder. Martin, I think. There wasn't any tree or location attached, so we don't know where he's from or anything."

Two Fingers looked absolutely stunned.

While Karen was still processing that, Seoul blurted out, her eyes wide on Two Fingers's face, "Santee. Santa. Oh my god." She hopped to her feet and went to Two Fingers. "Am I related to you?"

After an interminable moment, Two Fingers shook his head. "I don't think so, though a lot of Dakota are related in one way or another."

Karen frowned. "Why is that name familiar? Goodthunder, I mean."

"Chief Goodthunder," Marek murmured. "He called to let the Indian School know about Hunter's death, remember?"

"He's a chief?" Now Seoul looked stunned. "*The* chief, at Flandreau?"

Marek answered. "The tribal police chief."

Shaking a head obviously filled with feathered headdresses, Seoul laughed. "Guess it's in the blood, this job. Wow. Talk about Twilight Zone. I can't wait to meet him."

But Two Fingers said not another word.

CHAPTER 11

As Marek got out of the Sub at Spirit Mound, he wondered if there was bad blood between Two Fingers and the tribal police chief. Though since he'd been offered and almost accepted a job with the tribal police, perhaps not, unless the chief had only recently been appointed or hired.

Much to Seoul's bafflement and dismay, Two Fingers hadn't said anything more. And Karen had quickly ordered them to saddle up. Figuratively.

He and Karen weren't the only ones who'd made the trek to Spirit Mound at daybreak. The small parking lot was a gridlock. TV crews were trying to interview the more-than-willing protesters, as well as the field directors, who were shooing them away. The archaeology students were trying to carry their tools to the dig and being stopped by Kurt.

Karen let out a wolf whistle that pierced the air. "Listen up! Field directors, here." She pointed next to Marek and herself. "Dig students, there." She pointed under a tree near the restrooms. "Protesters, there." She pointed to another tree on the other side of the restrooms. "Media, stay put. No interviews until we're done with ours. This is an active homicide investigation."

"Free speech!" yelled one middle-aged man in an already-sweat-soaked T-shirt that proclaimed *Defend the Sacred*. Marek noted that some of the protesters had edged away from him, though a few stayed in his orbit. A few others in a quiet huddle appeared to be washing themselves, their faces, their hands, with air... until he saw the smoke. Smudge. He supposed that it might well be something to do after a murder had been committed on the grounds. Talk about clearing the air.

"You'll get your free speech," Karen told the protester. "After you talk to one of my deputies."

His chin lifted. "You can't make us talk to some white supremacist pig who'll try to pin a murder on us just for being Indians and having the gall to protest the theft of our culture."

Karen faced him down—and it was down, as the man was about five-seven—while the cameras rolled. "No, I can't make you talk. But I'd think you'd want to help us find whoever killed another Native American. And it won't be a white pig interviewing you. It will be a Native one." She beckoned to Two Fingers. "Take him first so he can exercise his right to speak to the press."

The protester opened his mouth, no doubt to spew more, but surprisingly, two of his fellows grabbed his arms and pulled him toward Two Fingers. They almost pushed him into the deputy's arms. Clearly, they either disliked him—or had better media savvy.

Marek had little doubt who the man must be. Tonto Hawks. Neither he nor Two Fingers looked thrilled to be thrown into each other's company.

"He's a twinkie. Ignore him."

Marek turned to find a woman in a floppy hat standing next to him. Stocky and suntanned with hills and valleys of wrinkles around her eyes, she looked to be in her sixties, but was maybe only in her fifties. And if they called her Doll, it was ironically. She was homely—and seemed entirely comfortable being so. Marek liked her on sight. "Twinkie?"

Her nose wrinkled—more, that is. "I know that's a slur.

But it's what my Indigenous friends call him. A twinkie, a fraud."

"A fraud in what way?" Karen asked, staring at the man's profile. "Is Hawks even Native? He doesn't look it."

But then, neither had Hunter. Marek was beginning to wonder just how many Natives had come and gone in his life without his ever knowing.

Doll shrugged. "No one really knows. Hawks started showing up at various protests a couple years ago. You know, things like the Dakota Pipeline. Whatever Indigenous Americans are protesting—and they have plenty of reason to do so, don't get me wrong—he's there. But he always seems to disappear when it gets to the sticking point, after he's bled sympathetic supporters dry. He doesn't walk the talk. In my part of the country, we call them all hat, no cattle. But lately, he's been showing up at digs. Writes a blog called 'Hawking Native.' Lately, he's been stoking a lot of backlash against my life's work, which is filling in the holes in Indigenous history."

"Which is utterly foolish and backward of them. Knowledge is power." A man strode up to them, obviously having heard the last. Marek guessed he was in his late sixties, perhaps even his seventies. He was slightly bowed at the shoulders but otherwise spry. "If they want power, they need to help us, not hinder us."

He sounded cranky and cross. Marek watched Karen force a smile. He imagined she felt the same way at the moment. Cranky and cross.

Through her smile, Karen asked, "Dr. Hardy, I presume?"

The professor apparently didn't pick up the Dr. Livingston reference. Or wasn't amused. His rather intense gaze below prominent brows focused on her without emotion of any kind. "I am."

Karen waved him and Doll to a nearby picnic table. Marek pulled out his minirecorder.

Doll stared at it. "You're going to read us our rights?"

Since she looked more thrilled than otherwise, Marek obliged. "Wouldn't hurt."

Doll proudly told the recorder that she understood her rights. Hardy, still cranky, did it far more snappishly.

Karen stopped the professor from sitting down. "Dr. Hardy, we need to speak to you each separately. Will you please take a walk until we call for you?"

"We don't want you to influence each other's answers," Marek clarified when the professor seemed ready to protest.

"Guess that makes sense. Unlike the rest of this mess." Reluctantly, he nodded but turned to Doll. "Don't lollygag. We only have one more week."

He strode off down the road toward the dig. Hopefully, he wasn't going to engage Kurt in an argument about access.

Doll waved a sun-speckled hand. "Don't mind Dr. Hardy. He's grouchy because we don't have enough yet to prove his theory of the site. We'll have to wait another year. Or more. Probably more. And this is a very small dig without much funding. Under the radar. I signed up because they wanted a codirector, as Dr. Hardy tends to be a wee bit pedantic with the students. I like a more informal style. And it's right up my alley. The transition from the prehistoric to the protohistoric period."

Marek was used to being considered dumb, so he asked, "Proto what?"

"Prehistoric is before the written record. Our written record, I must clarify. Protohistoric dates from first contact with Europeans. Not out here on the Great Plains specifically, as that was much later, but on the continent. That was the beginning of the end for the Indigenous peoples of America. And I truly mean end in some circumstances. There are, for instance, no full-blooded Arikara or Mandan left. A huge number were wiped out in smallpox epidemics starting in the 1780s."

Marek had heard about that somewhere. "Didn't the US Army deliberately infect them?"

Doll grimaced. "The researcher who put that forward had no actual evidence. When he was challenged to supply it, he just said it was common knowledge. He was later thrown out of his post for academic fraud. It's not impossible, but it's unsupported. By the time Lewis and Clark arrived, they found several abandoned villages along the Missouri River. The biggest smallpox epidemic in 1837 was caused by a hand on a steamboat from Missouri who got it, but the boat was allowed to continue on to Council Bluffs, where it spread like… well, wildfire. As they were a powerful trading tribe along the river, the Mandans went from thousands to an estimated one hundred and twenty-five people. The Arikara lost about half of theirs in that wave."

Marek couldn't imagine that level of devastation. What it would have been like to be a survivor, only a handful, of a once-vibrant culture. He glanced over at Two Fingers. "So our deputy is fairly rare to even have any Arikara and Mandan blood?"

"Two Fingers?" Doll's wrinkles waved upward in surprise—and a bit of awe. "I'd hazard to guess that's Mandan."

Karen asked, "What does Mandan have to do with his name?"

"The *Okipa*. Like the better known Sun Dance—which many, such as Charles Eastman from Flandreau, claim became much more sadomasochistic after contact with whites—it involved a ceremony where boys were pierced by the skin on their chests and suspended until they fell unconscious. When they woke, their little finger was chopped off."

Beside him, Karen flinched. "Ouch."

"If a man went through it twice, usually a great warrior, he lost two fingers. Your deputy has a distinguished lineage. I wonder if he knows the story." She looked like she would like to go talk to their deputy. Right now.

As if seeing the same, Karen said, "Now that the small talk is over, we need data, Dr. Doll."

Dead Spirits

With a sigh, she looked back at them. "Just Doll. It only gets more ridiculous with the title. Like Professor Barbie."

Marek imagined she'd been called a lot of things, but she seemed to take it in good humor. Or good resignation. "When did you last see Hunter Redwing-Digges?"

"Well, let's see. There was some excitement on the dig with a new find, so it was later than usual that I loaded up the students into the van. Not quite dark. Hunter stayed behind with Hardy and Richie to load up the finds for transport to the lab in Vermillion."

Marek glanced over at the swirl of students. "Richie?"

Doll pointed over to a shaggy-haired young man leaning against a white Corvette while he waited his turn. "Richard Anderson Legrange, Junior. Son of one of my esteemed colleagues. Or should I say, my new boss, as he just took over the department after the previous dinosaur retired in the spring." She gave them a wry look. "Richie's an ABD. All but dissertation. For the last several years, he's been treating field schools around the country as his personal hunting grounds. I'm supposed to be cracking the whip over him, but the only thing cracking is the whip. If I didn't have tenure, I'd be worried."

Marek didn't envy her. "Did Richie, Dr. Hardy, and Hunter have their own cars? Specifically, Friday night."

Doll pursed her lips then nodded. "Yes, I know Hunter did. He was gone for several hours earlier in the day. Personal issue, I heard. Dr. Hardy had the van we use to transport the finds. And Richie has his own wheels, too, to impress the girls." Her jovial face tightened a bit. "Not all are impressed."

Karen shifted on the hardwood bench. "Were there any protesters still here?"

"Yeah, I believe there were. Two for sure. Tonto Hawks and the NAS—sorry, that's Native American Studies—grad student that Hunter knew. I'm afraid I can't remember the name, if I ever knew it. I think he and Hunter used to be friends. Anyway, it looked like they were going at it."

Marek wanted to make sure he knew who *they* were. "Hunter and the grad student?"

"No, Hawks and the grad student. I was rooting for the grad student. Anything to get Hawks off the dig."

"Okay, so we had four cars left in the lot after you left?" Karen held up the fingers of one hand and ticked them off. "Hunter's, Richie's, the finds van, and the protesters'?"

Doll frowned. "I think so. Maybe one more, but I'm not sure about that. The protesters usually had three or four cars. They carpooled. I'm sorry. I was eager to head out, despite Hardy wanting to push until full dark. I was looking forward to the free day. And frankly, I will be glad when this dig is finished. Add a murder on top of it all, and I'm done."

Marek wasn't getting any feel for the motive. Yes, the protesters were upset. But they didn't appear to have done anything other than carry signs to flash tourists and motorists on the nearby highway. Didn't seem like a very efficient way to get support for their cause. Of course, now they had it in spades. He glanced over and saw Tonto Hawks was surrounded by microphones. Killing someone to get media attention, though, was pretty extreme.

Marek looked back at Doll. "Did Hunter have any issues with anyone that you knew?"

"Other than the protesters?" Again, she looked uncomfortable. "Well, he was a bit upset with me. More with Richie. Look, Richie is harmless, but he fancies himself a ladies' man. If you're going to be a woman in a job still dominated by ego-filled males, you have to grow a thick skin and let all the misogyny roll off." She sounded a little less certain now. "Maybe because I had to survive it—yes, even butt-ugly gals like me got hit on back in the day or told that men dig, women screen the finds—I expected too much of the younger generation. They didn't have to fight those battles as much. I might have been too... dismissive... of what one of the girls reported."

Doll looked truly troubled now. "Oh, my. If that's why

Hunter was killed, for defending Mariah, I will never forgive myself. But I simply can't see it. Richie regularly took digs at Hunter but only verbal ones. Not just over this one incident, by the way. But I can't see him bashing someone over the head."

Marek had heard the same thing said numerous times. "Does Richie drink or do drugs?"

Doll blew out a breath. "Drinks more than he should. Don't think he does more than weed." Then she frowned. "Is it illegal here?" When she got nothing but an exchange of looks, her head fell into her hands, dislodging the floppy hat. "I'm doomed."

Marek picked up the hat and handed it over. "Not really. It's just... complicated."

Karen explained further. "Technically, the voters okayed not only medical marijuana—incidentally, the biggest dispensary around here is in Flandreau, run by the tribe, along with the casino—but also recreational. The powers that be are doing everything they can to obstruct the will of the people. But as this is hearsay, it's not relevant unless it is."

Though the Flandreau connection might be interesting if that was where Richie had acquired his weed.

Karen asked Doll, "What did you do when you got back to Vermillion that night?"

"Dropped off the kiddos at the dorm, told them to enjoy themselves—but not too much." She winked. "And then I went to my hotel, got a big margarita, and put up my feet. I fell asleep about midnight, I think. I suppose that means I don't have an alibi."

After glancing at Richie, Marek looked at Karen. She nodded at his silent question. He went over to Seoul and Bork and told them to send Richie over after they took his initial statement. After Marek and Karen were done with Dr. Hardy, that is.

Richie of the fancy 'Vette was worth vetting.

CHAPTER 12

When Marek returned, Karen had cornered Dr. Hardy at the dig, or at least as close as the professor could get to the site. Kurt was courageously blocking him from access.

Marek looked down at the neatly dug squares separated by twine. He had a hard time figuring out what they were looking for. In New Mexico, the ancient peoples like the Anasazi were always in your face—their cliff dwellings dotted the sides of mesas, and petroglyphs marked the rocks across large swaths of the state. Pottery sherds and flints were a common finding when out for a hike. But he'd grown up in Eda County and never so much as seen a smidgeon of Native artifact outside a museum.

Even much more recent structures like homesteads never seemed to stay long—as if the prairies were eager to overthrow anything built on them. "What is there to uncover?" he asked. "I mean, weren't the Natives here nomads, traveling in tipis?"

Hardy gave Marek a long look and must have decided he was serious. And predictably, that told Marek he'd been slotted into the all-brawn-no-brain category.

The professor spoke slowly as if to make sure Marek understood. "The *Sioux* were nomadic. The Arikara, also known as the Sahnish, and the Mandans, who were here before them, were semi-horticultural, spending much of their time in villages. They lived in earth lodges, hence the pole holes." He indicated darker circles in the ground. "Most of the archaeologically surveyed villages are farther up along the Missouri River, around Pierre and then moving farther up into North Dakota. The surveys come almost exclusively from emergency digs for construction, many of them from dams back in the 1950s. This area has had very little surveying, but a few exploratory trenches showed the potential of the site."

Now Karen spoke up. "I always heard that the Indians were afraid of this spot. So why would any of them build anything here?"

"That is *precisely* the question." Hardy sounded like he wanted to give Karen a gold star. "My theory, which our finds to date support, is that this was an Arikara site. I believe that this particular band carried some strong magic, if you will"—he rolled his eyes—"against evil spirits that allowed them to stay here. Then the village was abandoned in a way that made subsequent tribes fear this place. Likely disease. Are you aware of the Mound Builders?"

Marek shook his head. Karen just remained silent. Which, knowing her, meant she had no clue. But Hardy turned to her. Marek had apparently been deemed unteachable.

"The prehistoric Mound Builders had large cities, one of the biggest being Cahokia in Illinois, across the river from Saint Louis. They were Caddoan Mississippian, as were the Pawnee and Arikara. I believe that, as a Caddoan people, the Arikara in this area got their 'strong magic' from Cahokia, whose priestly class abandoned the city there."

"How do you prove 'strong magic'?" Marek asked, genuinely curious.

Testily, the professor said, "You don't. It's bogus, of course. You prove their *belief* in it through the ceremonial trappings. But you didn't come here to solve that mystery."

True enough. "Run us through what happened after the students left with Dr. Doll."

The prominent brows drew down. "That obnoxious oaf with a poster kept yelling at us to get off his land."

Karen pounced. "Only one had a poster?"

"Two did."

Marek asked, "How many protesters were still there after the transport van left?"

"Only those two that I noticed. I stopped paying mind to them early on. Just noise. *Idiot* noise. They want to protest their own history? They're doomed to repeat it. Bogus magic. Bogus origin stories. No better than the 'Cherokee princess' stories they decry. All oral tradition, no science."

Obviously, this was a touchy point for him. "What poster did the oaf have?"

"It said, 'Get the F-U-K off our land.' Idiot can't even spell. The other one at least had some clue. It was the Lakota word for thief. Then there were a bunch of others who'd already left with signs about stealing, cultural genocide, all kinds of nonsense. We're in the business of documenting and preserving their history. I can't think of a more backward protest."

So it wasn't Tonto Hawks with the thief poster, assuming the oaf was him. "Do you know any of the names of the protesters?"

"Hawks is the oaf. It wasn't that bad until he got involved. He runs some blog that gets a lot of people outraged over one protest or another. The other one who was here, he's a grad student in Native American Studies." He snorted his opinion of that. "Jerome Stands By Him from Lower Brule."

"Lakota?" Marek hazarded.

"Sicangu Lakota. Burnt Thigh."

That confused Karen. "His thigh is burnt?"

Obviously, Karen's stock fell as Hardy glowered at her. "Sicangu means 'burnt thigh.' The story goes that they were trapped in a prairie fire and some were burned. So they were called the Burnt Thighs." His tone suggested some skepticism but not as strongly as before. "The French called them 'Brule,' which means 'burnt,' so you get Lower Brule."

Sounded like a logical reason to Marek. And they finally had a name to go with the poster. "Did Stands By Him have a car?"

"No, he hitches with others. I've heard him ask for rides."

"What happened after Doll left?" Karen asked.

Hardy shrugged. "Hunter and I packed up the finds. Hawks tried to stop us from loading them in the van, even tried to take one of them from me, but for some reason, Stands By Him didn't. Stand by his friend, I mean. Said their protest was nonviolent. Hawks said all the finds belonged to them, not us, and he had every right to recover his property. If he'd tried to take one again, I'd have called the police, but Stands By Him managed to drag him off toward the car."

Looking puzzled, Karen asked, "What did Hunter do during all this?"

A very good question. Marek hadn't quite gotten there yet.

"Nothing except tell Stands By Him to stop enabling a damn plastic."

That puzzled Marek for a minute. Must mean a fake.

The professor actually smiled. "That nearly gave Hawks an apoplexy. Then Hunter turned away and just kept loading the finds. Last thing Hawks yelled before they roared off was that they'd be back and they'd show us who was boss. I was thinking about calling you for some security for this last week at the dig when I got the news about Hunter."

"So when you left, it was just Hunter there?"

"That's right. I assumed he went home."

"You're sure that the protesters left?" Karen looked disappointed. "They didn't double back?"

The professor scratched at his salt-and-pepper hair. "I don't know. They could have come back. That Hawks guy had blood in his eye. And it wasn't aimed at me."

So only Hunter was left. Alone. "Hunter's car was still there?"

"Of course. I wouldn't have left him otherwise."

Somehow, then, Hunter had been killed and his car stolen. Was it that simple? Someone wanted his car? Maybe it had nothing at all to do with Hunter himself or the dig. Just an opportunistic snatch and kill. The poster board must have been at hand, either with Hunter or in his car, and was a convenient way to point the finger elsewhere. "Where did you go after you left?"

Hardy looked more impatient than insulted at the question. "I took the finds to the lab then went home. I had a talk to prepare for, so I spent Saturday doing that. Abigail called to let me know about Hunter. Such a waste."

Marek tried to imagine the scene. One person was missing. "What about Richie?"

"Oh, him. Legrange Junior left before we finished loading the finds. He and Hunter had some tiff over a girl. I told them to keep it off the dig." His brows rose. "Richie said he'd settle it with Hunter later. I didn't think anything of it. Richie talked big but rarely followed through."

"Are we talking his dissertation?" Karen asked. "Why did you accept him on the dig?"

"No way not to, with his father's clout in the archaeological community. I'm not saying he doesn't know how to dig—he grew up on digs. But he's lazy. He talks a good game. But all he really wants is the mystique." He snorted. "Indiana Jones wannabe. Attracts the girls."

Karen pressed on. "Did you know about some conflict between Hunter and Richie about one of the female students?"

"Is that what it was?" Hardy waved a dismissive hand. "Abigail takes care of things like that. She's their den mother. I teach them. Or try. Most won't make it. It's hard work. Physically and mentally. And it's often tedious."

As was an investigation. Marek knew he was missing

something. And it came just as Hardy started to turn away. "Where did Hunter go on Friday earlier in the day?"

Hardy was slow to turn, as if he wanted to jump into the dig and get to work, and hated being pulled back. "Personal business. I didn't inquire."

Karen didn't let him turn again. "You just let Hunter go? It seems to me you were hot to keep going with the dig. Losing one of your main diggers had to sting."

"He was a hard worker. If he said it was personal, it was personal. He knows I wouldn't put up with stuff like Legrange can get away with just because his father is a big name in the field."

Marek heard a bit of professional envy in there. But academia was just another field for humans to display their prejudices. He remembered that Hardy had given Hunter a hard time over his dissertation subject. "What about the winter count?" When Hardy stilled midturn, Marek clarified. "Why didn't you initially support it as a basis for his dissertation?"

Hardy blew out a breath. "Worthless. I told him that. It had no provenance." When Marek blinked, he sighed. "No one at W.H. Over knew where it came from originally. The owner's heirs gifted it to the museum. The heirs didn't know where their father got it, because he was a missionary who traveled to a bunch of reservations. He'd pay for things that interested him. Without written context from the keeper, and even that's suspect as it's oral tradition and often contradictory, a winter count is just pretty pictures. I told Hunter it might even be a fake. Some of the pictographs didn't match to any of the known Great Plains winter counts. People will pay for fakes, and maybe that missionary got taken."

All that sounded reasonable to Marek. "But you finally let Hunter use it?"

"I told him that as long as he explored and explained all possible avenues, including a forgery or at least a partial one, that it was instructional. But I wasn't very happy about it. Wasting precious years tracing oral traditions when he could be digging here?" Hardy gestured at the scarred earth. "That's science. It's like doing your investigation just based on what people say, with no evidence. Tracing legends is only for the Indiana Joneses of the world. That is, only in fiction."

CHAPTER 13

RICHIE SAUNTERED OVER TO THEM with a big grin on his sun-kissed face, probably because once Karen had given the green light, the other students had practically jumped into the dig at Hardy's barked order.

One olive-skinned girl, tall and hunched, with a glint of eyeglasses below a wide-brimmed straw hat, settled herself next to Doll, though stiffly. Karen would take bets she was the one Richie had offended.

A quick confab with Seoul confirmed and supplied a name: Mariah Mettis.

Mariah claimed that Richie had groped her in the parking lot of the dorm, and she'd had to push him off and run to escape him. She'd reported it to Doll but been told that Richie was harmless and wouldn't have taken it any further. Basically, Mariah was given to understand that accepting the ride with Richie implied liberties were to be given, not taken.

Karen had dealt with similar incidents in the Army. She'd survived. But they should never have happened. She had never reported any of those uncomfortable scenes, sure it would lead to her, not the perp, getting her career derailed.

But this was a new generation, with different expectations.

Karen led with it. "Tell me why I shouldn't have you arrested for assault."

Richie stopped in midstride. "What?! I haven't touched you or any of your goons."

Goons? Not the way to make friends and influence others. "Mariah Mettis."

Richie relaxed and gave an easy smile. "No harm, no foul. I thought she wanted some special handling. Awkward, gawky student. Typical nerd. Thought I'd give her some fun. But she reacted like a scalded cat when I touched her. I mean, she said yes, right?"

Was he that dense? Or just that entitled. "To a ride."

"Yeah," he agreed. "A ride. That's what it would have been. Her loss."

Marek said, "Hunter didn't see it as harmless."

"Hunter was an idiot. Gullible. And would do anything to get some action after he got dumped by his Viking goddess. Sorry to speak ill of the dead and everything." Richie sounded anything but sorry. "You hear what his dissertation subject was? Some fake winter count he found in a backwater museum. That's why I called him Little Beaver. Just kidding, of course."

Karen couldn't make the connection. Was Hunter buck-toothed? "Come again?"

"Oh. Guess you wouldn't know. He liked to gnaw on things, like Mettis, so that fit, too. But the name is from the legitimate documented winter counts like Blue Thunder and High Dog. The Little Beaver pictograph comes from the 1800s. A small white man who was inclined to stay in his house, and it burned down. Seemed appropriate. I mean, he looked white. Claimed to be Native, but I'm not convinced. Anyway, his dissertation wasn't anything serious like mine on radiocarbon dating the Woodlands cultures. Only reason he got away with it is holding up the Indigenous card. Hardy caved bigtime. But then, Hardy's got an off-the-wall theory, too. Priestly class from Cahokia ending up here?" He smirked as he looked around. Given he was from Boulder and the Rocky Mountains, his opinion aligned with the biker they'd met earlier. "Get real. No wonder Hardy could only get tenure at a backwater school."

Karen said in a very even voice, "I'm a grad of USD."

He just grinned at her. "Oh. My bad."

"You do realize you are a suspect in a murder?"

"A suspect?" Richie blinked at her. "Just because a girl rejected my advances and Hunter decided to play her knight in shining armor—or in feathered headdress? Get real. She's probably gay anyway." He looked irked. "I'm good with that, but she should have told me."

Now *he* was the victim? Karen wanted to shake him but doubted it would do anything. His head was filled with—well, himself. Empty that, and there would be nothing left.

Marek stirred beside her. "You told Hunter you'd settle with him later. Did you turn around and come back here?"

Richie shook his head vigorously. "I just meant we'd settle it. You know, smooth it over." His spread his hands out. When they looked utterly unconvinced, he shrugged. "Okay, so I was a bit upset. Said something I didn't mean. I'm not violent. Ask anybody." He flashed a grin. "Takes too much energy. And I wouldn't want to get in a fight and get a black eye." He swept back a hunk of sunny hair. "Not attractive. As for coming back to the dig, why would I do that? I assumed Hunter was already back in Vermillion or maybe in Flandreau, as Saturday was a free day. No, on Friday night, I went to the Char Bar and hit up a leggy brunette who was more than happy to take a ride. Believe me, I wasn't thinking of Hunter."

The Char Bar was the Charcoal Lounge in Vermillion. Unfortunately, that would likely check out. But she took the name.

Marek asked, "Did Hunter have any conflicts with anyone else on the dig?"

"Hell, yeah. Those protesters. That's where you're going to find your killers. Archaeologists dig bones, but only old ones." He shook his shaggy head sadly. "Never should've passed NAGPRA. It's set back archaeology in this country by eons."

Karen hated acronyms. Even if all occupations, including her own, had them. After all, she had a BOLO out on Hunter's car. "NAGPRA?"

Richie rolled his eyes. As if everyone should know it. With exaggerated slowness, he said, "Native American Graves Protection and Repatriation Act."

Karen knew this part. "You've found some remains here?"

Richie blinked. "Not yet, but I wouldn't be surprised if we do eventually. Especially if this village was abandoned because of disease. Of course, NAGPRA will likely prevent us from DNA testing so that we can determine just who they were."

Marek asked, "So if there are no remains, why protest?"

Richie rolled his eyes again. "It's not just remains. It's 'sacred objects,' which is subjective and allows them to claim whatever the hell they want."

Somehow, Karen didn't think it was that easy. "So what sacred objects have you found?"

"Nothing, despite Hardy's hopes. Tools and flints, mostly. Some pottery sherds. The protesters just want to stop us, period. Like they're afraid we'll disprove their religious beliefs, their origin stories, which a lot of them don't even believe anyway. They fear science. Not to mention, we are the big, bad colonial appropriators." Now he seemed to be truly passionate. "They don't own history. Native American history *is* American history. It belongs to all of us. We're all Americans. And without whites like George Catlin and Lewis and Clark or early missionaries who recorded the traditions and ceremonies of the Natives, they wouldn't even know their own history. Now they want to destroy it."

Sounded like a soundbite from someone. Perhaps his father? Karen didn't know much at all about ownership of stuff found in digs. "Who owns the finds?"

Richie glanced around the county park. "This isn't federal

Dead Spirits

or tribal land, so NAGPRA doesn't kick in unless they are accessioned into a collection that is federally funded. I don't know if that applies to either the university or the museum in Vermillion."

W.H. Over wasn't a large museum, but it wasn't a dusty, forgotten hole-in-the-wall. In fact, the collection had been moved to a new building since she'd graduated. If people were able to demand all their things back, what would be left? Was it better for everyone to be able to enjoy the collections or just those whose ancestors they belonged to?

Richie was still on his soapbox. "NAGPRA has kept us from even digging some places or rescinding permission to dig. That happened to my dad's dig in Colorado on federal land. Some peyote-smoking elders decided they weren't getting enough payment to 'monitor' the dig and shut it down. None of it makes sense anyway. They can apply to repatriate items in a collection that have been there for decades, even centuries. I mean, seriously? If my five-times-great-grandfather's diary ended up in a museum because some distant cousin donated it, I'd have no right to demand its return. I can see it, probably copy it, but it doesn't belong to me. It belongs to everybody."

Marek spoke up. "So you think they shouldn't have any say?"

Richie blew a raspberry. "Look at the history of warfare, of genetic mixing, of assimilation. I mean, the Natives are lucky that there were even treaties at all. I mean, the Normans didn't negotiate with the Anglo-Saxons. And UK archaeologists damn well don't consult the French when they dig up a Norman site, much less Anglo-Saxon."

"But they're descendants of both," Marek pointed out. "On their own lands."

"Natives can do whatever they like on their own lands." Richie made an expansive gesture. "This is ours. And they can keep their noses out of it. We won, they lost. Get over it."

Karen didn't think that advice would go over well with the protesters. "But NAGPRA does exist, and they do get a say. So... get over it."

To her surprise, Richie grinned back at her. "I'll let you in on a little secret. My dad and Hardy know how it works. Just tag the find as 'culturally unidentifiable,' and you're good."

Karen frowned at him. Not just the underhandedness but the pointlessness of it. "But does it do you any good? If you can't identify it, it doesn't increase the knowledge base, right?"

He shrugged. "Just use weasel words. You know, 'while this artifact cannot be absolutely identified, it is reminiscent of such-and-such tribe during such-and-such period.' Even big names like Harvard do it. It's how the game is played."

Karen liked games—when they were actually games. "Murder is not a game."

"Isn't it?" He smirked as he leaned in, a whiff of aftershave lingering in the air. "Oh, and by the way, you crack detectives haven't figured out yet that the protester who used to be Hunter's friend, Stands By Him, isn't even here today. Betcha anything that he's your killer."

Her phone went off. Brule County Sheriff's Office. Her daytime dispatcher must have given them the number. She took it. "Sheriff Mehaffey."

A man's loud voice assaulted her eardrum. "Yes, Sheriff. Good news. We found your car. And your killer."

Karen forced herself to ask, "Jerome Stands By Him?"

"You got it."

As the man's voice carried, Richie grinned widely. "Told you so."

Nobody liked a know-it-all.

CHAPTER 14

Kurt brought Jerome Stands By Him into the office while Walrus trailed with a sealed plastic bag. The young man stood tall and stone-faced in his orange jumpsuit. He was chained hands and feet, but Marek could see his lips tremble as he looked around the room.

The sheriff of Brule County had said they'd found the car first, out of gas, just north of Chamberlain. A state trooper had found Stands By Him walking by the road only a few miles from the boundary of Lower Brule.

Home. Marek got that. If things go bad, you want family.

And Stands By Him had none here. Not family, not culture, not the same rules or expectations. Marek tried to imagine if he himself were brought before a tribal court, not knowing how it worked, whether he would ever see the light of day again.

Karen nodded toward the interview room. Kurt and Walrus trundled their main suspect off. Then, to Marek's surprise, Karen called Two Fingers and asked him to stand in on the interview.

When Marek quirked a brow at her, she said, "You think I can't see it? He's scared down to his toes. He doesn't have a sheet. He's twenty-three, an adult, but he's got no one."

When Two Fingers arrived, in street clothes, he looked grim. He followed them silently into the room and parked himself in the far corner between two filing cabinets.

Stands By Him stared at Two Fingers then at Marek. "Is he a lawyer?"

"No, he's one of my deputies," Karen informed him. "I'm Sheriff Mehaffey. This is Detective Okerlund. And this is Deputy Two Fingers."

Stands By Him let out a breath, and his shoulders relaxed slightly, even as his mouth tried to sneer—then trembled and fell. "The token Indian?"

"He's no token anything," Karen snapped back. "He's a valuable member of my roster."

Stands By Him said something to Two Fingers in what Marek assumed was Lakota.

Two Fingers responded in English. "Santee Dakota. I am here if you have questions. I am a fluent Dakota speaker."

Stands By Him's nose flared. "I understand English. I am an American. I don't need a translator."

Marek watched Karen's face set, and he said, "It was merely a courtesy. To you. An assurance that you will get a fair hearing. Do you want us to send Two Fingers out?"

The young man struggled for a moment then shrugged. "He's here. Might as well stay. Look, I watch TV, I know how it works. I know you have to read me my rights. I know I can ask for a lawyer."

"Yes, you can." Marek pulled out his recorder and recited the Miranda. "Do you want a lawyer? The court will appoint one. You will be held until we determine whether you will be charged or not."

His lip trembled as his chin jutted. "Based on what?"

"Evidence." Marek tapped the plastic bag. "The car is being towed to Sioux Falls for forensic testing. This will all take time. It's not like the movies. It doesn't happen in an hour."

The dark head swiveled as he looked between Marek and Karen. Then he looked at Two Fingers and said something again in Lakota.

Two Fingers took a moment to respond. Again, in English.

"They play straight. They won't play games with you or pin a murder on you just to close the books because you're an Indian. They want justice for Hunter Redwing-Digges. That is also what I want. Justice."

Two Fingers's voice sounded empty, though. And justice often was, to those who had to deal with loss. Justice wouldn't bring back his friend. And it might put another Native American in prison. An educated young man with all his future ahead of him. Was restitution in the Lakota way better? It was certainly different. But Marek doubted that Jerome Stands By Him had the kind of wealth—in money instead of horses and blankets—to do justice even the Lakota way.

"Do you know there is no word in Lakota that translates directly as justice?" Stands By Him asked them. "My grandfather told me that the closest is *wowicake*."

Marek quirked his brow at the word. "And that is?"

With a strange look on his face, Two Fingers answered, "Truth."

"That is what we want," Karen said.

"The whole truth and nothing but the truth?" Stands By Him looked down at his chained wrists. "Add *sni* to the end of *wowicake* and it means *falsehood* or *to lie or deceive*."

If nothing else, Marek was learning more than he'd ever known before about his native state's Natives. Which was kind of sad. He wasn't sure that he'd ever learned anything in school about them other than Custer's Last Stand. And maybe the Wounded Knee massacre, but he wasn't sure about that. Maybe that had come later, through Dakotan osmosis.

"You need to decide whether truth is told here," Two Fingers told Stands By Him.

"You may lie to me. You may trick me. You have all the power."

Marek thought about that. "We have you in custody. For now. But we follow evidence."

Stands By Him crossed his arms, the chains rattling. "That sheriff that locked me up, he didn't even talk to me. I heard him call you, and he had this big satisfied grin on his face. That he'd found your killer."

Karen looked like she wanted to pace but was stuck in the small room. "He doesn't know anything about the case. Just that you had Hunter's car. And a bloody shirt that you discarded."

The chains rattled again. "He's a bigot and an idiot."

"Be that as it may, you aren't dealing with him." Karen leaned back in her chair. "You can talk to us. Or roll the dice with the system, get a lawyer, tell him or her the truth—or not—and we'll fumble around on our own, trying to confirm or deny whether you killed a man who died much too young. For us, this is all about Hunter Redwing-Digges. He had a hard life."

Stands By Him blew out a breath. "Hardly. Flandreau is like a first-world rez compared to mine. Besides, Hunter was raised white. Middle-class. Everything provided."

"You were his friend once." Reproach tightened Two Fingers's voice. "You know better."

That made Stands By Him look harder at Two Fingers. "You're the bestie. The..."

"Iyeska wasicu-loving cop? You wouldn't be the first to say it. Or much worse."

"Words matter." Chains jangled again as Stands By Him ran his hands down his face. "You know, when Hunter changed his name, people treated him differently. Suddenly, he got the Indian treatment. You know, shopkeepers watching to make sure he didn't steal anything. Snide remarks about how nice it must be to get free money and healthcare. Just once, I'd like everyone who says that have to survive a Dakota winter on a West River rez. Heck, just one day. At least Hunter knew. He lasted a winter. Barely. But it wasn't just that. Claiming his Indian heritage hurt him within the archaeology community. Colleagues starting to back away because he was no longer 'one of them' but one of *them*. The ignorant Indians who kept Native history from advancing. Oh, they won't say it that way. They say all the right things, but look at the dig Hunter was on. No one consulted the MHA."

Marek frowned. "MHA?"

Again, Two Fingers answered. "Mandan-Hidatsa-Arikara. What remains of those tribes banded together at Fort Berthold Reservation in North Dakota."

"Perfect example of why we don't trust whites." Stands By Him looked again like he was going to shut down. "Your word means nothing."

Karen crossed her own arms. "Because our ancestors brought smallpox that killed yours? How is that breaking our word?"

He stared at her. "I'm not taking about disease, which is bad enough, but the Pick-Sloan Dam."

When that got no traction with Marek or Karen, which seemed to floor Stands By Him, Two Fingers again filled the gap. "After losing almost all their people and their homes, the MHA settled on their reservation in North Dakota and tried to rebuild their lives. It was in the bottomlands, so they had some good farming land and also had coal deposits, which is more than many reservations could claim. They also came from an agricultural background, so they adapted and were basically self-sufficient. They had their sacred sites, their burial sites, and went on with their lives as best they could. But in the 1950s, Congress decided to build four dams on the Missouri River."

Stands By Him picked it up from there. "And guess who got shafted? To build a dam means you're going to flood some of those rich bottomlands. They carefully avoided white towns and hit on the Fort Berthold Reservation. Most Indians didn't even know what was going on until the Corps of Engineers showed up. Then they tried to palm off vastly inferior land as a swap, but the MHA weren't dumb. They rejected that proposal, and Congress, determined to go ahead, basically gave them a pittance in cash and removed thousands of MHA off ninety percent of their reservation. Fortunately, the MHA were smart enough to make the wasicus agree that they could still sue for future compensation. But it was never enough, as it took away their self-sufficiency. You want me to trust you, with that kind of history? Might makes right, then money makes right—that's your creed."

Stands By Him wasn't wrong. But it wasn't going to solve Hunter's death. Marek tapped the scarred table. "And just what do we gain here?"

That took a few long seconds to get an answer. "A win. Look at that—Indians are savages. A lot of you believe that. Just because we don't want your culture, you think we're backward. We don't live in the past, we live now, and we're finally finding our voice. It's just not *your* voice."

Karen said evenly, "You have to decide if you're going to use your voice or not. That's your right, here and now. All we want is Hunter's killer. Period."

Silence fell. Stands By Him stared down at the table, as if waiting for it to give him some sign. Finally, he looked up. "This is being recorded?"

Marek held up the pocket recorder. "It is."

"Good. I don't want anyone twisting my words." He took a deep breath then looked at Two Fingers, as if he were the only one Stands By Him trusted to hear his words. "I didn't hate Hunter or wish him ill. He actually agreed with me that the MHA should have been consulted, but that didn't keep him from doing the dig. So that angered me. But I didn't kill him. I don't know who did."

He finally looked at Karen then Marek. "Hunter was dead when we got there."

CHAPTER 15

In the time since Karen had first taken up the badge and worked her first homicide with Marek, she'd had to learn, time and time again, to curb her impatience. Not to assume. Not to jump ahead. It was hard, because her time on the hardcourts had trained her to act quickly or be left eating dust. Yes, patience was sometimes required, even on the basketball court, but that was still counted in seconds, not days, weeks, or even years of an investigation.

Rather than start with accusations, hitting hard with the car theft, the blood, she asked, "Who is 'we'?"

A bit to her surprise, Stands By Him answered without hesitation. "Me and Hawks. We found Hunter lying facedown by that last tent with his head bashed in. I'd seen a dead body before—my aunt, my grandfather. Both died at home. Natural causes, if you can call years of poverty and untreated illness natural. But this was... awful. Believe me, I want to know who killed Hunter more than you do."

"So that's why you fled rather than contact us?" Karen knew as soon as the words left her mouth that it wasn't the best way to keep Stands By Him talking. It didn't take Marek's wince to tell her that.

Stands By Him glared at her. "I was going to contact the police. The *tribal* police in Lower Brule. Have them contact you. They know how to deal with you people. I don't."

Marek's gentle rumble barely stirred the air. "Just tell us what happened."

Karen held her breath for a few seconds, then Stands By Him continued. "After we returned to Vermillion, I went to my dorm room to finish some research I was doing on cultural appropriation. That's my dissertation subject. Hawks knocked on my door sometime around midnight that night. He said that it was past time for action, or we'd never get any traction. The dig was winding down, and no one was paying any attention."

"What kind of action?" Two Fingers asked.

Chains clinked again as Stands By Him held up his hands palm out. "I said I wouldn't do anything violent. I told him that numerous times since he glommed on to our protest. He suggested we divert the creek to flood the dig. Kind of tit for tat for flooding the MHA."

Marek asked, "What were you arguing about earlier that day, you and Hawks?"

The bitter chocolate eyes closed. "Hawks wanted to dynamite the dig. I said no way. I don't know the laws on explosives, but I'm pretty sure using dynamite on public land is serious business. I wanted to bring more attention to the protest, yes, but not like that. It just feeds into the Indians-are-savages thing. Besides, it would have damaged or destroyed what was sacred to our ancestors. I didn't want to destroy it. I wanted to preserve it. For *us*." He pounded his chest. "That's *our* history. Not some wasicus' with an academic agenda. And it's not like they'd made any big finds. Hardy might get some footnote in some musty journal of academia out of the dig, but that's it."

"And flooding isn't destructive?" Two Fingers asked.

"Not to the ancestors whose bones may rest there. And not even to the dig. I told Hawks it would only be a token flood, just enough to make our point. That creek was almost dry, if you didn't notice. So it wouldn't have been much more than a trickle. The dig would dry out in the heat pretty fast. It was supposed to be more symbolic than anything."

Two Fingers spoke again. "To some Dakota, Spirit Mound is a sacred site. Any destruction is desecration."

Karen thought she knew her deputy well enough to infer that it was to him. What had he thought of the dig? She hadn't asked. Some things were touchy, and she tried not to cross his lines. Actually, she didn't know his lines, which made it even touchier.

Stands By Him nodded. "Archaeology itself is destructive. They get to take or destroy Native heritage sites without so much as a bye-your-leave, but we can't make a point that they need to consult the relevant tribe? Which they never did. *That* is what I was protesting."

"It's not the law," Karen said before Two Fingers could answer. "I looked it up. Federal or tribal land, or federal funding, none of which were involved here."

"It's the *spirit* of the law." Stands By Him looked like he wanted to pull his hair out. Which would be a pity, as it was thick and full. "Even Hunter got that. He argued with Hardy over it. Heck, Hardy gave him hell for years for following oral tradition, for wasting his time on dubious winter counts, and Hardy had no time or patience for indulging any Native spiritual nonsense. Even when that 'nonsense,' as he called it, could have helped him. But he never consulted the MHA. Maybe they know something about this site, somewhere in their oral histories, and he just dismissed it all out of hand."

Karen was still trying to gauge how deep the betrayal went between Hunter and his erstwhile friend. "So your beef was more with Professor Hardy than Hunter?"

"Ultimately, yes. But there are still those out there like Hardy, like the Legranges, who will do whatever they can to undermine NAGPRA. Many won't say it out loud like them, but their actions speak for them. In their view, it's their right to pursue our history without our interference. It's their science, their occupation. And only their version of our history is correct."

Karen recalled what Richie had said. "Native American history is American history."

"But few of you even know that history," he shot back. "And digging up stuff isn't going to change that. Because you think of *us* as the past, not living, breathing people with traditions that we live and breathe that they are trampling on. You might know a few Indians." He glanced at Two Fingers. "But you have no idea who I am, where I come from, my traditions, my culture, anything. Any more than you really know your own deputy."

She knew what she needed to know. "I know he's a good man. That he's dedicated to justice. That he loves his family. No, I don't know his religious or cultural connections. I am not sure he knows mine."

Two Fingers's lips twitched. "Lutheran. Scandinavian. German."

Zinger. But she wasn't the silent one. "Okay, so I have a big mouth, so he knows."

"He knows because you are embedded in your community. It's common knowledge. He is not in his community. He doesn't have the same practices, even religion, as yours."

Karen frowned at him. "How would you know that? Lots of Indians are Christians."

"And maybe he is, too. As you say, many are. But if he is, that's not all he is. I can smell sweetgrass. He smudges. I would have, too, plus a sweat as soon as it could be arranged, if I'd gotten home. It's a... cleansing, I guess you could say."

"Hunter smudged," Marek commented. "He may have gone home on Friday when he disappeared for several hours. Do you know anything about that?"

Karen hadn't gone there yet. There were too many angles to pursue this early in the investigation, and their most promising suspect was sitting in front of her.

Stands By Him frowned thoughtfully. "I do remember

when he came back. He seemed... excited... when he first got out of his car. He caught my eye. As if he wanted to rush over and reveal something. But then..." Stands By Him seemed to struggle for words. "He looked over at the dig and then back at me. Not as if he wanted to talk to me any longer, but as if I were an option that he was considering. I don't know if I can explain it any better. Just as if I'd reminded him of something. He sobered up a bit. Then he went to the dig, talked to Hardy. I actually thought he was finally going to quit, but no, he started digging."

Marek asked, "Was Hawks wearing the same clothes when you saw him as when he came knocking?"

Stands By Him blinked and frowned. "No, he wasn't. He'd been wearing a white tank top and khaki shorts, but was wearing a black T-shirt and jeans when he showed up. Clean."

Karen thought she knew where Marek was going. Hawks was definitely in play as a suspect. "Did he have shovels for this planned diversion project of yours?"

"I assumed he did. In the trunk. But I didn't see them."

If they could get a warrant for Hawks's car, that might be something to look for. But she wasn't ready yet to write off Stands By Him. Or, guiltily, her honeymoon. Maybe they could salvage a few days. "So what happened after you found the body?"

Stands By Him shuddered. "Hawks ran all out to the car, and after a few seconds, I followed. When I got there, he was in the car already. He said we had to get far, far away, or we'd be pinned. I told him running would just make it worse. That we could drive to Lower Brule and talk to the tribal police there. But Hawks said no way, no how, was he falling into *any* police hands." Stands By Him frowned. "He might have said *again*. You know, like he'd been falsely imprisoned before. Likely he'd been arrested before on protests. He did say they were all corrupt, that they'd lock up whoever fell into their hands first. Said I was a dumb Injun and deserved whatever I got."

The young man ruffled his hair with his hands. "Hawks left me there, spun out, and drove off. He never even gave me a chance to get in."

Because the whole plan was to leave Stands By Him holding the murder bag? The sacrificial Indian. That was one possible path. But Stands By Him still had a lot of explaining to do, especially the car and the blood. But she kept that zipped. They had him talking. They wanted to keep him talking. "What happened next?"

"I couldn't think. I was out there without a ride, it was after midnight, and I was alone with a dead body. A dead *friend*. At the very end, that's all I could think. We would never smoke the peace pipe together. He was so crumpled, so small, like a child. I couldn't leave him like that. Our people often left our dead high up in trees or scaffolds away from animals, in the past. A sky burial. I don't mean we do that now, but I was in shock, and I could only think, at least he died in the open, that his spirit could go to Wakan Tanka."

From somewhere, Karen knew those words. The Great Spirit. Or the Great Mystery.

"I didn't have a scaffold or a tree. So I picked him up, put him over my shoulder, and I took him to the top of Spirit Mound and said a prayer for him."

While it sounded like truth, even moving, Karen couldn't get past one thing. "Then you left your protest sign on his chest, calling him a thief."

"What?! Why would I do that?" His gaze flicked up to Two Fingers. "It would be traced right back to me." Then he stilled. "And a nice way to frame the dumb Injun. So much for truth. That's a lie."

"It's not a lie," Two Fingers said. "I was there. It was there."

Stands By Him shook his head, his dark hair shifting in

the light. "I put him on his back and straightened him, so he would be open to the sky. I didn't leave my sign. That would be monumentally stupid."

"Then how did it get there?" Marek asked. "When did you last see it?"

His dark head tilted back as he thought. "I ditched it on the ground—in the parking lot—when I dragged Hawks back to the car, after Hunter called him a plastic. That was a low blow. Twinkie, I expected. Not plastic."

Karen felt she was missing something. Apparently, Marek did, too.

"Doesn't plastic just mean fake?" he asked.

Two Fingers answered. "No, it's short for 'plastic shaman.' Someone, often a wannabe non-Native, but not always, who uses our spiritual traditions and ceremonies for monetary gain. Twinkies can also be plastics but are more likely the New Agers and Cherokee Princess people, those who claim to be Natives when they aren't."

"It's all about cultural appropriation," Stands By Him confirmed. "But for a Native to call another Native a plastic? That's serious stuff."

Karen's phone beeped. She took it out. A text from Larson. But not any lovey-dovey stuff. *Prints recovered from sign. One unknown. Other Tommy Knotts. Wanted in OK.*

Excitement bubbled through her. She showed the text to Marek.

"You ever hear the name Tommy Knotts?" she asked Stands By Him.

Stands By Him reacted like a scalded cat, almost overturning his chair. Two Fingers caught it before it could do so. "Hell, yes. I researched him for my dissertation. Talk about a plastic. He killed a tourist with one of his fake Sun Dances that he charged out the nose for."

Karen remembered Doll talking about the Okipa of the Mandan being somewhat like the Sun Dance. "Isn't that being hung by your skin? Why would anyone pay money to do that?"

"Wasicus are strange. They want what they don't have." His nose wrinkled. "Why are you asking me about Knotts?"

Marek was looking down at his phone. "Because he failed to show for trial on manslaughter charges in Oklahoma a couple decades back. His supporters got stuck with paying bail. There's an outstanding warrant for his arrest. No sign of him." He looked up. "Until his prints showed up on your protest sign."

CHAPTER 16

Marek wondered if Hunter Redwing-Digges had discovered Tonto Hawks's true identity. And that's what he was so excited about after returning to the dig on Friday. Because he could expose Hawks and get him off the dig. That would explain the strange look Hunter had given Stands By Him. Hunter knew that the news was going to devastate his one-time friend.

And it did. Stands By Him looked absolutely gutted. "Hawks is *Knotts*?"

Karen turned her phone so he could read it. "That's from the crime lab in Sioux Falls. Unless you can think of any other middle-aged man who might have touched your sign lately?"

Stands By Him shook his head slowly. "It can't be him. I saw pictures of Knotts. Slick dude. Nice suit, pricey shades, slim with dark hair. Hawks is an overweight, gray-haired, ugly dude with a ride that's barely hanging on, just like a lot of Indians on the rez."

"Living on the edge can do that to you," Karen said. "As will age."

Marek found an image of Knotts at his initial arrest. Everything had thickened, body and face, but he could still see it. The shape of the ears, one upper tooth overlapped slightly, a mole along his nose. When he pointed these out to Stands By Him, the young man still shook his head.

"What would Hawks possibly have to gain if he was Knotts?" he demanded. "You saw him. He's not rolling in dough. He's barely making it. Half the time, we have to pool our money for gas or food for him."

Stands By Him continued to stare at the image on Marek's phone, seeing the things Marek had noted. The mole was the most damning. "Maybe he had a change of heart. Maybe he's sorry for what happened. I mean, yes, it was really bad, but maybe he just didn't realize what he was doing." Stands By Him rolled with it. "Just wanted to help people. Stupid people do stupid stuff. Maybe with going to the protests, he was trying to pay back for what happened. Probably just didn't realize how dangerous it was, performing ceremonies like the Sun Dance without years of teaching by the elders. He always said he wasn't raised in the tradition."

Two Fingers finally spoke. "What tribe did he claim?"

"Cherokee. The standard tribe for wannabes." The young man pursed his lips. "But one night when he'd had a few too many drinks, he said he was from Broken Arrow."

"Oklahoma," Karen murmured.

Marek did a quick search. "Tommy Knotts was born there."

At least according to the Wiki article on him, to a single mixed-race mother who got knocked around one too many times and died of a brain hemorrhage. Tommy ended up in foster care. He claimed a feel-good rags-to-riches story, a poor Native soul lost in the system. Only by recovering the spirituality of his ancestors had he turned his life around— and he wanted to share it with others. But the rest of the article showed a much darker side—embezzlement, fraud, and the outrageous amounts he charged. The high life he led. The false claims he made about his ancestry—none of which could be verified. Despite his claims, he was not enrolled anywhere, as the Cherokees were quick to attest. The most he could claim was that he'd been honored early on by one of the tribes, but they were also quick to point out that it did not make him an honorary member.

Marek looked up after relating that. "He's unlikely to have changed his spots. But at least we know why he ran."

"And left you," Two Fingers murmured to Stands By Him.

Stands By Him slowly sank back in his chair. "You think he left me to take the rap."

Karen settled on the edge of the table. "We don't know yet. Maybe he just ran because of the warrant. Maybe you killed Hunter. Maybe you didn't. Maybe he did. Or neither of you did. We don't know yet."

He crossed his arms. "You don't believe me."

"I didn't say that," Karen replied with some heat. "You've given us your side. We need to check it out. That takes time."

A knock on the door heralded Walrus. "Sorry to interrupt, but thought you might like to know that Hawks was picked up by the Vermillion police for DUI. Tested 0.14. He's singing like a bird. Said he's ready to deal, that he knows who killed Redwing-Digges. Oh, and they found enough dynamite in his trunk to blow the dig—and all of Spirit Mound—to kingdom come."

Stands By Him's dark head thunked on the table, the strands of his hair sifting in the flickering fluorescent lights like a dark waterfall. "Not shovels. Damn him. He set me up."

While Karen went out to make arrangements for Hawks's transfer, Marek asked Walrus, "Why wasn't Hawks still at the dig?"

"He left after giving his spiel to the media. Said he was going to drum up more support with the increased media coverage, that he'd get the dig shut down faster that way."

Marek frowned at the dark head on the table. "Any idea where he got the money for the dynamite? Had to be black market without permits and licensing. Possibly thousands of dollars."

The head rose slowly. "Thousands? He didn't have any

money. He was broke. Slept in his car at that free camping spot in Vermillion. Lions Park. He'd rip off the toilet paper."

Knotts alias Hawks ripped off a lot of people. It's what he did, apparently. "Hawks had a website, a blog, you say. Did it have a donate button?"

"I guess. But..." The bitter chocolate eyes closed. "He's a user. Always has been, always will be. Wowicake sni."

Two Fingers spoke up. "You weren't deceived by us."

"No, I got snookered by a plastic. I always wondered how people fell for it. I mean, maybe tourists don't know better, but I should. *Especially* me. But he wasn't selling anything, he was protesting, and he looked to have nothing to gain." Stands By Him straightened. "What happens now?"

"You will be held pending inquiries." Marek watched the stoic face harden even as the lips trembled. "If we determine your story is true, you will likely be released on bail."

"I don't have any money for bail. It's all tied to my assistantship. My family has none. I don't have a car. I don't have anything, other than what I get from my assistantship."

"Maybe your friends or tribe can help," Marek suggested. "I can't tell you what will happen. That depends on our investigation." But he would tell the young man the truth. "The state's attorney may decide to charge you for obstruction of justice for disturbing a crime scene and fleeing the scene and not reporting a murder and car theft."

"Hunter wouldn't have seen it as theft," the young man insisted. "Those who have, help those with none. I was headed to LB to do the right thing. For him."

Two Fingers said something to him in Lakota, and the young man gave a huff of derisive laughter. "Yeah, right. Hawks—or Knotts—was right about one thing. I'm one dumb Injun."

When Walrus took him down to the jail in the basement, Marek asked Two Fingers, "What did you tell him?"

Lips twitched. "The truth will set him free."

Straight out of the Bible. Perhaps some dark humor? Or

perhaps it was said in all sincerity. While the road might be rocky, Stands By Him would eventually be free. Hawks was another story.

Karen returned with latex gloves for all three of them. "Let's see what we've got here." After unsealing the large bag that had come from Brule County, they found a couple smaller bags. One held an ancient flip phone and two sets of keys. One set, Marek guessed, was Hunter's. There was one wallet, which was Stands By Him's, along with a card that showed he was seven-eighths American Indian and an enrolled member of the Sicangu Lakota.

"Doesn't look like he had Hunter's phone or wallet," Two Fingers commented.

"It's still possible they're in the car or that he ditched them." Karen reached for the next bag. "Larson texted me that they've requested information on Hunter's phone from the carrier. And they've entered the phone's serial number into the system, so if it shows up somewhere, it'll pop."

Marek pulled out the white and red USD T-shirt that Stands By Him had been wearing when he'd been picked up. The front had a few blood smears, the back a lot more. The knee-length gray shorts were the same.

They all looked at each other. In disgust. But Marek wasn't yet ready to make it official. "We need to confirm that this is what Stands By Him was wearing Friday night."

Karen obligingly called Doll, who confirmed. She'd kept an eye on Hawks, and as Stands By Him was usually in his vicinity, Doll was firm on what he'd been wearing.

Two Fingers said it first. "Stands By Him didn't kill Hunter."

Marek nodded. No question.

"Not a spatter to be found," Karen agreed. "And the sheriff of Brule County is incompetent, lazy, or blind." Then she smiled. "But at least I can tell Richie Legrange he was dead wrong."

Marek reminded her, "Stands By Him could still be

involved as an accessory." Two Fingers's dark, brooding gaze landed on him. "But for what it's worth, I think he was telling the truth." You couldn't feign that shock—or that self-loathing.

Karen's phone pinged again, and she pulled it out. "They've started to print the car. Hunter's, I mean. But Larson reports no weapon, no wallet, no phone found. Hunter was fairly neat, so other than some research notes and the like, not much there." Her lips pursed as another text arrived. "They did find a torn-off piece of paper in the cup holder."

Karen paused a second to read the text then grinned at Two Fingers. "It had the name Tommy Knotts on it. Underlined three times and with a bunch of exclamation points after."

Marek barely saw it on the deputy's face, but the relief was there. Two Fingers would undoubtedly follow the truth, wherever it led, but he—and the rest of them—didn't want Stands By Him to be the killer. All the current evidence pointed at Hawks.

"You can go back off duty," Karen told Two Fingers as she pocketed her phone. "Or stick around for Hawks."

"To be fair, I should stay," he said after a minute. "If you wanted a Native here for a Native."

Karen leaned against the wall as they waited for Kurt to bring Hawks. "But that's the question, isn't it? Is he?"

Two Fingers's eyes dropped. "I hope not."

"Why?" Marek asked.

"It would be better for him, and us, if he isn't. Betrayal from within is always worse. Betrayal from without…"

"Is expected," Marek finished.

Two Fingers didn't comment. He didn't need to. It was true.

When Tonto Hawks aka Tommy Knotts arrived half an hour later, it was obvious he or his supporters had called the media. He walked up to the courthouse like a celebrity, not a prisoner.

Marek followed Karen out the double doors. On the top step, Hawks held forth to a respectable cluster of microphones. Unlike Stands By Him, who'd arrived unheralded and in chains, Hawks had only his hands cuffed in front of him and wore his own clothes. For some reason, the press hadn't picked up on Stands By Him. Not even Nails, but that could be because Stands By Him had been brought in from the back, not the front, where Nails could have seen him.

While Marek found Hawks smarmy and over-the-top, the man did know how to bullshit with a straight face. A necessary skill for a con man. And he'd adjusted to his audience, as he was considerably toned down from earlier. He sounded almost like a kindly professor, not the in-your-face protester from earlier.

"As usual, Native Americans are always the first targeted in any investigation where they are even remotely involved," he was saying. Though his eyes were rather bloodshot, he didn't sound particularly soused. "I was minding my own business, enjoying a rare day of pleasant weather, when I was pulled over. For what, I ask you? Driving while Native. That's what it is in this part of the country. Not many blacks, so they go after us. It's pure profiling."

The grizzled reporter from Sioux Falls said, "My sources say you were driving erratically. And that you failed the breathalyzer."

Hawks gave a big sigh. "That is false. I swerved to avoid a squirrel. Unlike many wasicu—that's whites, by the way—I have a reverence for all life. And I refused a breathalyzer."

Marek looked at Karen. That was an outright lie. Was he going to claim it was fudged? True, it did happen. It had happened to him. But that was well in the past and a special circumstance. Karen herself didn't know, and he never intended to tell her. That was between him and his half-brother, Arne Okerlund, her father.

Another reporter asked skeptically, "So you gave up your license for a year?"

South Dakota law for refusing a breathalyzer was license revocation. Hawks blinked but replied smoothly, "We all make sacrifices for our freedom. I served in the military at one time. I know how to sacrifice."

Marek had seen nothing in his bio that indicated that, but who knew. It was possible.

Blake Halvorsen piped up. "My sources say that you claim to know who killed Hunter Redwing-Digges."

As the other reporters murmured, Hawks nodded sagely. "Sadly, such information has come into my hands, and naturally, I'm here to make that information available to the proper authorities."

Marek had to admire how quickly Karen got in the picture. "Which is where we regrettably have to bow out of this impromptu media session. We want to protect the information from becoming public before we can act on it. We are grateful that Mr. Hawks has come to freely give us a hand. Mr. Hawks, if you will..." She made a grand gesture toward the double doors.

Perhaps appreciating the grandeur, though looking conflicted about the "freely" part, Hawks finally said with great magnanimity, "Always happy to help anyone find the truth. It's the only way to be truly free."

Marek hid his smile. The truth would not set Tommy Knotts free.

Quite the opposite.

CHAPTER 17

Karen knew she would get ribbed for that grand gesture, especially by Adam Van Eck, the master of the grand gesture, who trod the boards when not on the beat. He'd probably even critique her delivery, if she let him, which she wasn't planning to do.

But she wanted Tonto Hawks away from the cameras. Being aggressive with him would just look bad. And she wanted him talking. The more he talked, the more he lied. But she wanted it on record after the requisite Miranda warning. After that little scene on the steps, he had no leg to stand on if he cried lawyer before giving them his story.

After they got the Miranda warning done and the recorder turned on, Karen began simply. "Go ahead, Mr. Hawks. We're all ears."

He coughed. "I want a deal first. For immunity."

She widened her eyes. "Why would you need a deal, if you didn't do anything?"

He hesitated. "I may have, quite inadvertently, been caught up in criminal activity. I would just like some protection."

Deliberately misunderstanding him, Karen nodded at Marek. "No one is getting past him. You're protected. Though it would help if we knew who you need protection from, which is why you're here, as you told the press."

Hawks looked taken aback then slightly more relaxed.

He had this. Or so he thought. Dimwits. Karen was glad that they hadn't been the ones to take his statement earlier in the day. She and Marek had read over Two Fingers's notes. Hawks had known nothing. He'd heard nothing. He knew nothing. Yes, he'd been insulted by Hunter Redwing-Digges, but the young man was sadly assimilated and didn't know any better. "Nonetheless... there is some risk of legal jeopardy, not physical."

"If you tell us the complete truth, which I am sure you will, we can arrange something, I'm sure," Karen said blithely.

Hawks glanced at the recorder and apparently decided that was good enough. A good lawyer could likely argue the same. And she was fine with it. Because she'd already figured out that the man couldn't stop lying any more than a dog could stop chasing rabbits. As Marek didn't so much as twitch, she figured that he was of the same opinion.

Hawks smiled genially at them. He really did know how to slip into another character. Perhaps he should team up with Adam.

"I know I have the reputation of being, shall we say, somewhat abrasive. But that's show. It's how you get eyeballs. Same with my blog, which enjoys some modest success. I have never been violent or advocated for violence. What I found myself entangled in just makes my heart hurt, especially as it involves one of my fellow Natives."

He actually put his hand to his heart. Karen fought not to roll her eyes. "Do tell."

"You may have noticed, or perhaps no one pointed it out to you, that the student leader of the protest, Jerome Stands By Him, was missing for this morning's interviews."

"Yes, Richie Legrange mentioned it." Again, she made her tone deliberately offhand. As if they hadn't had time to even look at such things.

Hawks blinked. "Well, here's where things get a bit dicey. Jerome was disappointed by how little attention his protest had gotten. He wanted to do something big, to make a statement. He even mentioned dynamite." He made a horrified face. "I told him, of course, nothing violent. That just makes Natives look bad. We argued about it. Perhaps someone noticed."

Karen just looked at him expectantly. "Please, go on."

He folded his cuffed hands over his thick middle. "I'm older, wiser. You know how young men are. Hot, impulsive. Only age gives a man wisdom. That's why we Natives revere our elders. I tried to think of some alternative that would satisfy Jerome and finally get the notice that this protest deserved. If we diverted some water from the creek—not a lot, just enough to stall the dig for a day or two—we'd have made our point. I realize that this was still not ideal, but I was very concerned for what Jerome might do otherwise. I went to tell him about the alternative at his dorm room. He told me to sit down for a while, as he had to go get shovels, and he asked for my keys. Well, unlike the wasicu, we give. We always give. That's our way. I thought nothing of it. I was always helping out the students, giving them rides, paying for their meals, whatever I could do."

Hawks cleared his throat. "I am not quite sure of when he got back. I'm afraid I dozed off. Not as young as I used to be. But it was after midnight, I believe. I asked him if he got shovels, and he gave me this strange look at first but then nodded. And we went out to Spirit Mound. Such a lovely, spiritual place, with the moonlight spilling over the sacred land of our ancestors. It really was such a desecration, that dig, and I fully support the protest. But..."

Hawks closed his eyes. "It was absolutely horrible. I will have nightmares for the rest of my life. It's hard to even describe. I thought Jerome was taking me over to the creek, though I was curious why we hadn't gotten the shovels out of the trunk. Maybe, I thought, he wanted to figure out where best to make the diversion. Instead..." He took in a sharp breath, hard enough to be heard on the recording. "Instead, he led me straight to the sadly crumpled body of that deluded young man, Hunter Redwing-Digges. In a flash, I understood what had happened."

The obnoxious air conditioning was the only sound in the room. "And that was?"

"Isn't it obvious?" Hawks spread his hands as much as he could. "While I was dozing in his dorm room, Jerome had gone to get dynamite. From where, I have no idea, but he must have gone out to the dig to blow the place up. For whatever reason, Hunter must have been there, confronted him, and been killed."

For the first time, Marek spoke. He sounded puzzled. "But why would he bring *you* back to the dig to see the body?"

Hawks shook his head sadly. "I'm afraid you haven't met enough depraved minds in your life."

Karen almost choked. She covered it by clearing her throat. "What do you think his plan was, then?"

Hawks widened his bloodshot eyes. "I am absolutely certain that he meant to frame me for Hunter's murder. To kill me, set it up as if I'd killed poor Hunter, and then dynamite the whole place. Of course, I didn't realize that last part until this little misunderstanding with the police in Vermillion. I was truly shocked when I was told what they found in my trunk. I had no idea."

Karen was going to enjoy watching this bullshitter go down. "But you didn't know that then, when you saw the body. What did you do?"

"I ran," he said simply.

"You left Stands By Him there?" Marek asked, frowning.

"Of course I left him there." Hawks sounded a little testier now. "The young man was a killer. And I wasn't going to stay and let him kill me. It's clear he'd planned it out. I would have been pinned as the killer who'd sacrificed myself for the cause. One last grand gesture. A tidy ending." His mouth tightened. "You'd have closed the case. Just one more crazy Injun."

Karen gave Marek an admonishing look before turning

back to Hawks. "Do you have any idea where we might find Stands By Him?"

Hawks relaxed back into geniality. "You'll likely find him hiding out at Lower Brule. He may have even tried to tell the tribal police there—and I must regretfully inform you that they are heavily biased against white-passing Natives like myself—an entirely different tale. One that no doubt implicates me. Nonsense, of course."

After the reprimand, Marek had started shuffling through papers in a folder on the table. He didn't look up. "You told the press that you refused a breathalyzer."

Hawks hesitated again, looking harder at the file. "Well, yes, that was for show. It makes for good press." He cleared his throat. "After I left Jerome... I just didn't know what to do. He was a promising young man. He reminded me so much of myself at that age. Lost, angry. I admit I had to indulge in some Dutch courage to do the right thing. I was on my way when I was stopped."

So Hawks wasn't entirely stupid. He could claim whatever he liked to the press, but the stop had likely been recorded, as was the breathalyzer. A pity. But he'd already lied a dozen times over. At least, according to Stands By Him, he had. She had to remind herself that liking or not liking someone was immaterial. Only the truth mattered.

But obviously one man was lying. Rather than go for the throat, which is what she wanted, Karen asked with studied excitement, "Did you notice any blood on Stands By Him or his clothes?"

Again, Hawks hesitated. He squinted at her. "I'm afraid my eyes aren't the best. I can't afford to buy glasses. But he could have showered and changed clothes. I don't follow fashions, though. If pressed, I would say he was wearing a T-shirt and shorts, but I can't swear to it."

Hawks was canny, she'd give him that. "That's disappointing. Do you have anything to back up what you're saying?"

"Well... I don't know. I did sort of notice, that he no longer had his sign. For the protest, I mean. You may not have understood it. It's in Lakota."

Karen lit up. And not for the reason he thought. "Yes, that's it. It means 'thief.' At least that's what the other side said. It was found on—"

"Don't lead the witness," Marek snapped.

She shot him a nasty glare then turned back to Hawks. "Can you tell me why you think the sign is relevant?"

Hawks looked between the two of them. Seemingly satisfied by the level of conflict between them, he nodded. "When we walked out to the dig to divert the creek water, he had that sign in his hand. Like it was part of his plan, you know? To put it somewhere that it could be read and understood. Like I said, he wanted to make a big deal about the cause."

"For a backwater dig in a backwater county in a backwater state?" Marek rolled his eyes. "Who cares?"

"*We* care." Hawks pounded the table with his hand. "It's our land, our heritage. And by raising awareness, we can get a lot more mon—" He stopped. "More support for other causes."

More money? Just how much was Hawks raking in on his website for his various causes? That would be a good avenue to pursue. He was certainly passionate about either the cause or the money, and Karen would hazard to guess which it was. He didn't live like a king, true. But he had in the past. Maybe he was looking toward retirement.

"That sounds reasonable." Karen made a point of not looking at Marek. "But back to the sign—do you know if anyone else handled it, like other protesters?"

He opened his mouth, shut it, then shrugged. "We often just threw all the signs together into the trunk, so whoever took it out, they'd have their prints on it. Heck, I could have."

Karen looked over at Marek. The beating-about-the-bush tactic wasn't working. Other than the DUI, which Hawks had more or less acceded, they had nothing on the man to leverage.

Marek said, "We'll get your prints from Vermillion and check—"

"No, no, there's no need. I can give them to you." He stuck his hands out like a child wanting them washed after his ice cream cone melted. "Happy to help."

Happy not to have them run his prints through the system.

Marek said, "Good. We can check your prints against the dynamite at the same time."

Hawks's hands snapped back. He put them under his armpits. "No way. You're trying to trick me. You've got some beef with me." Hawks looked at Karen. "Your man's a bigot. You've seen how he treats me. He'll try to frame me."

"Oh, he wouldn't do that. Couldn't, in fact, as Vermillion had the car towed directly to Sioux Falls for forensic testing." After she got the slight nod from Marek, the go-ahead signal, Karen smiled quite genuinely at Hawks. "So you should be just fine and dandy if everything happened as you stated on the record... Mr. Knotts."

CHAPTER 18

Even in the unpredictable Dakotas, Marek had never seen someone so frozen in the middle of August. He was almost tempted to reach out and touch the man to see if he would shatter on contact.

Finally, Hawks managed to get out, "I don't understand. What did you call me? Mr. Not? As in 'not true'? I told you the truth. Mostly." His eyes darted away, back, away. "But... I, well... you have to understand how damned *scared* I was. And am." He held up his hands, which were indeed shaking. "Jerome *forced* me to go along with his scheme. I didn't want anything to do with it. But he had a gun. He *has* a gun. Don't you understand? He could kill me. He could kill *you*."

Karen just continued to smile at him. "That would be a little hard to manage from lockup."

That jolted the man. "What? When?"

"That doesn't seem relevant," Karen told him. "But you have no reason to fear him."

Hope dawned. "Then you've already charged him with murder? He'll never get out?" Hawks frowned. "But you asked me where he was."

"I was curious as to where you thought he was."

Hawks turned prim, folding his hands on the table. "You wanted to know if I was involved. I wasn't, at least not willingly."

Marek asked, "Who did you buy the dynamite from?"

"I didn't. I have no idea. He opened the trunk, told me to start unloading. Or else."

"So you didn't go right out and find the body as you stated."

Hawks looked briefly confused. "Oh. No, not right away. He had me take out the boxes. I didn't want to tell you before because I was so scared."

Marek continued to press. "Where did he have you put the boxes?"

"On... the asphalt. The parking lot. Then he forced me to go out to that last tent, showed me the body, and told me I was going to make the perfect sacrificial lamb for the cause."

Marek gave him a skeptical look. "So you ran back to the car and left."

"That's right."

Karen frowned. "He didn't try to shoot you?"

"He... He missed."

Marek crossed his arms. "Funny, there were no shell casings found on the scene. Nor any holes in the car."

Before Hawks could respond to that, Karen asked, "You never saw Jerome Stands By Him again?"

Hawks shuddered. "Never. And I never want to see him again. Unless... Unless I have to testify against him. I'll do that. I have to, as he's betrayed his people, all Natives, by what he did. It would be my duty."

Marek watched him. "You are now telling us the complete truth?"

"Yes, of course. I am no longer scared."

Marek shot back, "Give it time. You will be."

"What does that fucking mean?" Hawks was slipping now.

Marek often played good cop or dumb cop, but it was kind of freeing to play bad cop. "You left the boxes of dynamite in the parking lot. How did those boxes get into your car if you never saw Jerome again?"

Hawks's trembling fingers intertwined. "I... he... must've planted them there. Sometime in the night after he stole

Hunter's car. I was asleep at that park in Vermillion. Everyone knows I spend the night there. It's free."

"So we'll find his prints on the dynamite as well as yours?" Karen asked.

"Yes... no... you are confusing me! I am just trying to tell you the truth. He probably had gloves on. I mean, everyone knows about fingerprints."

"You'd think so," Marek muttered. "You didn't."

"That just proves my point!" His cuffed hands thudded on the table. "I had no choice. He had a gun."

"What kind?" Marek pressed.

"How the hell do I know? A *gun* gun. It shoots bullets."

"Handgun? Rifle? What?"

Hawks hesitated. "Handgun. Otherwise, I'd have seen it."

"Did he kill Hunter with it?"

"Yes... no... I don't know!" His face turned red as he yelled at Marek. "I didn't murder him! Hunter was dead. Dead when I got there, dead when I went back, dead, dead, dead. The only good Indian is a dead Indian—that's what you people think. Well, you got one, but you're not getting another."

Karen pursed her lips. "You went back to plant the sign?"

His mouth gaped. "What? I didn't go back."

"You just said you did."

"I... I misspoke. I didn't go back. Why would I do that?"

Karen leaned forward. "Good question. Then again, why would you go back to the park to sleep? I'd think that if I had to decide whether or not to turn in a young friend, especially one who'd threatened to kill me and that I was scared to death of, I'd be tossing and turning all night."

Hawks managed to look affronted. "I did."

"Yet somehow slept through Jerome driving up to your camping site to put the dynamite in your trunk? How did he get the keys?"

Marek thought the man might actually kill himself with apoplexy. His hands thudded again on the table. "I didn't murder Hunter Redwing-fucking-Digges. I can prove it. I was buying the damn dynamite when he was killed!"

The air conditioning kicked back on with a Dakota huff of a laugh, punctuated only by Hawks's gasps as he tried to grasp what he'd just said.

Rather than let him regroup, Marek leaned in. "Give us a name."

Hawks darted looks between Marek and Karen. When Karen just raised her brows, he slumped. "A guy named Dustin in Sioux Falls. I don't know his last name. He's got a hole-in-the-wall." Hawks rattled off the address. "He'll kill me."

Karen shook her head. "No, he'll be in prison. Though one hopes not in the same cell block."

"Jerome made me do it! He threatened me."

"How did he do that if he was killing Hunter? Oh, wait. Are you saying that none of the rest of your story was true?"

"Of course it was true. Well, except at first. I told you—I was scared."

Karen pursed her lips. "But you just told us that you didn't know about the dynamite, that you were forced to unload it onto the asphalt, and that Jerome then took you to the body."

"Okay, okay, I went to get the dynamite on my own, but that was before I saw the gun. I thought I could still talk him out of it. When we argued about it, about how much he'd made me get and where he wanted to do it, that's when he pulled a gun on me. He showed me what he'd do to me if I didn't follow through—what he'd done to Hunter."

Karen pursed her lips. "And then you ran."

"Yes, yes, yes!"

"So when was Hunter killed?"

"I don't know!"

"You said you were in Sioux Falls when he was killed."

As Hawks shook his head, trying to find a way out, Marek

went on, not letting up. "And Hunter wasn't killed with a gun. You knew that."

"I just meant... that he killed him. Not how."

"How was he killed?"

"How the hell do I know?" All the lies were starting to sink the man's bluster. "You're just trying to pin it on the most convenient scapegoat. An Indian."

"I believe you have the honor of doing that, not us," Karen said. No more good cop.

"My followers will rip you to shreds." Hawks crossed his arms. "And my lawyer will see you in prison, not me."

"What lawyer? You don't have any money, right? Good luck with your public defender. Once you finally get one, that is."

His chin jutted. "My blog followers have been generous."

"We will be looking into that. I don't think they'll be too happy to have been supporting a plastic shaman. They'll be clamoring for their money back."

He flinched, but there was real fear in his bloodshot eyes. "That's an insult."

"And if you claimed the money was going to support the various causes, but you instead used it for personal gain, I think there may be issues there with the IRS. What about taxes? Hmm? You can kiss any money you've raked in goodbye. It's as good as gone."

The fear of being exposed as Knotts seemed to dissipate. Hawks surged to his feet. "I've scrimped and lived like a damn Injun for *decades*. Spewed nonsense, walked miles in heat, in snow, for shitty backward people who should've died out eons ago. I was just one big protest from pulling in enough to leave their pathetic causes in the dustbin where they belong and sip mai tais in Borneo. You aren't taking that money from me. I *earned* it."

Hawks seemed to have totally forgotten the recorder. All to the good. For them.

Marek got to his feet, as did Karen, her fjord-blue eyes

wary. "And that doesn't, of course, cover any of the charges you are already facing."

"DUI is nothing. My first."

"That may or may not be true. Tax evasion is a big deal. Setting up, or failing to set up, a nonprofit and siphoning off the money for personal use might well fall under fraud or embezzlement." Karen leaned in. "But manslaughter is nothing to sneeze at, *Tommy*. I believe the minimum in Oklahoma is at least four years."

He breathed in then out, as if ready to spew fire, but only a mewling cry came out. "My name is Tonto, not Tommy. And I've never been to Oklahoma."

"Strange, you told others you were born in Broken Arrow." She leaned in farther. "You left your prints on the sign you left on Hunter's body. We've got you cold, *Knotts*. Hunter knew about you. He called you a plastic, and Jerome had to haul you away to stop you from attacking him right there with Hardy watching. Hunter had your name on a slip of paper in his car. So you confronted him, and you killed him. Then you went to Sioux Falls and bought the dynamite, got your sacrificial lamb in Jerome, and took him out there."

"I didn't kill Hunter! He was already dead when we got there!"

Marek chimed in. "We'll check your phone, your movements, everything."

"You do that. I went directly to Sioux Falls. I got the dynamite, and I had some beer at a bar. Got a room, took a shower, and had a roll with a willing ho—some gal with a cowboy tattoo. Then I drove back down to Vermillion."

"Via Highway 19." Spirit Mound was off that same highway.

"No! That was later. I was on I-29 then." The darting eyes stilled. "And I can prove it. I used Google Maps on my phone. I used it to find Dustin. You'll see."

Yes, they would. Over the man's protests, his demands for immediate access to the press and to his money for a lawyer, they booked him into the jail—in a cell that had no line of sight with Jerome's. And Marek called for a public defender.

That was all Hawks would get. While the statute of limitations may have run out on a lot of the charges against Tommy Knotts in Oklahoma, the charges in South Dakota would stick. Especially the sticks of dynamite. The money he'd collected as Tonto Hawks would be frozen solid.

Even in August in the Dakotas.

CHAPTER 19

Karen had little hope for a happy ending. For either her honeymoon or the investigation. After a check of Hawks's phone, they'd determined he had indeed gone directly to Sioux Falls after leaving the dig on Friday night and hadn't returned until he'd gone to Jerome Stand By Him's dorm room.

The change of clothes had been conducted in Hawks's car before his cowboy-tattooed assignation. As he'd said, protesting was sweaty work—attested to by his very smelly bag of laundry per Larson.

Yes, Hawks had gone back to Spirit Mound, no doubt to plant the sign to implicate Jerome. As he'd forgotten to turn off tracking, they'd also found that Hawks had stopped on Saturday at a pawn shop in Vermillion. A quick call yielded Hunter's phone, which was on its way to Sioux Falls, though Larson had already gotten access to the records via the phone company and had nothing unusual to report on Friday evening. No calls, no texts.

And they'd just heard from the highway patrol that a hitchhiker on I-29 had flagged a squad down because they'd found Hunter's wallet—without any cash, of course. So Hawks had not just planted the sign, he'd robbed the body.

All of that would put Hawks away. Hopefully for a good long time. But they were no closer to finding Hunter's killer.

At least her stomach rumbled happily as it digested one

of the party pack of tacos, burritos, and enchiladas she'd ordered from Mex-Mix after calling another incident meeting. She looked around the office, crowded with her entire roster except for Adam. The show must go on—summer musicals like *Sleeping Beauty* especially—and Adam needed his beauty sleep before opening curtain in another hour or two. Two Fingers and Seoul were on opposite sides of the room, studiously avoiding each other. Everyone else was studiously avoiding both of them.

After Seoul reached for her mug and slunk into the breakroom, Karen followed. The aroma of deep, rich coffee of Sisters Blend rose in the awkward silence.

"You okay?" Karen finally asked. "I mean, you and... Two Fingers." That got a gnarly look. But Karen had reason. "I need to know if you can work together."

"*I* can. I don't know about him." Then it burst out. "He won't tell me *anything* about Chief Goodthunder. Says it's up to the chief to decide whether to reply to my mom." Her young face was full of betrayal. "I mean, all I want is to get some *idea* of the man and of his family. I don't want my mom to be hurt. And she already is, that he hasn't bothered to respond. I mean, it's not like he turned up as a half-sib to my mom, like his father cheated on his mother. It's not *that* close. I'd think he'd be curious."

Karen knew something about the thorny issues involved. She'd been on both sides of it with Eyre. She hadn't told her parents, so her father was still mad at her and likely always would be. But Karen herself had not been told that she'd given up her child to her former basketball coach, the biological father. That had been a serious shock and betrayal. If she'd known, she likely would have been happy, but not once had he said a word, despite ample opportunity. "How much did your mom tell him?"

"Pretty much everything she knew. And she wrote again, after I told her about Santee instead of Santa."

"Maybe it's just going to take some time for him to process."

Seoul brooded over her mug. "Or he doesn't care to claim some Korean-Native relative."

"Or maybe your mom's dad is still living. That would change things."

"Oh. Yeah, I guess so. You think maybe my grandfather is married and has kids, that my mom has half-sibs?" She looked both torn and hopeful.

"I think that it's complicated. He may have been married when he went to Korea. That may be a good reason for Goodthunder to keep quiet. I honestly don't know what I'd do if I suddenly found out that a relative of mine cheated on his wife and had a kid."

"But Inyan isn't Goodthunder. And Goodthunder isn't my mom's grandfather. All I wanted was some idea of the family. None of us want to cause issues."

So it was Inyan now, even when at odds. "Maybe Two Fingers knows the family and it's not good. Maybe he's trying to protect you."

Her chin jutted. "I don't want or need to be protected. The truth is more important than any of that."

Karen was beginning to regret bringing it up at all. "To you and your mom, no doubt, but maybe not to him. He's caught in it, too, since he has to know Goodthunder. He almost went to work for him. If he had, you and Two Fingers... wouldn't have ever... gotten involved." The last came out pretty lame. She still didn't know if the two were a couple or not.

Seoul's lips twitched on the mug. But she didn't spill—coffee or details. But she did throttle back the hurt. "I get it. It's hard for him, not just the DNA thing, but that I'm something else than either of us thought. I wasn't raised Indian like he was. I don't know anything about the Santee, their culture, anything. I'd never heard of anything but the Winnebagos where I grew up." Her lips twisted. "WinnaVegas. Casino money. And here I turn up, a quarter Indian, not having a clue, and I could probably enroll. It doesn't make much sense to me. He's Indian. I'm German-Korean. That's my culture, my tribe."

And Karen's tribe was waiting. "Let's get the incident meeting started." She walked back out and clapped her hands for attention. "Listen up. We've cleared Hawks." She heard a number of groans. "Yeah, yeah, it sucks. He'll go down on a bunch of charges, but he's not our killer. Jerome Stands By Him looks to be cleared as well. His account rings true and aligns with the timeline that dovetails with Hawks's. What forensics we have so far backs him up as well."

"I thought Brule had him dead to rights," Walrus groused. "Wasn't he found in bloody clothes?"

"No spatter," Marek said quietly. "Just smears."

Walrus's jaw dropped. "Geez. Forensics 101. Where'd the blood come from?"

Karen shifted on her feet. "Stands By Him moved the body to the top of Spirit Mound out of respect, apparently to give Hunter's spirit access to the open sky. I can't say I understand. But Stands By Him took Hunter's car because Hawks stranded him there. He wanted to get to Lower Brule to contact the tribal police."

"It's our jurisdiction, not theirs," Kurt said, clearly disapproving.

Karen refrained from lecturing her straight-as-an-arrow deputy on the dismal history between whites and Natives. He would say it was irrelevant and be insulted. The law was the law. Right was right. Wrong was wrong. Period. The only colors he recognized were black and white—and that wasn't racial black and white.

She merely said, "He wanted to go home first. Whether he ends up paying for that misstep or for moving the body is up to the state's attorney." But Karen had already told Ed Martin that she was more than willing to deal with Stands By Him in exchange for his testimony against Hawks. "We need to move on. I need leads."

"Mmm. Just found out Richie Legrange has poofed."

She blinked at Bork. "Poofed how?"

"Doll said she let Legrange Senior know about the possible weed problem. His father sent him his marching orders. Richie drove straight south to Nebraska and then over to Colorado to avoid the possibility of being picked up in South Dakota."

Karen had more important things to do than track down the Richies of the world. Not that it wouldn't give her great satisfaction to see him behind bars. Of course, he was still a suspect. But not high on her list.

Out of the corner of her eye, she saw the movement of people in front of the courthouse. She walked over to the large bank of windows—transparency in government, her father used to say. "Oh, great. We've got protesters." She recognized a few from the dig, but there were a lot more that she didn't—and a fair number weren't Native. More were trailing out from cars parking along the main drag. She eyed a satellite van pulling up. "And media."

More groans. She turned her back on that circus. She had a job to do. Her phone went off. Nails. She took it only to say, "I can't talk right now." And she hung up before he could say a word. She might pay for that later, but she needed leads. As he could see the crowd from his windows, she doubted very much that he'd called with a lead. He just wanted a jump on the others. Well, not today.

"Anyone got anything from the interviews this morning?" she asked the room. Eyes snapped back to her.

Seoul piped up. "I talked to Mariah Mettis. She'd almost decided to poof as well, but her mom told her to stick it out. She'd come too far to let some jerk derail her dreams. Just told her to be careful to stay with the group in the future. Mariah confirmed that Hunter confronted Richie Legrange over what happened. She said Hunter was the only guy on the dig she really felt safe with. Other than Hardy, of course.

Not that she liked him particularly. She had liked Doll but felt betrayed."

And nothing there gave them any new leads. "Richie Legrange is still on the list. And poofing doesn't help his case. But he's just too…"

"Lazy," Marek finished.

"But we'll still follow through." Karen turned to her sandy-haired Minnesotan. "Travis, check his alibi."

Bork nodded and reached for his phone.

"Anything else?"

Seoul seemed to have shaken off her funk. "Several of those we interviewed said Hunter was distracted after he came back. Excited at first, then just distracted."

Karen nodded. "We think that's because he'd uncovered Tonto Hawks's true identity. The name Tommy Knotts was found on a scrap of paper in Hunter's car."

Two Fingers asked, "Did he tell Hardy that?"

Frowning, Karen looked at Marek, who shook his head. "The professor didn't mention it. He was pretty down on the protesters, so you'd think he would have."

Bork had put down his phone after leaving a message for the woman who was Richie's alibi. "Mmm. So maybe Hunter hadn't decided how to spring it on Hawks."

"Well, Hunter did call him a plastic."

"Opening salvo." Bork sighed. "Hawks was such a good suspect. Big-time motive."

Silence fell. A ping had Karen pulling out her phone. A text from Larson. He'd been digging hard on this case, no doubt hoping, as she was, for at least some white sands and blue water in their future.

Search engine report. HRD digging on Tonto Hawks and Tommy Knotts. And lots of Arikara stuff. Greek to me.

She relayed the news. Marek nodded.

Seoul was looking through her notes from the student diggers. "One gal said that she overheard Hunter say something about a bundle to Hardy. Maybe. She wasn't sure."

Two Fingers's dark head swiveled from where he'd been eyeing the growing crowd. But he remained silent.

"That mean anything to you, Deputy?" she asked.

After a pause, he said, "Not likely. A bundle could be anything."

Karen had to agree. "Yeah, a bundle of services like phone add-ons, a bundle of clothes, a bundle of artifacts. A bundle is always *of* something, and if you don't know the something, then it doesn't mean much."

Seoul continued down her list. "They did say Hardy seemed pumped. There was some excitement on the dig. Doll said it was a tool. A..." Seoul consulted her notes. "Maul."

A few heads nodded. A few tilted. Karen had some vague idea of a hammer but wasn't sure. "What's it look like?"

"I've got one in my truck." Marek got up, slipped out back, and returned with a tool. It had a rectangular metal head on both sides like a mallet and a wood handle like a hammer. Way too small, too regular, too rectangular to be their murder weapon. "Okay, scratch that. Any other ideas?"

Two Fingers opened his mouth, then his phone rang. He looked embarrassed then his face stilled as he moved to mute it. "Sorry, that's my mother. I have to take this. She texts first unless it's really important."

Karen gestured toward the breakroom. "Go ahead. Take it."

Seoul's gaze tracked him the entire way. Karen brought it back by asking for more ideas.

"How about a totally random act?" Bork suggested. "They do happen."

Walrus blew out his windsock of a mustache. "Yeah, that gets my vote. Maybe someone following the Lewis and Clark Trail stopped at the mound to take a picture. Got ticked off that their picture was screwed up because of the dig. People can get pretty upset about the weirdest things. My mother used to—"

Whatever his mother used to do was never revealed, probably for the best, as Two Fingers returned. Karen wasn't sure how to gauge his look. She rarely did. But this was more than conflicted. It was worried—and like he was being asked to do something he didn't want to do.

"Bad news?" Walrus asked. "Hope your family's okay."

"My great-grandmother wants us to come."

"Us as in… who?" Then Karen got it. "Seoul?"

He blinked then dashed Seoul's look of hope. "No, me. You. I guess Marek."

"Because…?"

"I don't know. I didn't ask. My mother didn't ask."

Karen tried not to snap at him. "We're trying to solve a homicide here. Your mother, as I recall, was very insistent you—and we—do our best by Hunter. I would be happy to meet your—what was it your mother called her? Unci?—when things settle down. I'd be honored."

Two Fingers started to speak, sat down, then looked down. Karen opened the floor again to ideas, which got more and more bizarre. But Two Fingers got more and more antsy, until he finally got to his feet, his eyes avoiding hers. "I have to go. I'm sorry."

She let out a frustrated breath. But Marek put a hand on her arm. "We'll go."

Karen turned on her uncle, about to demand why, but what she saw was understanding—and a plea. And she was reminded of an incident meeting when he'd also been antsy… and had left without a word. To pick up his traumatized daughter from her first day of school.

Responsibilities.

Karen threw up her hands. "Sure, it's not like we've got anything else to do." She started toward the back then cursed when she realized that wasn't where she'd parked. "Sub's out front."

They all looked out. Karen sighed. "The media will want a statement anyway. Let's get it done. All of it. The rest of you are dismissed to your duties or home. If you have any bright ideas, send a smoke signal to Flandreau."

CHAPTER 20

THE DECIBEL LEVEL ON MAIN Street had to be at a harmful level, Karen thought, as she pushed out of the double doors, flanked by Marek and Two Fingers. What with the protesters' chants to free Hawks warring with pickups honking their horns, it was chaos.

A reporter she'd never seen before boomed out with a voice like a megaphone, "You have a Native American in custody. Tonto Hawks. Is this correct?"

Marek got her a bit of space to stand on the top step. "I have two Native Americans in custody. Tonto Hawks is one. Jerome Stands By Him is the other." That lessened the noise considerably. "Neither man has been charged with homicide. Stands By Him is being held pending inquiries and will likely be released on bail. Hawks is being held on more serious charges. We are continuing our investigation."

A young white woman shouted, "You mean you're going to make up some evidence to pin on him! Hawks was right. You're just a bigoted bitch with a badge."

Not bad alliteration. "You might like to know that Tonto Hawks is being held, among other charges pending here in South Dakota, with manslaughter on an old but still current warrant from Oklahoma." She paused just enough to make sure they were all listening. "For killing a tourist during a fake Sun Dance that he charged five thousand bucks for. Under his real name: Tommy Knotts. He's on Wiki. Go look him up if you don't know him. He should also be under the definition for *plastic shaman*. He's a fake and a fraud."

Faces—and signs—fell. Betrayal ran over those who knew of Knotts or at least knew the actions of a plastic shaman.

"Can you prove that?" yelled one holdout with a sign that read Hawking Justice: Free Tonto!

"Hawks already admitted it. On record. And yes, it's all there, the Miranda warning, waiving a lawyer, everything. He incriminated himself several times over on lesser but still serious charges than homicide. That includes buying dynamite with the intent to blow the dig—and likely Spirit Mound—to smithereens."

The protesters were absolutely silent now. It was eerie.

"The state's attorney will make the final determination on those. But I can tell you that, unlike Jerome Stands By Him, Tonto Hawks aka Tommy Knotts, wasn't in this for his people, assuming he is even Native. He was in it for the money. He was going to go out in a blaze of glory, blow up the dig, blame Stands By Him for it all, and no doubt rake in money for a defense fund for the deluded young man. Then he had plans to skip the country to escape—and I quote—'shitty backward people who should've died out eons ago.' If you want to help anyone, I suggest you get a fund going for Stands By Him so he can make bail."

The outrage was only an echo of earlier. "On what charges?"

"That all depends on how it plays out. But the most likely would be obstruction of justice." Karen moved forward. "If you don't want to join him, I suggest you let me and my people get down these steps so we can continue the investigation. If you haven't forgotten, the real outrage here is the death of Standing Rock–enrolled tribe member Hunter Redwing-Digges."

While the protest had nearly died, no one moved.

Marek started to step forward when Two Fingers said something in Lakota. No, Dakota. Whatever. She'd been told they were the same language, just different dialects. It was as if Moses had spoken. The protesters parted—Natives pulling confused whites aside—and allowed them to leave unhindered.

The same couldn't be said of the reporters. But she ignored them after a quick "No further comment" and stalked toward the Sub. "What did you say to them?"

Two Fingers's dark eyes were at half-mast. "We've been called to wacipi by an elder."

He turned to go to his own squad before she could get words out. "We're going to a freaking powwow?" Seeing one of the protesters turn, her brow furrowing, Karen let out a breath. "Whatever it takes. We're going. But I swear, it better be relevant."

The drive to Flandreau took forever. But they finally rolled into the small town, which appeared to be pretty deserted, even for a Sunday evening. Nor did she see a single sign about the wacipi or directions to it. When she followed Two Fingers's squad up Highway 13 north on to the reservation, which also wasn't marked, he almost immediately turned left into a treed area on a bend of the Big Sioux River. The road down was blocked off by golf carts and orange cones.

After a short conference with the cart drivers, who appeared to be volunteer security, they parked their vehicles and were allowed to walk down. Karen had the distinct impression that security would vastly prefer that they also change out of their uniforms and ditch their weapons. Not happening. But she got it. It was likely crashing a town parade loaded for bear. They would think the sheriff's office was looking for a killer or something. And yes, they were.

But she didn't like being immediately placed in the position of being the "other," the outsider, or the enemy just because of her badge. Yes, she was used to that reaction when confronting miscreants in Eda, but not during a festive event in unfamiliar territory. She could hear drums and high, keening voices that immediately said Indian music, and some kind of jingling or jangling sound.

As she walked down the paved road, Karen could see a large number of tents, RVs, and cars—none of them held up by stereotypical baling wire, though a few had bales in the back—that were obviously camping out for the duration. A few kids and adults were crisscrossing between the tents, but otherwise, the people all seemed to be at the center of the grounds under a circular wooden canopy. An arena? That was the closest word she could come up with to describe it.

A number of booths selling fry bread and Indian tacos, jewelry, blankets, and clothing were set up in a larger circle around the arena, separated by a circular road. One booth had a bunch of what were advertised as jingle dresses. Hmm. Now that she looked, she saw several women and girls, including young ones, wearing brightly colored skirts with metal cones attached. The cones jingled as the women walked.

Two Fingers led them under the canopy to the closest bleachers—only three benches high—which were under a white-painted section. Others, she could see, were painted red, yellow, and black. She knew that from somewhere. Medicine wheel. That was kind of cool. Each section had an opening between bleachers to get from the outer circle onto the grounds.

In the middle of the circular grounds, two flagpoles stood high, flying the United States flag and presumably the tribal one at equal heights. A reminder that each tribe was its own nation, sovereign—at least as much as whites had allowed them.

As Karen sat down and a woman reluctantly slid down, she got several nasty looks and a few puzzled looks. Karen raked the crowd and felt very much out of place with maybe only half a dozen other whites in the whole arena. Then those nearby saw Two Fingers inch his way forward to one of the folded chairs in front, at the edge of the grassed grounds totally enclosed by the canopy. The looks turned guarded but not as hostile. She didn't really blame them for it, as this was obviously not just what had initially had the feel—but not the look—of a combination of family reunion, heritage days like Valeska's Czech Days, but also an outdoor church service.

Crashing the wacipi really wasn't the place or time for whatever she and Marek were here for. Maybe they were here simply to attend the wacipi, but that made little sense to her. They certainly weren't going to be honored like the long row of mostly camo-wearing veterans who were being given various items like sweatshirts and blankets as their war was announced. Korean, Vietnam, Desert Storm, Iraq, Afghanistan. The list went on and on.

The ceremony went on far longer than any Reunion veterans' event she'd been to. She got a clue when the emcee said something about warriors. As the drums started up again, a small cadre of singers raised their voices. The veterans separated into rows and started around the grounds in lockstep—or dance—clockwise. They tapped or bounced on one foot twice before doing the same with the other foot. The oldsters did more of the tapping. It was infectious, making her tap her own foot, which she immediately stilled. Was that disrespectful, coming from an outsider, a wasicu?

The woman next to her started clapping—but only some of those gathered did the same. Was she supposed to do that, too, or would that be offensive?

Next came two women in fancy dresses, followed by a number of younger women and girls wearing beaded headdresses... crowns? All in bright colors. Some wore the jingle dresses, and others had shawls trimmed with long ribbons that they flicked around as they danced. Their dance steps were more complicated than most of the others. Maybe their version of heritage days royalty, like Valeska's Czech Days queen and princess except a lot more of them?

Karen felt like she had as a teenager when she'd gone

with a friend to Catholic Mass for the first time, unsure of what she—Lutheran to the bone—should and should not be doing. Or could or could not be doing. Her friend's mother had hushed her for asking too many questions during a sacred ritual. And that had at least been in a Christian context, where she had some concept of what was going on. She had no clue here.

Two Fingers returned and said quietly, "Unci will talk to us after the Grand Entry."

Okay. Karen looked back out and saw that the veterans had moved to the middle of the grounds. Three were holding up long staffs adorned with single feathers—she guessed eagle feathers. She'd picked up that much, at least, in her years as a South Dakotan. Eagle feathers were a huge deal. Not given or taken lightly.

Now dancers streamed in from the four aisles between sections of the arena. Some of the men wore full feather headdresses, some long bone-beaded breastplates, others with bells attached to their ankles. While most followed the two-tap bounce or hop, others added whirls, dips, and crouches, but there didn't seem to be any rhyme or reason to Karen. Though she'd bet that those watching could give each style a name. The dancers seemed to have their own unique outfits, and some had little to none, with some kids in sneakers and jeans. She was startled to see a couple of African Americans, who she presumed also had Indian blood.

As the women and girls started in, closer to the bleachers in a clockwise circle as they danced, Karen recognized first Jaydyn then Shania, Two Fingers's sisters. Then, with a shock, she realized the woman dancing energetically just ahead of them was Winona, their mother. Gone was the hard rocker look. Rather than jingles or shawls, she wore a white dress with colored bands on the skirt and a large metal-worked belt. And she looked entirely comfortable doing so, as if she'd done it for years.

She likely had, starting as a child, just as Karen had dressed up for Easter or the like. Had Two Fingers done this as a boy? If this investigation hadn't pulled him in, would he be here, dancing? She honestly didn't know. He had occasionally asked for time off, most recently back in June, but she had no idea what he did with the time. Unlike her other deputies, he rarely talked about what he did on vacation. The most he usually said was that he'd spent it with family.

As her gaze fell once again on the veterans, who still did the two-tap if a bit less energetically, she wondered if Two Fingers would normally be part of that group. So much she didn't know. She always thought of him as a man apart, but here, where he should be part of the whole, he also seemed apart. Was it just the uniform, or something more? Was he excluded because of not being enrolled? But she didn't think so, because from what little she understood from the emcee, other tribes had been mentioned as participating. Or was it the blood-quantum thing?

After fretting for a while over the loss of time, Karen let herself relax into the throbbing beat, the color, and the movement. She remembered the painting at the Diggeses' that was called Grand Entry. It had indeed captured the spirit of the wacipi. As all the dancers filled the circle, the sun broke through the clouds and cast a shadow over the grounds. An audible *ahhh* went through the crowd.

Did the Dakota have some kind of sun-worship thing going?

"Eagle shadow," the woman next to her said. "It's a good sign."

Karen squinted for a few seconds before she saw it. The upswept wings in a half-circle, the blocky head and tail, cast onto the grounds by the shape of the arena. Almost like a blessing. That was truly amazing. It seemed every bit of what looked like a fairly flimsy canopy with bleachers had been constructed to remind its attendees of their traditions.

With no more dancers arriving onto the grounds, the Grand Entry seemed to be over. Karen took a deep breath. Almost done. As the dancers streamed off the grounds in a jangle of sound that echoed over the grounds now that the drums had stilled, Karen slipped off the bleacher. Marek followed. Karen noted that the woman she'd been sitting by gave them a hooded look, but Karen didn't know if it was because their leaving was an offense—another ceremony seemed to be starting—or if she thought they were going to arrest one of the dancers.

But when Two Fingers slowly followed with a tiny woman holding on to his arm, the woman nodded respectfully before turning her attention back to the grounds. The drums started up again.

"You will take us home, Inyan," the tiny woman announced in a surprisingly clear voice. She wore a beautifully beaded and fringed buckskin dress and midcalf moccasins. "I cannot hear myself think here."

Karen decided that if there was any offense to leave in the middle of the wacipi, it was negated by the elder.

But as they walked up the road back to their vehicles, a Native man in a tribal police uniform confronted them at the top, though he did drop his eyes as he saw the elderly woman. His voice was soft-spoken as he addressed Karen. "Just when were you going to give me a heads up that you are investigating a homicide on tribal land, Sheriff?" Then his hooded gaze went to Two Fingers. He nodded slightly. "Son."

CHAPTER 21

It didn't take a detective like Marek to deduce that the man in front of them was Chief Martin Goodthunder. He was slightly shorter and stockier than Two Fingers, but to Marek's eye, they both looked equally Native, though not related. Goodthunder's face was wider, for one, and his gaze of a lighter brown.

But that the chief was also Two Fingers's stepfather answered a great deal.

Talk about being between a rock and a hard place. No wonder the deputy had been unwilling to answer Seoul's questions about Goodthunder's family. Two Fingers *was* the man's family, the father of his sisters. Was there some kind of taboo about dating Seoul now that she was part of his stepfather's family? Marek knew the Navajo had very complicated dating and marriage rules that had to do with their born-to and born-for clans.

The tiny woman holding on to Two Fingers's arm was the first to break the frozen tableau. "I asked them here, Martin. If you had told me earlier that young Hunter had been killed, I could have spoken to them when they were here before."

Though her voice held no bite, Goodthunder dropped his head. Marek was beginning to think that this wasn't just a show of shame but a difference in cultures. He'd noticed during the wacipi that children would approach an adult and just wait with eyes downcast without speaking, until the adult deigned to notice them. Not all of them. But enough that he'd noticed. And in a like way, many of the adults deferred to their elders.

But as Winona—apparently Goodthunder, if she used her husband's name—rushed up, holding her skirts to show intricately beaded moccasins that went up to her knees, Marek decided she was likely an exception to all rules. "What's going on? Is someone being arrested?" Her flashing dark eyes pinned her son. "Do you realize how bad it looked for you to be there at the wacipi with the wasicu police, Inyan?"

An almost melodic sigh escaped the elderly woman's lips. "Winona."

Winona stared right back. "Grandmother."

Goodthunder looked faintly amused at his wife's unchastened response but made no comment.

While exasperation filled the old woman's face, her eyes twinkled with amusement, which told Marek that despite their obvious differences, there was love there between grandmother and granddaughter.

"You always were a contrary soul," the elder said to Winona. "You know very well that they are here because I asked them to be here. They need to understand something of us, to understand what I tell them, and I wanted them at the wacipi before I took them home to tell them what I know."

Winona actually put her hand over her mouth, no doubt to keep from arguing. Maybe it was bad to argue on this day or on these grounds. Or in front of wasicu.

The elder peered up at Marek and Karen. "I am Delma Two Fingers."

Karen nodded politely, started to move her right hand as if to shake, then hooked her thumbs into her belt instead. "It's good to meet you, Mrs. Two Fingers. I am Sheriff Karen Okerlund Mehaffey, and this is my detective, Marek Okerlund."

The steel-gray brows lifted. "You are related?"

Karen smiled down at her. "I know, it doesn't look like it. But yes, he is my younger half-uncle. His father was my grandfather."

Delma's still-bright gaze darted to her great-grandson. "You see, it can be done, Inyan. You do not even share blood with Martin. There should be no problem."

Contradictorily, Winona bristled. "Unci, he is a man. He makes his own decisions. Even when we don't agree."

"Have I said otherwise?" her grandmother replied mildly. "Inyan speaks of conflicts of interest, of nepotism, yet these two are closely related."

Karen said, "Marek actually works for the county commissioners, not me, so there's no nepotism or conflict of interest."

That didn't seem to make anyone happy. Before what obviously was still a raw family argument could continue, Karen glanced at her watch. "But we are happy to have him in Eda County for as long as he wants to work for us. And as you know, we have a murder to solve. We don't have a lot of time to—"

The elder held up an imperious hand. Karen immediately stopped speaking, though she looked incredibly frustrated.

Delma gave her granddaughter a significant look, as it if to say—see, even a white can learn, why can't you?—before turning back to Karen. "You wasicus are always ruled by your clocks. I have never understood it. Why give such a thing power over you? There are important things to learn, to hear, and these take time. Inyan, you will take me in your car. The others will follow."

And of course, Two Fingers complied, his dark eyes glinting with clear relief. His great-grandmother had to be well into her nineties by Marek's mental math, but she had no problem making it up the hill to the squad car, though she did hold tightly to Two Fingers's arm.

Marek murmured to Goodthunder, "You stayed out of that."

"Delma's a force of nature," Goodthunder said. "And while times have changed, it is traditional for the son-in-law not to speak directly to his mother-in-law but only through his wife. Technically, Delma is my grandmother-in-law, but she stood in as mother to Winona, so the same applies as far I'm concerned."

Winona snorted. "Good excuse for bowing out of the line of fire. Coward."

"I am merely withholding judgment," her husband said in his soft-spoken voice, as they all walked up the hill toward the little huddle of squad cars and SUVs behind the golf carts. Marek decided that Two Fingers got much of his personality from his stepfather, not his mother or grandmother.

When they reached the top of the hill, Karen's gaze darted between the Sub and Goodthunder's sleek black SUV. "Nice," she commented.

Goodthunder glanced at the Sub, his lips pursed, and said nothing.

Karen sighed. "Yeah. Not much to say."

Marek slipped into the passenger seat, and Karen headed the Sub north. Prepared for something different than the usual rolling farmland, Marek was disappointed. They passed fields of corn and beans with mud-spattered pickups parked in pulloffs and irrigation systems lazily spraying fields. The houses were just houses, with no indication that Natives lived there. Several had basketball hoops and a mishmash of rotting vehicles. Just the usual.

They passed an auto repair shop then hit some land that had been left fallow, the Big Sioux River snaking through it under a hill. Or possibly a bluff. Marek was used to his own bluff, a gentle slope down into the bottomlands of the Big Jammer, but this was more prominent and steeper. On the top of the hill were a cluster of trees and a couple houses with outbuildings.

Karen followed the sleek SUV and parked beside it on the gravel pulloff at the top.

The larger house, a ranch with light-blue siding, looked to be maybe ten or fifteen years old. Two Fingers went into the smaller, older house, a cabin with a porch where a hickory rocker sat. The cabin looked out to the south, where the Big Sioux flowed in lazy curlicues below. Marek could hear all kinds of birds even if he couldn't see them. Woodpeckers tat-tat-tatted warring patterns against their chosen trees while others warbled cheerfully.

Beside him, Goodthunder said quietly, "We should wait until invited."

Silence fell until Karen apparently couldn't take it anymore. "Did you live here before you married Winona?"

Goodthunder shook his head. "No, I lived a few miles to the southwest." He seemed to fall back into memory and spoke as if without realizing it. "I fell in love with Inyan first. He was such a lonely little boy. Sitting at his great-grandmother's feet on the porch. Fishing on the bank of the river, as quiet and placid as the water, and as deep. He fed his family for years. He is probably closer to the land than anyone I know. A special knowing from living on it so much, watching it, waiting for it in all its seasons. He's an old soul. I thought he would farm this land. But he wanted to be a warrior. He wanted to learn. Both drove him away from us." His eyes hooded. "Along with the rejection of the tribe."

"With Delma around, I'm surprised they didn't enroll him just on her say-so," Karen commented, her gaze also on the twisted river. Not an easy river to navigate. And only slowly. A canoe, a kayak, but not a motorboat.

"Even she has her limits. Inyan feels that he's neither fish nor fowl. If he was straight-up wasicu, he'd be okay. If he was enrolled, he'd be okay. But being everything Indian except the blood quantum, not to mention being my son, he feels that he'll be more hindrance than help to the tribe as a policeman. I understand his reasons. I don't think it will be

Dead Spirits

as hard as he thinks. I almost convinced him to join us until you were reelected. I don't understand it. But then, I have never lived in his skin."

"You're full-blood?" Karen asked, then looked uneasy, as if it were an offensive thing to ask.

If it was, Goodthunder took it in stride. "Santee Dakota through and through. Descended from Little Crow and one of the thirty-eight."

While watching the Grand Entry, Marek had counted the eagle feathers on the staffs held by the veterans at the wacipi. Same number. That couldn't be coincidence. "Thirty-eight?"

Goodthunder turned his head to look up at Marek with a searching look, as if trying to determine either how he didn't know or how to relate it to a wasicu. He closed his eyes, as if by doing so, he wouldn't see what he was saying. "After the Dakota War in 1862, thirty-eight warriors were hung at Mankato, the largest mass execution in US history."

Marek didn't know much about wars, but soldiers who participated weren't usually executed by the winners en masse. At least, not afterward. War itself was the largest mass execution in the US.

His voice tight, Goodthunder went on. "Two of them were, even by the standards of the rigged show trials, completely innocent. One was even white, a boy raised by the tribe, who'd been acquitted. We honor all of them and will never forget."

Or forgive? Yet today, they honored the same flag, the same country, who'd done that. Marek wanted to ask more about the Dakota War—what started it, how long it lasted, who'd been killed—but he sensed that this wasn't the time.

But Karen asked bluntly, "What exactly was the Dakota War? People keep bringing it up as if we're supposed to know about it, but it's the first I've heard of it."

Goodthunder pursed his lips. "It's probably better known in Minnesota, which is where our lands were."

Marek blinked. "This wasn't your land? I mean, not this particular spot, but the Dakotas?"

"No, we were thrown off what remained of our lands—our treaty-protected lands—in Minnesota after the Dakota War. Afterward, some of our people were sent to Nebraska. A small number of Christian converts there, including my ancestors, decided to homestead here in Flandreau, along with the wasicu. They even attended the same Presbyterian church together. It still stands. You passed it on the way to the wacipi. Our history is very different than the more well-known tribes like the Lakota because of that."

"But you came from Minnesota originally?" Karen pressed.

"My band of the Santee, yes. According to our traditions, the Mdewakanton came from Spirit Lake—now called Mille Lacs—north of the Twin Cities. But by that time, we had been pushed out of that area and were living on reservations more near the border of what became South Dakota. Pipestone was ours and finally is ours again."

Goodthunder nodded when he saw that they at least knew about the place where the blood-red rock that was pipestone was quarried to be made into sacred pipes. The town of Pipestone was just over the border into Minnesota, not far from where Bork had been born and raised. Marek wondered if Bork knew about the Dakota War.

Goodthunder cleared his throat. "Having lost many of our traditional ways to survive, we relied on payments and food rations from the government."

Hence fry bread and sopapillas.

"The Sisseton and Wahpeton bands of the Dakota on the Yellow Medicine reservation especially needed it. When our people there showed up at the warehouse for our rations, the traders refused to give them to us until our payments arrived as well. We were starving and desperate. We could not wait."

Marek hadn't learned much about Native history, but

Dead Spirits

he did know what else was going on during the year 1862. "Supply issues from the Civil War?"

"Probably. Money was hard to come by. But that was no help to us. The warehouse had the flour, the sugar, but they would not release it to us. And we already felt that the traders were taking all our payments for little return in goods." He spoke very carefully. "The warriors attacked the warehouse, and there was a skirmish. At a council afterward, one of the traders said to Little Crow, the chief of the Mdewakanton Dakota, 'Let them eat grass.'"

Karen pursed her lips. "I bet that went over as well as Marie Antoinette saying, 'Let them eat cake.'"

Goodthunder nodded, though he appeared to still be choosing his words with care. "Four young warriors, perhaps less than wise, raided the farms of white settlers in Minnesota for food and ended up killing five of them. Put in the position of having to disavow or support the young men, Little Crow and several hundred Mdewakanton warriors went to war on August eighteenth. The war lasted five weeks and left hundreds of settlers and Indians dead. Many terrible things happened. It was a fierce and bitter war. Its aftermath for my people was even fiercer. Little Crow unleashed the fury of the wasicu, not just on the Dakota but the Lakota and Nakota and many other tribes."

Marek wondered how it felt to be descended from the man who'd led that war. "What happened to Little Crow? Was he one of the thirty-eight?"

Goodthunder's face stilled. "No, he was not. About a year after the war, he and his son went on a raid into Minnesota on their old lands. Again, not a wise decision. A white settler and his son saw them and exchanged fire. Little Crow was killed, but his son escaped. The settlers scalped Little Crow, dragged his body down the main street, put firecrackers in his nose and mouth, and lit them. Then they dumped the body into a slaughterhouse pit. Later, it was decapitated then dug up by the Army. In 1879, the Minnesota Historical

Society put his remains on display. But after several decades of protests, they removed them from view. In 1971, they finally returned what was left of his remains to us. He is buried at the First Presbyterian here on our lands."

So much for Indians being the savages. It also explained a lot of the anger over displaying remains, or anything of value to them, in museums. There really wasn't anything to say.

Apparently deciding the same, Karen asked, "Has your son ever been honored with the other vets at the wacipi?"

His stance relaxed only slightly. "Inyan participated in the wacipi as a boy. He longed to be one of the warriors, and he went with a warrior's heart to Afghanistan. But not all wars, not all battles, are honorable. He felt that being used as a tool, even if unknowingly, to kill innocents in bombing that small village based on faulty information of a rival had forever barred him from that honor."

Marek heard the ambivalence. "You disagree?"

"My son followed orders, as did the warriors under Little Crow, as did the soldiers in the Army. Some fought with honor, some did not. Inyan has a very strong sense of honor. Delma taught him that. She knows more than most of what a warrior was. Perhaps less than what a warrior is. Inyan is exactly what our tribe needs. He should have been my son. He is in all ways that matter but blood."

Two Fingers emerged from the little house and beckoned.

CHAPTER 22

WHEN KAREN STEPPED FROM THE porch into the cabin, she walked straight into a living exhibit. Not a dead, musty place, but a lived-in place, a living history. The first thing that hit her was the rich smell that she now associated with smudges, though she couldn't name the ingredients.

The walls were covered with all kinds of fascinating things: a stunning star quilt on one wall behind a cabinet with a number of intricately made dolls of Natives displayed in various dress, some clearly warriors, others dancers, some looking quite old. Another wall bristled with everything from pipes to dreamcatchers to beaded moccasins to little pouches that awaited time to explore. The last wall was what drew her, though, despite her impatience.

Rather than lined up in regimental lines, the framed pictures were arranged in circles, starting on the outside with old black-and-whites of men and women in traditional dress. Perhaps parents, grandparents, even great-grandparents. Each generation became successively more standardly American. Stiff young Natives in starched dresses and suits stood in front of a very formidable stone-built institution that she recognized from Dana's office as the original Flandreau Indian School. A young man in a uniform posed with a beaming young Delma in front of a church. Perhaps the Presbyterian mentioned?

So Two Fingers's great-grandfather had been in the Army. Given the ages involved, Karen had to think it was World War II. Had he been sent overseas?

Karen could see a strong resemblance between him and her Two Fingers.

"He was a handsome man, my Christian. I lost him in 1959. He was never the same after the Bataan Death March in the Philippines. But he lived longer than anyone expected. He was strong in spirit. Inyan takes after him. He will make some woman a fine husband one day."

So Two Fingers hadn't told his great-grandmother about Seoul. Was it casual, then, at least on his side? Or was it because he didn't want to break his great-grandmother's heart and tell her that Seoul was Korean and German? Oh, and Santee. Wasn't that a kicker and a conundrum. Would that make it better or worse?

The last in that circle of pictures showed a young man brooding by the Big Sioux, wearing a white T-shirt and jeans, looking like a Native James Dean. This must be the young man who'd lost his heart to the young white student teacher and killed himself. Karen wasn't sure she would be able to keep such a photo on her wall without screaming. Or blaming. Or hating.

The innermost circle started with a young Winona dancing in a shawl dress, looking like she was ready to take wing. Next was one of her in black leather looking mad and bad with a drum set at her feet, holding a guitar like a rifle. That jarred against a black-and-white photo, which must have been deliberate to set the mood, of a young Two Fingers sitting cross-legged on the bank of a misty Big Sioux, a remote but concentrated look on his face, obviously unaware he was being immortalized.

Karen recognized that look. She'd seen it enough these past couple days.

A uniformed Goodthunder—Flandreau police this time, not military—and a white-dressed Winona were kissing at their wedding, followed by one of them with their two daughters between them, holding hands, obviously at a wacipi. They looked happy. And like a family. No Two Fingers. But the very last was of him in his Air Force uniform in front of a bomber. He was showing one of his rare flashes of a smile.

Karen ached for that young man who wanted to be a warrior and honor his people and country, but had come back a self-loathing killer, even if that killing had been in the line of duty. What had broken that circle, she wasn't sure, but something had.

"I hope to add a few more pictures." Delma shot a pointed look at Two Fingers. "Before I walk on into the Wakan Tanka."

Winona came in with a tray of cold drinks. "Unci, stop embarrassing my son. He will find his own wife in his own time."

"Indian time," her grandmother said with a straight face but a twinkle in her eye.

Karen took a raspberry-flavored bubbler with her thanks. "Speaking of time..."

"Yes, yes, you want answers now. I don't have answers. I only have questions."

They'd come all this way to answer questions? Karen bit her lip. But it escaped anyway. "We don't need more questions. We need answers. We need to—"

Beside her, Two Fingers deliberately stepped on her toes. She was miffed for a few seconds. He was her deputy. He'd just—if very mildly—assaulted a superior officer. But she refrained from either commenting or reacting. It was just another reminder that she was out of her culture, out of her country even, in ways she'd never understood before, with different rules that she could easily trespass.

"We were given two ears, only one mouth," the elder counseled.

Karen felt her face burn. It wasn't like she'd never been reprimanded to speak less, hear more, because she had, but rarely had it stung so much. No one made any other comment, nor did anyone else react, and silence fell until Delma finally broke it.

"This is my question for you. How could young Hunter's death be related to the winter count of my tiospaye?"

Karen remembered Two Fingers struggling to define *tiospaye*. Community. Extended kin. But she had no clue what Delma was talking about. Nor was she about to open her mouth.

After a short pause, Marek asked gently, "Why do you think it does? Have anything to do with Hunter's death."

Delma's tiny frame slumped. "Because Hunter came to see me the day he was killed."

Everyone stared at her.

"Why didn't you say so?" Winona demanded.

"I just did." Delma looked affronted. "You did not tell me he died—or *how* he died—until today. You say to spare me, to not shock me, but little can shock me at my age. I have seen many come and go." Her gaze lingered on the circles of life—and death—on her wall. "We of all people know that life is not fair."

Marek asked, "When did he come?"

"I do not keep time like you. It was after lunch." She held out a hand. "Inyan?"

Obviously already primed, Two Fingers handed over a rolled document. When Delma unrolled it on her lap, Karen recognized the winter count that Hunter had pinned up on his wall that had so fascinated her.

Delma's worn hands hovered over the pictographs as if they were too precious to be touched, even on a photocopy of a photocopy of the original. "Hunter was very excited. Very happy. Because I knew it. I knew its history. All these years, his teacher said it was worthless because it was just pictures with no words. That it was even a fake because some of the pictures were not like any others ever found." She shook her head. "No tiospaye is the same. So why should the winter count be? It is what is important to the tiospaye; they decide every winter what should be recorded."

Her fingers danced over a man speckled with spots. "But many pictures are the same for all. Smallpox, it killed so many. So very many."

Delma looked up, her faded dark eyes glazed with memories of darker times. "Hunter did not know where the winter count came from. He had never shown it to me before. So I could not tell him. All those years he searched." She shook her head. "My father was Santee Dakota, but my mother, she was a Rockboy from the Yankton Dakota. She left her home after being forced to go to Catholic school, where the priests abused some of the girls, including her elder sister. When her parents learned of this, they sent the rest of their children to Flandreau, even though it hurt them for us to be so far away. I have not been back to the Yankton reservation since I was a child, but my mother took me many times."

No one spoke, no one moved. It was kind of eerie. But for once, Karen was not moved to speak. She wanted to hear this, if not for the case, for a slice of history that only a living, breathing person could give.

Delma had obviously gone back in her memories—overlaid with the reflection of time. "So much heartache, so much lost. The children, learning white ways, not our own." Her gaze went to the big stone building and its stiff children. "My great-uncle, a great medicine man who was feared by the wasicu, was sent to an insane asylum in Canton. We never saw him again. My grandmother tried. So much grief. All of us who survive, we are dead spirits." Her hand hovered over a fallen warrior with a red circle at his heart and an inverted red triangle dangling from it. Blood. "A wound inflicted, so deep, so wide, that we have never recovered."

Her hands spread out over the winter count, still not touching. "But this winter count... I recognized it right away. When I was a little girl, when my mother went to visit relatives that she did not want me to meet because they had gone down the wrong path, she would leave me with my uncle, who had lost his wife. He was lonely because his children did not care for him properly and did not care about his traditions. He was the last keeper of the tiospaye's winter count. So I would sit at his feet, and he would tell me what all the pictures meant. The story of us."

A single tear streaked down her face. "But the winter count was lost to us, to my family, after he died. His eldest son sold it to a wasicu for *money*." She spat out the last. "My mother did not go back to Yankton after that or speak of her family or allow us to speak of them. My younger siblings, they did not go as I did and did not learn the stories. I learned not to speak of them, but I held them in my heart."

Delma dashed the tear before it could drop onto the winter count. "Hunter made me very happy that day. For the first time, I could speak of those stories. I was eager to tell him. And he said he would be back, so we could record it all, so it would never be forgotten. And that he would do everything he could to see the winter count returned to me, to us."

Karen sucked in a breath. Was repatriation at the heart of this case? Was it that simple? Maybe they needed to talk to someone at the museum.

After a long silence, Karen opened her mouth, but Delma shook her head. "There is more. Be patient." But this time, it was said with amusement. "Hunter was excited, yes, but then there was this..."

Her hands moved back to one of the first pictographs, closely following the first with a spotted man, so if Karen remembered right, the 1780s smallpox. Delma's index finger, trembling now, hovered over a man—obviously a warrior per the feather—holding hands with a woman in a dress. "This one was special, my uncle told me. A spirit woman came among us wearing a white dress."

But the dress was uncolored. Still, Karen took her word

Dead Spirits

for it. Perhaps white wasn't an easy color to paint, or heck, perhaps it was a sacred color or something.

"Hunter said that there were several known winter counts with this woman in white. No one really knows who she was or what it meant. Only that it was very significant to many Sioux tribes. But this pictograph for our tiospaye, it was different. It made his teacher think it was fake. But it wasn't. It was special to our family."

Grasping her husband's hand, Winona, her voice barely audible for once, asked, "Why?"

"My uncle told me, I should remember this one. To never forget it. Because this was our family, our many-times great-grandparents. The warrior was Yankton Dakota and lived along the Missouri in the area of what is now between Vermillion and Yankton. The warrior married the woman in white, and they had children of great spirit, great power, among their people. Great-uncle Willis Rockboy, who was sent to Canton, was one of them. After that, the power faded, my uncle said, and has not returned. He said that as a boy, he was to be trained to follow in his uncle's footsteps, but that his parents forbade it for fear of losing him. All he was allowed was to be the keeper of the winter count."

This time, when silence fell, Karen didn't speak. She waited. But she knew it was far easier for Marek than for her. He thought by thinking. She thought by talking. It was killing her not to ask questions, to talk it out. But perhaps Delma was done.

Then the trembling hands moved one last time to the last of the pictographs. To a small hill with a creek running at its base and what looked like a small uncolored pouch drawn under the hill. "Hunter asked me about this one. My uncle was always very quiet when I would ask. Mostly, he would say that some things are better left buried. It was painful for him. But one time, he said, Inyan Ska. He said it twice. Then he wept."

Startled, Karen looked at Two Fingers. She'd seen his full name. Inyan Ska Two Fingers. What did it mean?

But Delma went on before Karen could find the courage to ask. Her hands spread palm up. "It's as if the world revealed itself to Hunter. He looked stunned and awed. Then he laughed. When I asked him why, Hunter said something I didn't understand. That my great-grandson was the key. That all this time, the answer to everything was right under his nose."

CHAPTER 23

MAREK OFTEN WISHED THAT PEOPLE who had revelations wouldn't speak in such vague terms. Then again, most who had such had to be vague, because they usually didn't know what they were talking about. Prophetically speaking.

When he and the rest turned to Two Fingers, the deputy shrugged. "I wasn't even born then. I'm not the one who named me Inyan Ska. I don't know how I could be the key to anything."

As Karen looked like she wasn't willing to break any more silences, Marek did. "Does Inyan Ska mean something in Dakota?"

Delma looked at Winona. "This is your story."

Winona slid her hands down her white dress. "You know what happened to me. I was so young, and I thought my life was ended. All I could think was, it was hard. A hard thing to have a child thrust on me, unchosen. Unci reminded me of Inyan Hoksila." She paused, as if trying to describe something that might take days, but she had only a few words to do it. "There are many stories about him, but only one that you will hear from me. We don't speak much of our beliefs to wasicu any longer. Too much gets taken from us already. You get the CliffsNotes version."

When her grandmother interrupted with a sharp Dakota question, Winona said wryly, "The short version. While our oral traditions vary, they are the same in essence." She glanced sidewise at a bookcase. "Some have chosen to tell some of these stories, at least in part, to help you wasicu understand. That was mostly in the early days, though. Like Zitkala-Sa of the Yankton Dakota. Unci knew her."

Delma nodded with a faint smile. Obviously, it was a good memory. "You may know her as Gertrude Simmons Bonnin."

Marek nodded, though Karen looked puzzled. Marek's mother had a book of Zitkala-Sa's writings. Though Janina Marek Okerlund had left her Catholic faith early on, she still had some appreciation for the mystical, the mystery, of life and death. She'd often quoted, "I seek the level lands where grow the wild prairie flowers," as she'd walked with him below the bluffs. A kindred spirit of the land, she'd said.

Delma told Karen, "Zitkala-Sa was a strong woman, a storyteller, a musician, the daughter of a Frenchman. She went off to a Quaker boarding school in Indiana, only to be told to forget her people. She never forgot." Her voice lowered, as if she were speaking to herself. "We never forget." Then her head rose, and she looked at her granddaughter. "Go on."

Winona took a deep breath. "I am going to tell you the version that Unci told me that night I knew I was pregnant."

Goodthunder held out his hand, and his wife grasped it again.

"You have to understand that to us, spirit is in everything, not just people, not just animals, but rivers and rocks, too. Inyan means 'stone' or 'rock' and is a very powerful spirit."

Winona took a deep breath and launched into the story. "Once, there was a young woman who had four brothers. Times were hard, and they were starving, so the brothers went hunting. One by one, they went out, and one by one, they disappeared. The sister was left all alone. She was so hungry that she picked up a stone and swallowed it. From that stone, a child was born named Inyan Hoksila or Stone Boy. He grew very fast inside her and into a boy. Just days.

She didn't want him and turned him out, but he kept coming back to her. He asked her why she was alone, and she told him about her lost brothers. He went to find them, but instead found a witch who sat outside a tipi. She tried to kill him, but he stepped on her back and, being heavy as stone, killed her. He found four bundles inside the tipi, all that was left of his uncles, whose spirits whispered to him. Following their instructions, Stone Boy built the first inipi—that's a sweat lodge—and with it, he brought his uncles back to life. He took them back to his mother, who ever after rejoiced in her son."

The last, Winona said directly to Two Fingers. "And I have." Her lips twitched. "Mostly." Her amusement faded. "If I'd known how the kids at school would bully him, though, I would have just called him Stone or maybe Rock, not Inyan."

Karen apparently decided talking to Winona wouldn't get her reprimanded. "I think Inyan's a pretty cool name."

Winona just sighed. "Most of the teachers in the public school were white, and on the first day of class, they would read out the names. They would pronounce his *in-yahn*. I think you can guess what they called him."

"Oh," Karen murmured. "Injun."

"As the kids say, my bad."

"It is a good name," her grandmother insisted. "A warrior's name. Wasn't it I, who told Inyan what he should do to heal himself, when he came back to us wounded? It was the inipi—the only way to bring the spirits back to life. He was well named."

Two Fingers didn't move a muscle.

Marek waited a long beat then asked, "What does *ska* mean?"

"White," Winona said, and her son relaxed—marginally.

Because his father was white? A hard man, a hard stone to carry?

"The color white," Winona clarified, as if to distinguish it from wasicu.

Delma clarified further. "On the medicine wheel, white is north, which brings the cold, bitter winds of winter. It reminds us how we as a people have endured many hardships."

Winona's nose flared. "And there was another reason to call my son White Stone or Inyan Ska. You've heard of Wounded Knee? Yes, you would know from the 1970s standoff there that destroyed the village, but maybe not the original massacre in 1890 when unarmed men, women, and children were killed. But few know that even more were massacred, women and children included, at Whitestone Hill in North Dakota in 1863—just one more vengeful reaction to the Dakota War."

Winona nodded toward the circles of old photos. "Unci's Rockboy ancestor fled there after the Army went after the Sioux after the Dakota War, even though he took no part in it. He was only a boy and barely escaped Whitestone Hill with deep scars that he carried—real and figurative—to the day he died. He made it back to the Yankton reservation and managed to escape the schools until soldiers came and forced him to a boarding school far away. He escaped again on the railroads. So few made it back or with any sense of their Native traditions. Some died there. Recently, the remains of nine children who'd died at Carlisle were returned to Rosebud. We all honored them along the way."

Again, there was nothing to say. Marek had never heard of Whitestone Hill. He barely knew that Wounded Knee had been a massacre. Many white Dakotans in the 1970s had taken the American Indian Movement's violent actions as proof that the Indians were lawless savages.

Delma weaved her trembling hands together. "Inyan Ska reminds us we survived hard times and endured, as the bison facing the north in bitter winter survive. Some of us. Not all. You have your war wounded, yes? My great-grandson, he almost took that path, before the inipi."

What Marek knew about sweat lodges could fit in a thimble: sauna with religion. Only much deeper, more meaningful. Like the Tewa kivas, though, it was reserved for the men. At least as far as he knew. Maybe that, as other things, had changed.

Delma's eyes had faded into memory, into pain. "The wounded wander. They live homeless, like Hunter did, without family or friend, and kill themselves with drink or drugs like Hunter's mother did." Her gaze went to the circle of ancestors. "Now think generations of wounded—and without many of our ceremonies, our sacred things, to heal."

Her hands spread out again over the winter count. "Hunter said it was a very, very good day, for him, for everyone on the dig, for all Natives, and that he'd fight to bring the winter count back to my family. He wanted the knowledge. He said that was power enough. We should have the healing of having our own back. You want to know why we protect what we can? Because it's what little we have left after all the hurt." She pointed to the wall with some pouches. "We may not know what all these sacred things are, but they are sacred and demand our respect. We have gotten very little respect from wasicu."

She said it without personal blame, but Marek felt it. He dropped his head.

"Times change. We change. Nothing stays the same. To try to only hold to the old ways is unbalanced. We can hold the old in one hand but bring the new in the other. The old must clasp the new." Her gaze went to the dolls. "You see those dolls with the buckskin dresses? In my day, that is how a proper young woman dressed to dance at wacipi. Traditional. I displeased my mother when I chose to dance in non-traditional regalia. A jingle dress. It was not even a decade before I was born, after the 1918 flu epidemic, when the Ojibwe—our traditional enemies—began using the metal cones on their dresses, claiming they had cured a young girl. The fancy shawl dance"—she pointed at the doll with the ribboned shawl—"came even later. I did that, too."

"You rebel, you," Winona teased her grandmother.

Rather than a reprimand, that got a smile—and for the first time, Marek saw their resemblance. A rebel did live in that small body. The amusement faded, and Delma's hand swept down her own buckskin dress. "But now, I go to the old ways. I am old. I remember when there were still tipis, still warriors, still songs, and dances that are no more. I don't want them forgotten. But one day, they will be, except to some historians like Hunter, and I, too, will be an old picture on the wall. My time is soon gone. You wasicu, you think of us like that—" She pointed at the old photos, the dolls, and the wacipi. "But today we are farmers, doctors, lawyers, musicians, soldiers, and yes, policemen. Some here, some all over the world. Here, many work in the casino or in the marijuana store. We survive. That Hunter did not, after finally confronting his devils, is a great grief to me, to us, and a loss to our tribe and his own."

Now she looked fierce. "You will find who did this to him. All of you, Indian and wasicu."

"Yes, ma'am," Marek said as she seemed to demand an answer. "We will do our best."

Delma seemed to take that as a given and slumped back in her chair. She rolled up the copy of the winter count and gave it to Two Fingers. "I am blessed to see it again." But she looked sad, perhaps because she felt she would never see it in the flesh, so to speak, again. Or because of all the loss of its keepers that went before.

With a tired wave, she dismissed them.

They all went out single file, last being Marek and Goodthunder, who held his silence until they were outside.

"Did any of that help you?" Goodthunder asked.

As Two Fingers went to his squad, no doubt ready to make a break for it before he was embarrassed any further by the women in his life, Marek said honestly, "I have no idea. Our two main suspects are pretty much in the clear. If we don't find anything soon, it might end up going cold."

"Not an uncommon ending for one of us," Goodthunder

murmured, but whether that meant Natives or law enforcement, Marek wasn't sure. But as he watched Karen and Winona talk, Marek decided one Native mystery might be solved.

"You ever take a DNA test?" he asked Goodthunder.

The man's eyes widened, clearly taken aback by the question out of left field. Marek got that a lot.

But Goodthunder answered. "Many don't. We've been burned too many times by the scientists. A DNA study on Native American diabetes was used to argue that we came to America through the Bering Strait. That's not what we did DNA for, and we were not told. But Flandreau is different. I did it when Inyan did, to support him. We all did in the family, even Delma. Interesting results. Inyan had more Indigenous American than his family tree would have predicted. Well over the twenty-five percent blood quantum. But as of now, the council won't accept it."

Marek chose his words with care. "Have you checked the DNA site lately?"

Goodthunder frowned. "No, why would I? It told me nothing I didn't already know."

"Matches can message you there."

He shrugged. "I sometimes get an email from the company saying I have a message, but the people I am related to, I know. I ignore the messages. I may share some small amount with wannabes. That's not a headache I want to bring into the tribe, much less the person, explaining why they cannot join."

Sensible. But... "You might want to check your latest messages."

Startled, Goodthunder looked at Marek, searched his face, and sighed. "You could be a Dakotan. You do have a mouth, you know, not just two ears."

"Not my story to tell," Marek answered.

Which Marek spent the rest of the trip back to Reunion explaining to Karen, who had wanted to be more direct with

Goodthunder. That is, in between Karen getting tagged by a disgruntled Nails and trying to come up with a game plan for the investigation.

That, of course, didn't take a great deal of time. First up on tomorrow morning's agenda: field trip to a museum.

CHAPTER 24

In Karen's day, the W.H. Over Museum in Vermillion had been housed in what was now the National Music Museum, which had been the Shrine to Music. As Delma Two Fingers had said, the old and the new joined hands.

Karen shook the hand of the curator, one Dr. Osirus Grant, as she stood with Marek in the lobby of the relatively new brick building only a stone's throw from the venerable Dakota Dome. Which was where she'd rather be: sports was her thing. Museums, not so much.

The curator looked like he could have wandered right off the football field next door. True, he was bespectacled like a typical nerd, but that did little to diminish his size or muscle. He wasn't as tall as Marek but well over her six-one, and he had them both outweighed in muscle. His dark hand smothered Karen's but was gentle and warm. Still, it wouldn't take much exertion from that hand, that arm, to shatter a skull.

"I was very sorry to hear about Hunter," Dr. Grant told them in a deep voice that hinted at origins farther south than South Dakota. "He was as persistent a researcher as I have ever met. Against some stiff headwinds, too."

Karen gave him a wry smile. "Would one of those blowhards be called Hardy?"

The laugh boomed out, startling a pair of tourists rifling through postcards in the gift shop. "Hole in one. I've got nothing against the man personally, but he sure rode Hunter hard. Said the boy was obsessed with nonsense. Wish I could say otherwise, but I can't say he was wrong."

"We can," Karen informed him.

Caterpillar eyebrows wriggled up toward Brillo-pad hair. "Seriously?"

Intending to find somewhere private, Karen turned to Marek, only to find he'd wandered over to a framed print outside the gift shop. Against a blue background, a woman in buckskin was being held by a large eagle that, at first sight, looked like a shawl the woman had raised over her head. At her feet were two toddlers.

Following her gaze, Grant said, "That's an Oscar Howe. *Origin of the Sioux*. It was after the flood—so many origin stories have a flood—and an eagle saved the woman and gave her two twin boys who became the Sioux Nation."

Karen knew of Oscar Howe, as he'd once been the artist in residence at USD. Marek had one of his prints on his wall called *The Woodgatherer*, an old woman with kindling on her back, a picture of endurance in a hard winter. He'd told her the story of it. His mother had bought the print while an education student at USD and had, with much trepidation, as she'd been in awe of the artist, knocked on Oscar Howe's door and asked him to sign it for her. He'd done so without a word, but with a smile. "I know his work. It's powerful."

"That it is." Grant nodded sagely and seemed to slip into curator mode. "Fewer know that he broke the mold for Native American artists. He entered one of his paintings in a national competition, and it was rejected as 'a fine painting— but not Indian.' It reeked of the abstract style of Modernism. Despite being a very gentle and quiet man, Howe fired off a furious letter that had to have been years, even decades, in the making."

Walking over to a wall of the gift shop, he pointed at a poster with the words blown up: "Who ever said, that my paintings are not in the traditional Indian style, has poor

Dead Spirits

knowledge of Indian art indeed. There is much more to Indian Art, than pretty, stylized pictures. We are to be herded like a bunch of sheep, with no right for individualism, dictated as the Indian has always been, put on reservations and treated like a child, and only the White Man knows what is best for him."

With obvious pride, the curator said, "There's a new exhibit of Howe's work in New York right now called 'Dakota Modernism.' People are finally taking note."

Karen thought of Delma and her jingle and shawl dresses. "The old holds hands with the new."

Dr. Grant nodded. "A good summary. Now, what was this about the winter count?"

Marek asked, "Is there somewhere we can talk privately?"

"Sure, sure." Dr. Grant led them through a maze of exhibits—a tipi, a settler cabin, and a truly amazing collection of Native American dolls—and back into an office that displayed a PhD from the University of Oklahoma, along with a picture of a young Osirus next to legendary football coach Bobby Stoops.

When Karen paused in front of it, he shook his head sadly. "Ancient history. Bummed up my knee freshman year, got stuck with work-study in a freaking museum, and found my passion. But it was fun while it lasted. This is funner. I don't have to break my bones in this job, just dig old bones."

Karen glanced at Marek then back. "You are an archaeologist as well?"

Laughter boomed. "No, 'dig' as in 'like.' And don't you be looking at me that way. Talk about an evil eye. We've returned all identifiable remains to the tribes. I made it a priority when I came here seven years ago. You may not believe it, but I have Cherokee ancestors. I know, I know, everyone's got Cherokee ancestors these days. But my people were slaves to the Cherokee. We walked the same Trail of Tears from Georgia to Oklahoma. Got me some Cherokee in there, Choctaw as well, but they kicked us off the rolls. Though I think we're back on after some court case. I haven't looked into it because, to me, I am who I am. Trying to quantify race—from the one-drop rule for Blacks to blood quantum for Indians—just leads to heartache and loss."

"But back to NAGPRA." His gaze went to a stack of papers teetering on top of a file cabinet. "I can't say we've made as much progress on inventorying all the rest of our holdings that could be returned to the tribes, but we're short-staffed, mostly volunteers who don't have the expertise to evaluate what is and isn't relevant under NAGPRA. Just take the winter count that Hunter worked on. He's spent years on that, consulting other winter counts like the Blue Thunder variants and Lone Dog and High Dog, writing to museums across the country to see if they have any of the novel variants found in the one he was trying to identify."

"Novel variants?" Marek asked.

"Unique to that particular artifact. You say that he did it? Hunter found its origin?"

Rather than answer directly, Karen took a different tack. She'd been learning from Marek, a master of misdirection. "What would you do with it under NAGPRA, if it was identified?"

"Well, that's the tricky part. It has to be remains, funerary objects, sacred objects, or objects of cultural patrimony. I am not entirely sure a winter count is sacred in the religious sense. There are no ceremonies that I am aware of that are attached to them. Cultural patrimony may or may not apply, depending on the circumstances."

So Dr. Grant would be reluctant to part with it. Still, that seemed an extreme motive to kill someone over. Well, people killed over less, that's for sure.

Marek asked, "Can we see it?"

"Sure, sure. Let me bring it out to you. It's in a secured area." Dr. Grant led them back to a large open room where a number of workers—or, more likely, volunteers—were chatting. Then he disappeared through a door. A few minutes

Dead Spirits

later, he emerged carrying a large flat box, which he placed on a standing table. He lifted the lid.

Karen took in a quick breath. The colors on the tanned hide were still bright, the reds especially. That hadn't come across in a color photocopy. It was beautiful. Almost awe-inspiring. "What kind of skin is this?"

"Buffalo." Dr. Grant's face was alight with curiosity. "It's ironic that while it is a pretty thing, we couldn't display it for lack of provenance, of its origin, its historical context. We don't even know if it's genuine or a fake. Hunter was the one who found it stuffed into a mailing tube along with the name of the collector who'd died. The heirs just didn't want to throw it in the dump. If it is genuine, it is much more valuable—to us, Natives, the public, academics. So it would be hard to let it go. But I wouldn't block a genuine claim."

Karen watched him carefully. "The winter count belongs to the tiospaye of a Yankton Dakota woman who lives in Flandreau. Delma Two Fingers. Willis Rockboy, her uncle, was the keeper."

Dr. Grant pursed his lips. "Does she have proof?"

"You only need to talk to her," Marek said shortly. "She said her uncle's eldest son sold it for money. Delma never expected to see it again."

Dr. Grant nodded but was still cautious. "I don't suppose that eldest son is still living and knows the history? A winter count needs context. The pictograph itself is just a mnemonic device, a prop to memory. It's the stories that go with it, the oral tradition, that is so often lost. Without them, any variants that aren't found in other winter counts of the area remain a mystery and add nothing to the knowledge base. Of course, the quality of oral tradition degrades over time, and by now, there may be little actual knowledge to impart."

Karen wondered how Delma would respond to that, to hear its value limited to a knowledge base. "Her mother often left Delma alone with her uncle, who told her the stories. So far as I know, Delma is the only living person who knows them. She is well into her nineties."

Excitement finally flickered. "Is she willing to have them recorded?"

"Hunter was going to return and do so." Her gaze fell on the pictograph of the man and woman holding hands. She didn't know what was key, what wasn't, so she didn't mention what Delma had said about the two variants Hunter had asked about. "Hunter also said he wanted to see the winter count returned to her, to her people, her tribe."

For a long moment, he was silent. Then he burst out, "It's just so unfair that Hunter didn't get to do that himself. I've been to repatriation ceremonies, and they are something else. Like you'd returned the Holy Grail to Rome. If all you said is true, I am willing to see it returned, as long as we have a high-quality copy and the associated stories. In fact, I'd love to do an exhibit on it. And I would be very eager to speak with Delma Two Fingers. I admit I was rooting for Hunter against all odds. I am glad, at least, that he died happy. That would have made a very interesting dissertation, even Hardy would have to admit, with this news."

Marek's brow quirked. "Hardy is not well liked?"

A few snorts rang around the room, but Dr. Grant laughed. "Well, I wouldn't go that far. He is very knowledgeable. He's helped us out a number of times to identify or give context for some of our collections and exhibits. No one can say he hasn't been a friend of the museum. If you're willing to learn, you will learn. But he can be very cutting to those who do not meet his exacting standards. I believe that is why Dr. Abigail Doll of Colorado was added to the field school." His smile broadened. "Now, she's a lady who knows how to have a good time. She's also a damn good digger. You'll also learn from her, but you'll have more fun doing it."

Having no idea where to go next with the investigation, Karen asked, "Was there any friction between Hardy and Doll, or between either and Hunter, that you know of?"

"No, not that I recall. I mean, Hardy thought the winter count was a dead end, but he didn't actually stop Hunter from studying it." Then he laughed. "And Doll did say over a few beers the other night that she thought Hardy must've, um, taken a male enhancer, if you get my drift, the way he was suddenly gung-ho to dig this last week."

Marek asked, "What is the monetary value of this winter count, now that its origin is known?"

The room went quiet. Dr. Grant said, "Are you suggesting that someone killed Hunter merely so they could repatriate the winter count and then sell it?"

"No, I am asking, what is its value on the open market?"

"The last winter count that I saw for sale was about seven years ago. A later copy of Lone Dog, a Lakota winter count. It had pictographs going from about 1800 to 1870." He tapped the table beside the Rockboy winter count. "This one would likely sell for more, as it's older and has a better provenance. But that one sold for a little more than three thousand dollars. I wouldn't put it beyond ten thousand."

Karen stared at him, dumbfounded. She'd been expecting tens of thousands, if not hundreds. "Is that all?"

The curator smiled then. "You've seen its cultural value. As the ads say, priceless." The smile faded. "If you have any inkling at all of a scheme to claim the winter count and then auction it off, I will do everything I can to keep it here."

Marek shook his head. "We have no such inkling."

Karen reinforced that quickly. "We're just looking at all possible angles."

"Well, that one sucks. Now, I can see that Tommy Knotts character you arrested doing something like that. I was a kid when he was arrested in Oklahoma. A lot of bad blood there. He worked his way into getting the blessings of some pretty powerful tribes, got chummy with councils, did some charity stuff, wrote an inspiration book. Then he started up with the Redman Ripoffs, as my mother used to call them, selling repackaged spiritual ceremonies to whites. If you want to bilk them for gambling, she'd say, that was all good—payback. Greed took our lands, and greed is giving us back some of what was lost. But selling what is sacred? That crossed a hard line. I still remember her screaming at the TV."

Dr. Grant gently replaced the top of the box, and the beauty faded from view. He disappeared with it then returned, making an "after you" gesture, and they walked out through the exhibit room.

"It guts me that Hunter will never return here," Dr. Grant said. "He punched above his weight, y'know? He had a way about him, despite his size. He'd seen things, done things, few his age had. He'd talk sometimes with the staff or volunteers, just shooting the breeze, about his life on the rails. Funny things but also sad things. He understood how dark the heart could be."

As they passed the tipi exhibit, Marek suddenly stopped. Karen pushed at his back. "We don't have time for the tour, Marek. We have to get back to the dig, talk to people, find clues."

Marek pointed down at something she couldn't see. "What's that?"

Sidestepping her uncle, she looked, too. And stilled.

Dr. Grant peered down and looked disappointed. "Nothing all that unusual. We've got a few more of these in the back. But this one's the best of the lot."

"Lot of what?" Karen was almost afraid to hear the answer. Because what she was looking at was a big round rock with an indentation all around in the middle where the hide-bound handle was attached.

"Oh. Sorry." The curator shrugged. "It's just a maul."

CHAPTER 25

JUST A MAUL.

Marek closed his eyes. Assumptions. They always came back to kick your ass. "Didn't Natives have iron or some other metal?"

"Open your eyes," Dr. Grant said with amusement. "Do you see anything metal here?"

No, he didn't. He'd never even considered that a maul wasn't a maul as he knew it, but he should have known better. Things changed, tools included.

Dr. Grant went on. "Like horses and smallpox, metallurgy on the Great Plains—though not in some other areas of the Americas—came over with the Europeans."

"Horses? But..." Karen gestured to a painting along the wall with Lakota warriors on horses of varied color.

"That's post-contact. Not-so-funny fact: the Arikara were the premier traders along the Missouri River and sold the Sioux horses. The Sioux then used them to drive the Arikara out. Payback's a bitch."

Marek remembered Two Fingers saying once that someone was always kicking ass out on the Plains. He couldn't imagine the Sioux without horses. Did they farm like the Arikara? "They weren't nomadic before horses?"

"They used dogs."

Karen looked horrified. "They rode *dogs*?"

Grant's booming laugh startled a cranky toddler into

silence as his mother hurried him away toward the exit. "No, they walked. They attached their bags to travois—a drag sled—and the dogs pulled those." Dr. Grant searched their faces. "Somehow, I don't think Native transport links are what have you floored."

He wasn't a stupid man. Unlike Marek.

"If it pans out, you'll hear about it," Marek said shortly. After thanking him for his time, they left the curator staring down at the maul with his caterpillar brows wriggling in thought. He might suspect, as they did, but without evidence, there was nothing.

Karen slammed herself into the Sub and burst into words as soon as Marek slid in. "Hot diggity dog. A maul. That's exactly what we're looking for. A large round rock. And the big find of the day on Friday was a maul. I bet it was dirty. But where is it?"

Some of Marek's elation deflated. "It may have been dumped."

"Spoilsport. Where was it that they took the finds? We need to check." She got out her phone then hesitated. "Who should we call?"

Marek pursed his lips. Hardy was still in play. Though he couldn't imagine what motive other than messing up the dig would get a whack on the head with a maul. But they hadn't eliminated Doll, either. "We need someone with access to wherever they lock up the finds after each day."

"Hardy, it is." Karen sighed and called her dispatcher for the number. A few minutes later, she was talking to the professor, who, judging by Karen's increasingly clipped replies, wasn't at all happy to be dragged off the dig. Karen didn't tell him why, just that she needed access to the finds. No need to tip off the man if the maul wasn't there, though he would likely notice himself if it wasn't.

When Karen said they would be happy if someone other than Hardy, especially someone on campus, could give them access, he'd caved. Did Hardy have the only access? That seemed hard to believe, but who knew. Hopefully, they'd soon find out.

Karen parked on the east side of campus and walked to the aptly named East Hall, an overwrought castle-like stone building that Marek guessed was built around the same time as the Eda County Courthouse and the original Flandreau Indian School in the late nineteenth century. Richardsonian Romanesque. An imposing but also fanciful place. The stone glinted pink and was, he guessed, some variant of quartzite, perhaps Sioux, but it was detailed with something closer to the color of pipestone.

"It used to be a woman's dormitory," Karen commented as they waited inside, as the heat was already rising on a day that would have the diggers jumping in the creek. Assuming there was any water left in it.

When Hardy finally arrived, he looked red and hot. Whether from the sun, anger, or both, it was hard to say. "I don't appreciate having to leave the dig for a fishing expedition."

Wasn't archaeology itself a fishing expedition? But Marek knew better than to say that out loud.

Karen, on the other hand, was not so shy. "We all dig in our own ponds."

Air hissed out between his slightly uneven teeth. "Yours is plumb dry if you're looking at any of us. It's those protesters. Has to be. Dig deeper there and leave us in peace. At least the protesters finally gave up after you exposed Hawks. Are they still hawking you? Is that why you're here, to get away from them?"

"We're here to look for anything connected to Hunter Redwing-Digges's murder, Dr. Hardy."

The professor let out a breath, this time not through his gritted teeth, as he let them into the lab that was prominently labeled as ARCHLAB. "Yes, of course. Poor Hunter. I'm sorry if I seem less than cooperative, but losing Hunter has been a hard blow to the dig. Richie, too, though he's just returned, for whatever that's worth. We'll see."

Marek looked at Karen, who asked, "Returned? Why? I thought he was worried about getting tagged for weed."

A glow of satisfaction appeared on the professor's face as he switched on the lights in the room, showing rows and rows of shelving and large tables. "His father read him the riot act. No weed, no booze. He gets his act together, or he's on his own. No more money."

His tone said, "About time." Marek could only agree.

Marek looked around at the computers and other equipment. "It's not just a storage room."

Dr. Hardy looked at him as if he were less than bright. Not an unusual look from an educator. Dumb Pollack. "No, the dig is the easy part, the quick part. It's what happens here that takes the longest and has the most impact. Analysis, cataloging, reporting. It can take years. Now, what is it you're looking for?"

"The finds from Friday," Karen said.

The heavy brows lowered, caging the man's eyes. But he sighed and went to a shelf. After perusing what was written on them, he pulled off a carton and brought it to a table. Then he handed white gloves to both of them.

Marek's didn't fit.

"You just won't be touching the finds," Hardy informed him, sounding like he'd already had his doubts about Marek anyway and was happy not to have his valuable finds broken by clumsy hands.

Pulling on her gloves, Karen peered down into the carton. Marek peered as well but kept his hands in his pockets. Lots and lots of Ziploc bags. Gingerly, Karen began taking them out.

The first was a large piece of pottery. A sherd? Marek thought that was what the diggers called them. It had a number of slightly wavy horizontal lines near the rim and some smoother strokes below.

"Stanley Cord-Impressed along the rim and Stanley Tool-Impressed below. A good if fairly common example of the type." Hardy looked happily down at the sherds. "Firmly identified with the Arikara roughly dated to the Post Contact Coalescent or possibly late Extended Coalescent Variant."

Marek didn't ask what actual years those spanned, nor did Karen, as she gradually emptied the carton and let Hardy drone on about La Beau, Talking Crow Ware, and other arcane terms.

It was obvious fairly quickly that the maul wasn't there. At least, nothing like the one in the museum.

"Well? Are you satisfied?" Hardy demanded when she'd finished, glancing at his watch.

Marek asked, "Is that all?"

Dr. Hardy pointed at the date on the carton and "Box 1 of 1." It looked like they'd struck out in one sense. But they might very well have identified their weapon. That was progress of a sort. The question was, how did it escape notice that it was missing when the van was unloaded?

Karen pursed her lips. "From what I heard, you had a big find on Friday that caused a stir. Something called a... What was it, Marek? He's the tool guy in the family."

Marek took a beat. Let the man think him slow. Most did anyway. "A maul."

The man's eyes widened. "Oh, yes. Sorry. I thought you were looking for the *fine* finds. Everyone wants to see the ceramics. Lithics like the maul are stored separately. They can't be stored with more fragile finds."

So a stone tool was a lithic? Everything kept coming back to stones, it seemed. Stone Boy. Rockboy. Inyan Ska.

Hardy brought out another carton marked with the date and "Box 1 of 1" from high on the opposite shelf labeled Lithics. He opened the top, and his eyes lit up under the heavy brows. Though smaller pieces of stone and arrowheads were in sealed bags, the maul was not. Hardy reverently lifted it from the carton and put it on the table.

Marek remembered Dr. Grant's indifference. One man's maul was another man's gold.

Hardy tapped the maul lightly with one gloved hand. "The stone itself is characteristic of the Mound Builders of Cahokia. Further testing will confirm the actual geological classification, but I have studied enough artifacts from Cahokia to be sure that is its origin. The handle work is distinctly Arikara. It is one more tie from Cahokia to the Caddoans of the Arikara and Pawnee who spread out over the Plains."

The maul looked pristine. As if it had been in use yesterday. Or Friday. "Was it cleaned on site? Why isn't it in a bag?"

"Hunter might have cleaned it, but I can't say why it wasn't bagged. Perhaps he didn't have any bags large enough available. He was working the finds tent that night. He often did. Not the strongest of men. His contribution was between his ears, not with his hands, though he was a careful digger. His biggest failing was always to put his traditions ahead of the science. That's not how it works if you truly want to find answers."

Hardy sounded like he fully expected that most Natives did not want answers. Marek was still trying to figure out how it had gotten into the carton if this was their murder weapon. Maybe Hardy himself was their killer. "When you dropped off the finds here, did you notice the maul?"

Hardy tilted his head to look up at Marek. "No, I didn't open the cartons. I just put them on the shelf."

Karen stepped in. "Did the... lithics... carton feel heavy?"

Hardy considered. "Now that you mention it, not very. It should have. That's a very solid artifact there. But I was in a hurry to get home and finish adding notes on Friday's finds for my talk on Saturday night. I assumed Hunter had put everything where he should in the cartons. Perhaps he was distracted, though, by Hawks and Stands By Him. Congratulations, by the way, for getting them off the streets—

or should I say, the digs. It could be that the maul was still at the finds tent when I left. But... how did it get here?"

"Someone obviously returned it," Karen said. "Who has access?"

Hardy looked concerned, even alarmed. "Obviously, I do. All the professors in the department, Dr. Doll, grad students, the dean, facilities management, perhaps the departmental secretary."

Marek thought that at least narrowed the list. Though there was another possibility. "How hard would it be to get a copy of the key?"

"Not terribly hard, I'm sorry to say. Oh, NAS grad students also have access besides those in anthropology. I've suggested a badge system as more secure but..." He shrugged. "Money. It's always money, isn't it? We have to fight for our small slice of the budget. I'd rather spend it on digs, on knowledge. Knowledge is power."

True enough. "Do you have a bag big enough to hold that?"

"Certainly. It needs one." He went over and pulled out a bag from a roll. Then he carefully placed the maul in it and sealed it. "There."

Marek reached out. "We'll need to take that with us."

The professor looked horrified. "You can't. It's evidence."

"Yes, it is. Ours," Karen answered. "We need to test it."

He looked baffled. "For what?"

"Blood," Marek said.

He gaped at them.

As Marek took and cradled the bag against his brawn, much to the dismay of the professor, Karen said, "Don't worry, Dr. Hardy. None of the tests will harm your artifact. Surface only."

What she didn't say, Marek knew, was that if the maul was used in a homicide, it would not be returning to ARCHLAB any time soon.

CHAPTER 26

AH, WEDDED BLISS.
Just the two of them snuggled together in the dark. Well, okay, Marek and Larson's DCI sidekicks Jessica and Blue were here as well. But Karen would take a quick kiss. And did—just as the ultraviolet light flicked on.

"Take it outside," Blue growled in a perfect mimicry of Larson.

Jessica stifled a giggle then didn't stifle a gasp. Blue aka Arvo Sininen had turned the UV light on the maul, which had been carefully dowsed with luminol and set on the table in the DCI crime lab in Sioux Falls.

Karen and Marek had driven straight there from Vermillion. Without evidence of blood, they were at a dead end. Breaking off the kiss, Karen turned.

And smiled broadly. "I love blue." Then as muffled laughter rang out, she realized what she'd said. "I meant the *color* blue."

"Uh huh," Blue said out of the blue-tinged darkness. "That's what all the girls say."

"Watch it, Sininen," Larson growled. "You're disposable."

But all of them, Karen knew, were grinning madly. Because of the smears, swirls, and spatters of blue that outlined the maul on the table. A glowing gotcha. "We've got a winner."

After lifting a camera off the counter, Jessica snapped a photo. "And somewhere, a loser."

"More like, losers. One of them will be Professor Hardy," Karen commented. "He's not going to be happy that his precious Mound Builder-Arikara maul is locked in evidence."

After the photoshoot was finished, Jessica flicked on the lights. The only blue left in the room, other than several blue eyes, was Blue's blue-tinged fair hair. Larson went over to the table and picked up the carton of swabs he'd taken before using the luminol, which could damage DNA. He handed it to Blue. "Send off for DNA analysis."

Though it would take considerably longer to get results than the luminol, it was a necessary step to make sure the blood belonged to Hunter. If they were really lucky, the killer's would be there as well, but Karen doubted they'd find any. Unlike a knife, the maul had no sharp edges to cause the killer's hand to bleed.

Blue gave a smart salute and marched out.

Jessica shook her head. "Blue's like your Adam Van Eck but on steroids. Never a dull moment." But her gaze lingered on the door Blue had disappeared out of.

Was another romance in the offing? That reminded Karen again of Seoul and Two Fingers. Had Goodthunder contacted Seoul's mother? Or had he decided not to? Had he even checked for messages as Marek suggested? It was maddening. Goodthunder had to know who Seoul's grandfather was. Even if he was a bad egg, wasn't it better to know?

"Report," Larson barked at Jessica, who blinked.

"Oh, yeah. The cars." Jessica dragged her hand through her long blond hair, pulling it away from the scar on her face from an assault. "Larson filled you in on some already, but I finished this morning. Plenty of prints belonging to Hawks aka Knotts on the dynamite. Which, by the way, I am glad is finally out of our hands. I was afraid some random spark—or even the heat in the garage—was going to shoot us all to Mars."

Blue had come back in. "Only us guys get shot to Mars, the god of war. You gals are headed to Venus, goddess of loooove. You know, I wonder if Native Americans have gods and goddesses like the Greeks? Or was it the Romans? Or is it all just everything is a god, so to speak, and—"

"Stop wondering, stop speaking." Larson turned back to Jessica. "Go on."

Karen's lips twitched as Blue zipped his mouth shut. He was one of the few people she knew who could out-talk her. Fortunately, he seemed to be okay with being reprimanded in public, just sitting in mock dejection.

Eyeing him sardonically, Jessica opened a folder. "Okay, Hawks's car first. He had a nice bundle of cash stashed in the toolbox in the trunk. About five thousand. I found a couple receipts in the glove compartment for some really swank places in various cities like Denver and Omaha. Seems he likes to take some breaks from the protest circuit and blow some dough."

After a knock on the door, a tall, pasty white guy stuck in his head. "Heard Eda was here. Finally busted through the firewalls. Your Hawks guy had almost five mil stashed. Details to follow." He shut the door before they could even thank him.

Karen stared at the closed door. "Who was that unmasked man?"

Her man from Mars replied, "Smith. Forensic accountant."

"We only let him out of his computer cave once in a blue moon." Blue zipped his lips shut again as Larson gave him a look.

Jessica cleared her throat. "Well, then, five K was just pocket change to Hawks. If he'd put some of that money into fixing his car, he might not have been pulled over. Some serious issues, the guy at the garage said."

"It was all about keeping up appearances," Karen told

her. Seeing the puzzlement, she explained. "He had to look the part of a poor rez Indian with a heart of gold."

"Check. Instead, he was a gold digger with a heart of cold." Jessica looked back at her notes. "But we've got him cold on the dynamite. The Seasons scooped up the guy Hawks referred to as Dustin." With the resident FBI agents in Sioux Falls on the case, Hawks was going to spend the rest of his days living as the dirt-poor Indian he claimed to be. "Dustin's real name is Milo Hansen. He's singing like a canary. Willing to deal on several outstanding cases where he supplied the ammo. He ID'd Hawks right off and said Hawks told him to watch the news—it'd be big and public—but not to worry. He'd arranged for someone else to take the fall."

That shot Hawks's story to the moon—and beyond. Saturn, perhaps?

Jessica went on. "We found no blood in the car. No indication from Hawks's phone that he knew of or was planning Redwing-Digges's death. There's no mention of him at all, actually, until after the homicide was widely known. Then he sent one text to Stands By Him that read: 'Why did you do it? Redwing was harmless. I told you to cool off. No violence, remember?'"

"That would be the frame," Marek said. "If not for the crime he planned."

Karen made a mental note to herself to talk to Ed Martin again about springing Stands By Him in exchange for a deal against Hawks. He'd taken the heat for too much.

Jessica shuffled papers. "Okay, next car up. Redwing-Digges's was last driven by Stands By Him. That car was in much better shape. It just ran out of gas. Not even fumes left. There was some blood that transferred from Stands By Him onto the seat. The clothes you submitted are consistent with those transfers. As for what else was in the car, other than the torn-off note on Tommy Knotts, there were some annotated topo maps from the Hub City and Vermillion quadrangles. Those two cover Spirit Mound, so presumably, that was for the dig."

Jessica took them out and spread them over the table, joining the two maps, as the mound straddled both. There were some notations about finds and some measurements, and the creek was circled, along with a couple exclamations.

Karen looked at the map. "What is that creek?"

"A small tributary of the Vermillion River. I figure that they were worried about the water levels at the site. Maybe that's why they conducted the dig in the peak of summer. I can't imagine trying to dig in muck. Yuck."

Jessica folded up the maps and put them back into the folder. "As for the glove compartment, Redwing-Digges had the usual stuff: auto insurance cards, emergency supplies, some old prescription meds that were likely there for a backup if he ever got stranded somewhere. But also a lighter, a small ceramic bowl, and a bag of some kind of herbal mixture." She turned, opened a drawer, and lifted a Ziploc bag with the said contents. "Not weed."

Karen was happy to be able to impart some multicultural knowledge. "Smudge bowl and mixture of probably sweetgrass, tobacco, and/or cedar."

"Oh. Cool. Here I thought he was a dealer or something."

"It's for cleansing," Blue said unexpectedly. "A purification ritual. You know, sort of like sweat lodges, only on a small scale. You know, my family has a sauna that my Finnish great-great-grandfather made, and we still use it every time we go to the old homestead. It was always fun to throw the bucket of water onto the hot stones. But freaky to see all the old guys in their birthday suits. And, boy, when you get out of there, you almost have to crawl, you're so weak. You think, never again. Then you jump into the cold stream outside, and it's like you're born again."

"Isn't that a shock to the system?" Jessica frowned at him. "You'd think people would get heart attacks."

"Nope, we Sininens are very long-lived. Centenarians all

except Great-Uncle Tuomo, who was killed by logs that fell off a lumber truck. Even Great-Aunt Emmi, who smoked a pack a day since she was fifteen, lived to be one hundred and three, and then there's my—"

"Enough." Larson gave Blue the stink eye then opened his own folder. "Hunter's computer activity. In the last week, Hunter did searches on Tonto Hawks, his blog, his life. Lots on the Arikara, too, and various objects associated with them: tools, sacred objects, rituals, secret societies. Also some on Cahokia. Two days before his death, Hunter started researching Tommy Knotts. Then, on Friday, he, or at least someone who used his computer, linked the search words for Hawks and Knotts. He hit on websites where they used the very same wording, same stories about their origins. Then he brought up images of both Hawks and Knotts."

Karen nodded. "That's when Hunter must have made the connection. Or at least strongly suspected they were the same man. He must have jotted that down on that legal pad there, ripped it off, then taken it with him and stashed it in the cup holder when he went to see Delma Two Fingers."

Larson went on. "No activity for seventy-two minutes and thirty-nine seconds. Then searches for *Arikara, Spirit Society, sacred bundles, Inyan Ska*. Last means—"

"White stone," Karen finished. "It's also Two Fingers's name."

Marek asked, "What are sacred bundles?"

That had gotten by her. Bundles. Seoul had mentioned a student digger who overheard mention of bundles between Hunter and Hardy.

Larson shrugged. "Some kind of ceremonial collection of artifacts. Ask an expert."

Either Hardy or Doll. Karen had no desire to consult Hardy right now, given she'd have to tell him his maul was in lockup indefinitely. Thinking of lockup, she asked, "What about the keys that Stands By Him had?" They'd taken an impression of the ARCHLAB key before leaving Vermillion. She pulled it out of her pocket. "Do any match this?"

Larson got up, went over to a drawer, and pulled out the keys. Both Hunter's and Stands By Him's bundle of keys contained a match.

"So no one took theirs since Stands By Him took the keys from Hunter's body. And we know Stands By Him didn't kill Hunter."

Jessica chimed in. "But could Stands By Him have taken the maul back? I mean, he moved Hunter to the top of the mound as a matter of respect, you said. For the same reason, he might have cleaned up the maul and returned it to the lab before heading for Lower Brule. He'd know where to put it, right?"

Karen blinked. "As an NAS student, yes, he'd know." He might also know about sacred bundles. That would be something to find out.

But Marek shook his head. "Stands By Him was there protesting the dig, so why would he return the dig's biggest find to the enemy, so to speak?"

"Good point." Karen pursed her lips. "But let's go ask him."

CHAPTER 27

THE NEWS THAT THE PROTESTERS had been taken in by a plastic shaman had considerably diminished the crowd outside the courthouse. No media. No honkers. No protesters other than a few diehards who sat on the courthouse steps, using their signs as fans.

As Marek waited for Karen to finish talking to Ed Martin, he went out the double doors to get a better look. He and Karen had parked out back. One of the three protesters was an older man and clearly fading in the heat, even though it wasn't yet noon. "Want to come inside to cool off?"

The man turned. His sign read: We'll Stand By Him! Free Jerome NOW! "I'm not going in until my nephew comes out. You'll have to arrest me to get me off these steps. I promised the family I'd bring him home."

The young woman to his right, white to all appearances, tugged his arm. "Come on, Carl, you're going to have a heatstroke. That won't do Jerome any good."

"I survived Vietnam. I'll survive a Dakota summer." He wiped his brow with a bandana. "Told that boy to join the military, go to war, not college. Told him books wouldn't do him any good. Looks like I was right."

The third protester didn't look up, nor did he contradict the older man. But eyes down, the younger man said, "We need lawyers to go to war these days. We can't win otherwise."

The older man humphed. "Jerome's innocent. He was

never trouble." He lifted his war-haunted eyes to Marek. "If you can't see that, you're blind."

"I've often been called dumb, but not blind," Marek answered mildly. "I'll be right back."

When he came back with a bucket of water and paper cups, he was half afraid they'd be thrown back at him. But all three thanked him and drank deeply.

Waving his cup, the vet said, "Y'know, I went to war with a man looked like you. Big man, quiet as a mountain, a farmer from Mobridge. White as snow. He had my back more'n once. He got shot to bits right beside me one dark night in the jungle. Figure it was 'cause he was so white. Never forgot him. Name was Don Drover. Any relation?"

Marek shook his head. "My people were all from here in Eda."

The vet shook his head sadly. "So were mine, once upon a time." He looked out at the main street with its solid buildings—more than a few were vacant, though it had improved some in the last few years. "My people just picked up and left in minutes when we had to. We had to, a lot. Lived easy on the land, just followed the hunt. You whites killed the bison almost to the last one, so we'd starve. Shooting them out of railroad cars until the bones and skulls littered the land. Still doing that. Just killing for sport, I mean, like outta helicopters. Crazy."

Marek thought of Walrus and pheasant hunting. "Not all of us."

"You eat what you hunt?" the girl asked.

"I don't hunt. Except bad guys."

"Jerome isn't a bad guy," the young man said, finally lifting his head. "He's my cousin. And he's why I'm going to be a lawyer."

The older man glared at him. "You're going to the military."

"First, yeah. Then college and law school." His chin jutted. "Beat them at their own game."

Had this boy gone to Flandreau, perhaps? Taught by Armon Ladeaux?

"Maybe," the older man conceded grudgingly. "Stupid game."

The doors opened behind them. "We're ready, Marek." Karen eyed the three. "You want to come in?"

Before a repeat, Marek answered. "They're not leaving until Stands By Him is released."

She opened the doors wider. "Then they might as well come in and wait. He'll be sprung after we talk to him, assuming he's smart enough to take a deal."

The cousin eyed Karen suspiciously. "What kind of deal? Good for him or for you?"

"It's called a win-win. He testifies against Hawks, all charges dropped."

The girl fist-pumped. "Yes! I told you he'd be released!" The girl did a little dance... right into the office. The two men followed more slowly, as if expecting a trap.

Marek picked up the bucket and cups and walked back into the welcome coolness. Josephine, their some-time secretary, pulled chairs over. "About time you got sensible. You were frying like scrambled eggs out there."

"Nothing scrambled about us," the vet muttered but took the chair, and as was her way, Josephine soon had the man chatting about his war experiences. Being the widow of a soldier killed in Korea gave her a pass, apparently.

But Marek felt dark, cynical eyes on his back—from the younger man. Presumably, he was the man's son but possibly grandson or some other relation. Just how the young woman figured into the equation, Marek didn't know, but he suspected she was their ride. Stands By Him had indicated his family was dead poor.

That same dark, cynical gaze hit him when he and Karen went into the interview room. Straight on. "Don't tell me." Stands By Him plucked his orange jumpsuit. "The new red is the old orange. You've always imprisoned us."

"Different times," Marek told him.

"And I don't think orange is your best color," Karen followed.

As Stands By Him froze, Marek switched on his recorder. "Do you want a lawyer?"

"I want a lot of things I can't have. I haven't heard a lick from my public defender. What do you want?"

"It's more what you want." Karen placed a sheaf of paper on the scarred table in front of him. "If that's to put Tommy Knotts in prison for the rest of his unnatural life, then we have a deal you can't refuse."

His eyes hooded. "What's the catch?"

"No catch. But—"

"Yeah, but. There's always a but."

"We need information," Marek told him. "You don't have to give it to us."

Karen nodded and tapped the paper. "The state's attorney just signed off on a deal to drop all charges in exchange for your testimony against Hawks aka Knotts. I'll warn you ahead of time that there may be multiple trials on multiple charges in multiple jurisdictions."

Stands By Him looked between Marek and Karen, then at the wall where Two Fingers had stood, as if he wanted confirmation from a Native that the deal was real. Finally, he said, "I'll follow his lying, cheating ass to the ends of the earth if I have to."

But Stands By Him took the time to read the entire legal document. They waited. He asked a few questions. He signed. But he still looked like the deal might disappear in the next breath.

Good. Step one. Now to the rest.

Karen asked him, "You have a key to the ARCHLAB, right?"

"I did until that sheriff in Brule County took it off me with everything else." The cynic was back, and he crossed his arms. "Why? Was something stolen?"

"No, something was returned."

He blinked. "Returned?"

Marek shifted, and his chair protested. "We need to know if you returned anything to the lab before you headed for Lower Brule."

"Are you kidding? I got the hell out of Dodge. Why would I go there? I was wearing bloody clothes, if you'll recall. I was trying to avoid anybody and everybody until I made it to LB."

Karen glanced wryly at Marek. "So much for that avenue."

"What avenue? What was returned? Something from the dig?"

"We can't answer that at this time," Marek told him. "It's part of an ongoing investigation."

"And part of that is why we need your input," Karen went on. "You're a Native American Studies student. How much do you know about sacred bundles?"

Shock filled his face. Even horror. "They found a sacred bundle? Hardy has it? Did he open it? Of course he did." He slid his hands down his face and stopped there, shutting out the world, as if his worst nightmare had come true.

Marek hadn't expected such an extreme reaction. "So far as we know, no sacred bundle was found at the dig."

The hands slid slowly to show dark eyes wide with shock. "Then why ask?"

"Hunter did some searches about sacred bundles that day, the day he was killed."

He relaxed. "Oh. Well, that's Hunter all over. He *studied* the culture. I *know* it. Down to my bones. The origin stories, the ceremonies, the sweats, the smudges, all of it—it's bred into my very being. It's academic to him. *Was* academic."

Marek thought about the smudges. "Not all of it."

"Maybe not all. But sacred bundles... That's something we don't really talk about, at least not in my tribe. Too much has been stolen, literally and figuratively, of our sacred things."

Karen said, "Talk generally."

Stands By Him seemed to struggle to do even that. "Look, either of you Catholic?"

Karen looked at Marek.

He said, "Mother was lapsed. My wife was." Perhaps his biracial daughter was, with her pictures of angels and retablos that hung over her bed, especially the one of her mother and brother.

"So you know about the whole host thing—the bread and the wine are supposed to become the actual body and blood of Jesus Christ." He shook his head. "And you think *we* have weird beliefs. Anyway, what if an Indian on the rez stole them after they were blessed and started selling the wine, the wafers? Having tourists come and set up fake Communions that they don't really understand and selling the whole experience for money? Or putting the bread and wine on display like some trophy—like taking a scalp of your religious culture. How would you feel?"

Marek knew what his wife would have felt. She'd have reacted like Stands By Him had. "Violated."

Stands By Him nodded. "If Hardy found one and opened it, that's how I'd feel. Sacred bundles are kind of like holy relics of the Catholic Church. Venerated. Believed to have special powers, especially for healing. But also for victory in war and other such things. Sacred bundles are a collection of sacred items. All have a pipe, but the rest is different, and like pictographs, they are often a prop to memory of events and rituals, so that the stories that hold us together as a people are not forgotten. Some bundles are for the entire community, some for special societies, and some are personal. Ceremonial and society bundles are never, ever to be opened without the proper ritual, usually feasting and dancing and a giveaway. When a bundle belonging to the entire tribe is lost, it's as if... well, as if we were barred from going to Mass if we're Catholic."

Marek thought any such items would be protected at all cost. "How are they lost?"

"Many ways. War, disease, theft, ignorance, even sale or gift, especially when the associated rituals were lost or the descendants want or need the money. Even though a keeper is not the owner, so has no actual right to sell it." He paused. "And it's not always that they are meant to be lost. Like Crazy Horse's personal sacred bundle. Before he died, he gave it to an old friend, Fast Thunder. It got passed down to his grandson, who, with many at Pine Ridge, worked the potato fields in Nebraska. When World War II came around, things were pretty dicey, so the grandson buried the bundle near a place called Minatare. By the time anyone returned for the bundle in the 1960s, everything had changed, including the landmarks, so it's been lost. Some say Crazy Horse's spirit wants it that way."

Marek asked, "But museums end up with some of these bundles?"

His lips tightened white. "Actually, the first known repatriation involved a sacred bundle of the Hidatsa. The keeper suddenly died, and a relative sold it to a missionary. The bundle, which was a tribal one meant to bring the rains, ended up in a New York museum. During a drought in the 1930s, the tribe tried to get it back. They had no success, including with Congress, until it hit the newspapers. Then the museum reluctantly agreed to trade it for artifacts of equal value. The Hidatsa gave them a stone hammer and a bison horn." He grinned unexpectedly at them. "Hardly equal, but the museum thought so, so the trade was made with great fanfare. The Hidatsa were even treated to a meeting with President Franklin Roosevelt."

His smile faded. "Of course, when the museum tried to open the bundle for newspapers to photograph, the Hidatsa immediately shielded it from view." He shook his head. "That's why we say that museums don't respect our ancestors, our sacred objects."

Karen asked, "Isn't it better, with NAGPRA?"

"Better but hardly perfect. The Spirit Mound dig is just an example. The MHA should have been consulted from the very start. Instead, whatever is found, depending on whether it ends up in a collection with federal funding, the finds may or may not ever be repatriated. That's what I feared most. That's why I protested. And that's why I argued with Hunter."

Stands By Him shuddered. "If they'd found a bundle? That would've been the worst. If Hardy had found one and opened it, that would have been not just disrespectful but, according to our beliefs, disastrous for the tribe involved."

Marek began to understand just how thorny the issue was for both young men. But sacred bundles weren't the only thing Hunter had searched for. "Have you heard of the Spirit Society?"

Stands By Him frowned. "What tribe?"

"Arikara."

He shook his head. "Sorry. You have to understand—there are five-hundred and seventy-four recognized tribes, not counting bands within that. Trying to learn all the bundles and ceremonies and societies, much less the beliefs, of all of them would be impossible for one person. Even within our tribes, we've got our Native versions of the First, Second, and Third Reformed churches that line the streets of many of your East River towns. And that's just one denomination for you. As for politics, divisions, whatever, we've got all that, too. In spades. I almost didn't get financial aid because of tribal politics. One thing about Natives almost universally, though, is serving the family, the tribe, the people. But sometimes... your service isn't supported."

Marek had an idea of where Stands By Him's thoughts led. "Your uncle is sitting in the office, along with a cousin, waiting for you to be released."

Stands By Him stared at him, his eyes welled, and he looked down. "That would be my mother's brother, Joseph

Brave, and his grandson, Mason Boy Elk. Uncle Joe isn't happy with me for encouraging Mason to go to college." His head came up, with a hint of betrayal. This time, at least, it hadn't come from wasicus. "No one else in my family ever went to college. I had no mentors, no role models, just my grandfather telling me before he died that times have changed, and so must I, to help our people."

He rubbed at his eyes. "I almost didn't make it through my first semester. Hunter helped me, because he knew how to deal with financial aid, how to fill out forms, make a budget, deal with professors and classmates, and find the cheapest books. Now I try to help out the younger Native students. But it's hard. Many drop out. They have family who need them back home. They don't adjust well. All kinds of things. Some are actually told, 'Who do you think you are? You trying to be better than us?' I want to be that role model, so more of my family, my people, can make it. Not out. But inside out. Or outside in. It's a circle. Life's a circle. We're about family, about the tribe, about giving back."

Stands By Him dashed away a tear as if it offended him. "Some are afraid they won't be welcomed back or they'll change and won't or can't go back. I want to go back. I want to teach at the high school at Lower Brule and give young boys hope—too many kill themselves, one way or another. I want to keep the language going, the culture, the traditions... all the good things that made us strong. And some will do that off the rez. Most don't see any Indians in the white world except as fodder for old westerns. I ask my younger cousins what they want to be when they grow up, and I get blank stares. We need doctors and nurses. We need teachers, writers, actors, and sports figures. And yes, soldiers, but we need to be ourselves as we do all of that. Maybe the wasicu will learn something from us, because right now, we're mostly just invisible."

"Some of us think your elders are quite wise," Karen commented. "I do."

His lips twisted. "Yeah, we're either savages or wisemen, nothing in between. Look, we're just people. Good and bad. We're flawed like everybody else."

Marek got to his feet and fished out the key the jailer had given him.

When their prisoner rose, Karen told him, "I'm looking at a good man, Jerome Stands By Him. In the end, you stood by Hunter, despite the cost of a few days in jail. I hope you do just as you say, finish your degree, and help your people."

As the chains fell off, Stands By Him gave them a shaky but genuine smile. "No way up but out."

CHAPTER 28

WHEN THEY GOT TO THE dig, Karen took the bull by the horns and went directly to tell Hardy the bad news. When informed that his precious maul was now Exhibit A in a homicide investigation, he stalked off, leaving Doll to deal with them at the dig site.

"Whoa, whatever you told him, it must have been big and bad news," Richie said, his shaggy hair matted with sweat and hanging in his tired eyes. "I've never seen Professor Sobersides so pissed. That should make us one big happy band of diggers. Not."

One of the girls groaned and flopped back on the grass. "He's been pushing us like galley slaves ever since he found that maul."

Doll upended an empty white bucket—a bunch of them were scattered around and were outnumbered only by water jugs—and sat heavily on it. "I officially declare a break."

Those still digging desultorily immediately dropped trowels and brushes. A heavy boy shaking a sieve-like structure, which Karen decided must be used to catch anything overlooked in the dirt from the buckets, stopped what he was doing. Red-faced, he grabbed bottled water from a cooler and started lobbing them to those who lifted a hand.

"It's only noon, guys," said one of the floppers, shielding

his eyes from the sun with a hand. "Sundown isn't for another eight hours—or more."

"Spoilsport."

A girl with a body like a small tank rolled her shoulders. "I'm good to go."

"Yay, girl power," said another girl, raising a fist.

Richie snorted. "Brawn belongs to the Y-chromosome."

"And brain to the double-X," tank girl shot back.

Doll held up a hand. "Please. No gender wars on my watch. But I will say, that in Arikara culture, the women not only built the earth lodges, they were the farmers."

Karen's ears perked up. She would like to tell some of her bigoted Forsgren relations that, as they liked to say that a woman farming—or policing, for that matter—was like bringing a steer to stud. A steer was, she knew, a castrated bull. "What kind of crop?"

"Maize," Doll said as another girl called out, "Corn!"

"Mother Corn was an Arikara creation story," Doll said.

"And the men went out to hunt. Big risk, big gain. We provided defense." Richie made a muscle that trembled. That got a few titters. He reddened. "I'm just jittery, that's all. You try driving all night across Nebraska. Took a boatload of caffeine."

Mariah Mettis, the girl who'd accused Richie of groping her, spoke for the first time, her eyes on the distant figure stalking up Spirit Mound. "Why is Dr. Hardy so upset?"

Karen looked over at Marek, who nodded. Might as well get it out there. Hardy wasn't likely to keep quiet over its loss. "First of all, both Tonto Hawks aka Tommy Knotts and Jerome Stands By Him have been cleared in Hunter's death." That apparently wasn't news, though Richie seemed less than satisfied. "The maul that was found on Friday at the dig was the murder weapon."

A few of the floppers sat up as if electrified. Doll looked completely blank, her wrinkles slack, while Richie whistled. Others looked horrified, intrigued, or a combination of both.

"No great loss," Richie said into a silence broken only by the wind and birdsong. A red-winged blackbird lit on a bucket and seemed to berate him, along with a passing grackle.

Mariah's head snapped back to Richie. "Hunter was a great loss."

Richie rolled his eyes. "The maul, I meant." He paused. "Though it's always dicey to have an Indigenous archaeologist on site. No objectivity. Just too damn close to it. Their religion gets in the way of science."

Mariah seemed to have found her voice. Good for her. "That's not true. It's better. He could explain the cultural context better than anyone else on the site. And he always reminded me that these were real people, not just things to study."

Richie shook his head. "Hunter took everything personally when it was just science. He'd get defensive if one of his precious creation myths was challenged."

Once again, Doll held up a tired hand. "It's always better to have different viewpoints. But I will say this. In my experience, the cultural aspects often informed the dig, as some nugget from their oral tradition would lead us to the right place or the right approach. But it doesn't come without cost—and I don't mean NAGPRA. It weighed on Hunter. And on all the Indigenous archaeologists I've worked with. They carry a weight that none of the rest of us had to deal with. These were Hunter's people—generally, if not specifically. I'd say Hunter felt he had a great responsibility to honor and respect every find. And that his desire to know sometimes conflicted with his desire to respect. Enough so that he often failed to have fun. I mean, it's hard work, digging, so you have to have some fun with it. That Hunter had to deal with protests from within his own community made it doubly difficult for him."

The boy next to Mariah said earnestly, "Our country

would be a lot better off if we'd adopted Indian ways instead of forcing ours on them. All take, no give."

That got a raspberry from Richie. "Oh, come off it, Norton. You can't get through Anthro 101 without knowing that Indians had no trouble with human sacrifice, torture, and massacring their enemies long before we got here. Not to mention after. Don't forget, Hunter's Sioux massacred the Pawnee, including women and children, at Massacre Canyon in Nebraska in 1873. You're whitewashing history. It's like people today going after Lincoln for the thirty-eight hung at Mankato after the Dakota War. Totally ignoring that the settlers were clamoring for the extermination of every last Sioux man, woman, and child. Not surprising after Little Crow's band of brave warriors finished kidnapping, raping, pillaging, and killing innocent settlers. And there were three-hundred-and-three Sioux sentenced to death. Lincoln got enormous pressure to rubber-stamp the tribunal, but he pardoned all but those thirty-eight. Look at the actual record. Lincoln said, and I quote, 'I could not afford to hang men for votes.' Yet PC idiots knock him for saving them from the mob. That's the kind of lopsided history you get if you listen to Natives like Hunter and his erstwhile friends. That's why they need to stay the hell out of digs."

"Your opinion is noted," Doll said, though her face had hardened. "As in most areas of human endeavor, a balanced view is what is needed. The largest mass execution in our history was also the largest executive clemency on record. On balance in post-contact history, Natives got the very short end of the stick. That's also on record. Consulting them on digging up their history, their ancestors, is the least we can do."

Richie waved away a mosquito that buzzed around his head—and the whole discussion. "Back to the maul. Hardy was busting his balls over that. Claims it's Mound Builder, but the handle is Arikara. Just repurposed in my father's view. Doesn't mean what Hardy thinks—that it proves the two are linked. Arikara were big traders. Probably got it that way. Jumping to conclusions isn't the mark of a good scientist."

Doll eyed him with barely suppressed impatience, if not active dislike. "Sounds to me like someone was jumping to conclusions without actually seeing the item in question. Whatever else he may be, Dr. Hardy is an expert in Caddoan artifacts. That's not Dr. Legrange's area."

That jerked Richie up. "My father has more American Indian artifactual knowledge in his little pinky than Hard Hardy has in his little dick."

"Talk about defensive," tank girl noted.

When Doll started to say something, Karen held up a hand. "I'd like to talk to you personally, Dr. Doll. And maybe to some of the others, if needed."

Doll nodded with clear relief. "All right, crew, go for the gusto. It's lunchtime."

As if rejuvenated by talk of food, the young leapt like antelope for one of the vans.

Doll snagged a couple more buckets and made a grand gesture. This case was rife with them. "Please, come into my parlor."

Said the spider to the fly. But Karen sat and gratefully accepted bottled water that Marek retrieved after getting a nod from Doll. "Not my drink of choice, but it'll do. What do you want to know? Hardy is the expert on Caddoan artifacts. I'm fluent but not an expert."

Marek asked, "Do you have a key to ARCHLAB?"

Doll blinked. "Yes, I have one." She dug it out.

Karen compared it to the impression and nodded at Marek. It matched. "Have you used it at all during the dig?"

"A few times, yes. I mean, I'm here solely for the dig, not processing the finds, as that's a huge time sink. That's the agreement with the school. I'm only a field director. But I was curious about some of the finds, not just in this dig but others they have in their collection, that align with my specialty, which is ceramics."

Marek asked, "What about this past weekend?"

"No, I'd had enough of the dig and the drama by then. Like I said, I spent Friday night in a margarita haze in my hotel room. Saturday, I took a float down the Missouri River on my kayak—yes, alone—and had supper and a drink with Osirus Grant from W.H. Over before Hardy's presentation. On Sunday, it was back to the grind."

Her wrinkle-bracketed eyes tracked Richie and Mariah. She seemed relieved they were at different picnic tables. "I've had a think about a lot of things since I talked to you. Archaeologists tend to be an informal and gregarious lot, the Hardys and Legranges notwithstanding, but this dig has been a real challenge for me in several ways. I had a long talk with Mariah Mettis. I think we both understand better where the other was coming from. I'll be more proactive in reporting incidents in the future. Mariah is from a fairly protected environment—not of the mind, but of the body. She didn't see anything unusual in getting a ride from a fellow digger. Now she knows there's a whole code-switching for gender relations that she wasn't aware of."

That stopped Karen. She'd heard of Native code talkers used to confound Nazi codebreakers during World War II and was aware that included Lakota as well as the more well-known Navajo. "Code-switching?"

"Sorry. Hazard of talking to anthros. It's not just history. It's behaviors and cultures. Just as an example, I'll bet you talk and act differently around your parents versus your friends versus anyone in authority. Your posture, your tone of voice, even the words you choose might be different in different circumstances."

Karen thought of Judge Rudy, a name she would never call him to his face. She was always at attention in his presence. And she chose her words very, very carefully. "Oh, yeah." She thought a minute. "So Mariah hadn't picked up that accepting a ride meant... a ride."

"It's not quite that cut-and-dried, but yes. Richie went too far, too fast, and he had to know she wasn't experienced. He was one of the two grad students on the dig and should have known better to fish in that pool anyway, which I made sure he understood. Too much has been let go in the past. Things aren't like it was in the good ol' days when men like his father felt they got first dibs on anything with breasts. It wasn't always easy to discourage them, but it can be done."

Marek cleared his throat. "Anyone ask to borrow the key?"

"A few, yes. Mariah Mettis, Aaron Jacobsen, and Kyle Norton."

Karen suspected that Mariah had used the key to escape Richie. "Any that weekend?"

Doll thought for a moment. "Yes, I believe Mariah did ask for it over the weekend, and she didn't return it—nor did I ask for it—until Sunday. Why?"

"It's just part of the investigation," Marek told her.

Karen suspected that with a bit of thought, Doll would figure it out, so she hastened to the next question before they became the questioned. "Do you know anything about a bundle that Hardy and Hunter might have discussed?"

"No, I haven't heard anything about a sacred bundle." Doll looked conflicted. "That would be a serious find, but one with some serious cultural sensitivity issues as well. Are you saying they found one but withheld it from the rest of us?"

Karen assured her, "No, so far as I know, they were only discussing a bundle, not that they'd dug one up."

"Oh." She shrugged. "It may have been any number of possible contexts then. Haven't you asked Hardy?" She watched their gaze flicker to the summit of Spirit Mound. "Oh, yeah. He's ticked off at you."

Karen asked, "What about the Spirit Society of the Arikara? What can you tell us about that?"

Doll's eyes widened to the point that she actually resembled her name. "Very little. Not because it's culturally sensitive, though it is, but because very little is known. The Spirit Society is extinct and has been for centuries. Are you saying... you think Hunter believed he'd found a bundle belonging to the Spirit Society?"

The awe on the woman's face made her almost pretty.

Karen hated to pop her bubble. "All we know is that he was researching sacred bundles and the Spirit Society on the day he died."

"Did he search for a location?" Doll demanded.

Karen exchanged a glanced with Marek. "No."

Her awe faded. "So just another wild-goose chase. You had me going for a minute there."

Karen still hadn't gotten an answer. "What are these societies? Spirit, ghost, whatever."

"Okay, there were several mystic or spiritual societies of the Arikara. Spirit was one of the founding societies that we're aware of, along with Ghost, Buffalo, Owl, and Bear. But more may well have been lost to time. I can't think of an exact analogy to anything you'd know. But think of the popular legend of the Knights Templar and the Holy Grail. The societies were the keepers of a power embodied in the bundle and held their secrets close."

"Gotcha. Like Freemasons."

"Sort of, yes. Much of what we know of Arikara mystical societies comes from the research papers of ethnologist Melvin Gilmore from the early twentieth century, which probably wouldn't have seen the light of day today, as he described the ceremonies, the contents of the bundles, in a way that would be highly offensive today. But back in Gilmore's time, so much was being lost that I can only think that, on balance, it's best we—and the MHA themselves—have some record of what was. In fact, at the time, the

Arikara much appreciated his help and gave him an Indian name and allowed him to take part in their ceremonies."

How times changed. But Karen understood why, with the Tommy Knottses of the world profiteering off the sacred, it had stopped. Sacrilege. Much how she felt about televangelists raking in money from poor widows to use on their mistresses and fast cars. "So how do bundles and societies connect?"

"The way Gilmore put it, each spiritual society had a bundle used to fix the attention—say like on a stained glass window in medieval times—on a certain sacred legend, stories that convey the doctrine, wisdom, and morality that are to be passed down. Put them all together, and you have what Gilmore called the 'unwritten bible of the Arikara.' I probably don't need to remind you that common people in Western societies did not have access to their Bible until the Reformation."

"Only a priestly class had access," Marek murmured.

"Yes, exactly. So the Spirit Society was just one of several, but many think it was the most powerful, because it dealt with the spiritual world. Gilmore said nothing about it."

"What would its value be?" When those doll eyes opened wide, Karen hastened to add, "Not monetarily, not spiritually, but archaeologically?"

"Oh. Immense. Priceless."

"Say a departmental chair? Prestigious journals and the like?"

"For those that care about such things," she said evenly. "Certainly, it would get a lot of buzz. But it's the knowledge gained that attracts most of us. But you have to understand, the Arikara bible is unwritten. Many legends are lost. What is left in the sacred bundle for the Spirit Society in particular may give us clues, gives us associations to like bundles, but it won't bring it back, not to the MHA."

Karen asked, "But they would want it anyway?"

"Oh, certainly. Wouldn't you want the Holy Grail back, even if you'd lost all knowledge of how it was used, of what

Communion actually entailed? Sometimes, the sacred object is really all that is left. And it has power."

Marek swatted and smeared a mosquito on his forehead, leaving a red mark. "So any bundle of the Spirit Society would be returned to the MHA?"

Doll pursed her lips. "That depends on the spirit or the letter of the law. The spirit of NAGPRA, yes, though hopefully with some knowledge gained. The letter... debatable. No federal land or funding involved. Though if the press got a hold of it, it'd cause an unholy stink." Her gaze went to Hardy and back. "That's just one of many reasons why it's best to involve associated tribes at the very beginning."

Marek asked, "Why wasn't that done here?"

"Because Hardy is an old fart," she said baldly. "And the letter of the law says he's good." She shook her head. "He probably didn't notice, but I saw a couple of MHA at his presentation on Saturday. They want to know about their own history, but they could also sense that he viewed it as something entirely unconnected to anything other than scholastic knowledge. So none approached him or asked him any questions afterward, which I think was sad. One did ask me some questions. I did my best to answer them while Hardy answered those who had no cultural stake at all. I also learned a few things. Hardy had some things wrong. I don't think he'd appreciate hearing about them, though."

Karen nodded. "Right. Oral tradition is bunk."

"That about sums up his view, which isn't mine. Again, balance. I don't know why it's such a hard concept for people to wrap their heads around. Humans make for fascinating study, that's for sure."

In Karen's line of work, *fascinating* wasn't quite the word. More like *appalling*. What human beings could do to others. But apparently, killing was as old as the hills. Or in her cultural reference, as old as Cain and Abel.

CHAPTER 29

According to Richie Legrange, he hadn't used his key or loaned it out. Which, if true, came as no surprise to Marek. Legrange wasn't a serious student. Student diggers Norton and Jacobsen also claimed they hadn't made copies or loaned Doll's key.

Marek waved Mariah Mettis in to their makeshift parlor. Doll had gone to have her gusto.

"Dr. Doll said you wanted to talk to me. I told Deputy Durr about Richie Legrange and Hunter." She looked vastly uncomfortable. "But I don't want to press charges or anything. Dr. Doll and I talked it all out, then Richie left. I was so relieved. When he came back, she talked to him, and he's stayed away from me. It won't happen again."

Marek agreed it was unlikely, at least with Richie. He thrived on adulation. Sexual assault would be bad for his Indiana Jones image. "You know what to do if it does happen again?"

Mariah nodded and reddened a bit.

Karen gestured at the vacated bucket. "Okay, have a seat. We want to ask you about this past weekend. Not the confrontation between Hunter and Richie but the key to ARCHLAB."

Her jaw dropping, Mariah sat down heavily. "I didn't steal anything. Did someone say I did? Did Richie?"

"No, someone returned something."

"Oh. I didn't steal or return anything. I just went to..."

Marek knew the answer, but Karen supplied it out loud. "Get away from Richie?"

Her dark head bobbed. "And to learn. I *want* to be an archaeologist. Not Indigenous American archaeology, I don't think, but you kind of have to take what you can get. Dr. Doll told me that it'll be hard. I mean, not just the people part. But it's hard to get an academic position anywhere. Years and years of work with no guarantee you'll get a job, much less tenure. But that's what I want to be. I have since I went to Greece with my grandmother when I was twelve. We saw a dig that was going on there. I'm part Greek. I'd like to go back, and the people at the dig said I'd be more than welcome."

A Greek doing Greek archaeology wouldn't lift an eyebrow. But apparently, an Indigenous man doing Indigenous archaeology was questionable. Did the Greeks feel the same weight of responsibility Hunter had, or was it just the weight of trauma? The answers to which would not help the investigation. Marek asked her, "Were you at ARCHLAB on Friday night or anytime on Saturday?"

Mariah pulled at her lip. "I was there Friday night. Late. I didn't want to go back to the dorm. Or out anywhere because..."

This time, he supplied the answer. "Richie might be there."

She bobbed again. "I just hid out. I was a mess. I was thinking maybe I'd have to give up my dream of being an archaeologist. Because of the Richies of the world and so many digs being remote places where you can't get away. And that really, really hurt. I expected Dr. Doll to stand up for me, and that hurt even more. Anyway, I was there a lot that weekend. Why?"

Marek held his breath. "When you were there, did anyone return the maul? Or have either of the cartons from Friday's dig out on the table?"

Mariah shook her head. "I only saw Norton once on Sunday. And an NAS student looking at some ceramics from another dig years ago. That was Saturday morning."

Karen asked, "Were you there on Friday night when Dr. Hardy returned with the finds?"

"No, I'd left by then."

Marek felt the usual fall of disappointment. This case seemed to be rife with them.

"But I saw him in the parking lot," Mariah went on. "I was going to ask if he wanted help because the cartons were heavy. But he seemed, I don't know, weighed down. Not by the cartons exactly, though those, too. But like... well, like I felt. Really disappointed and sad and just wanting to avoid everybody." She shrugged self-consciously. "Maybe I was just projecting."

Perhaps. Why would Hardy look disappointed? He'd made what he thought was a big find. Or at least one that supported his theory. Marek glanced over at the man on the mound. He certainly wasn't happy now or eager to return to the dig.

Karen asked, "What time was it?"

"I left the ARCHLAB about ten thirty."

That was kind of late. But Marek didn't know the process of securing the finds or who all was involved. "Was Dr. Hardy always the one to bring in the finds?"

"So far as I know. He drove the finds van by himself. He said it was the only way he could hear himself think."

Karen shifted on her bucket. "Are the finds, like that maul found on Friday, thoroughly cleaned at the dig before being brought to the ARCHLAB?"

Mariah shrugged. "Depends. At least a quick brushing, more if there's time. If not, that can wait for when it's processed at the lab. Last I saw the maul at the finds tent before we left, it was still pretty dirty."

That made sense, since the maul was still dirty when it was used to kill Hunter. But that didn't answer the critical question of whether the maul had been removed from the lab and returned or if it had been taken from the finds tent and then taken to the lab. In either case, the killer must have cleaned up the maul afterward. Along with himself or herself.

Marek asked, "When you saw Dr. Hardy in the parking lot on Friday night, was he wearing the same clothes as he was at the dig that day?"

"I... I don't know. I mean, he always wears a white dress shirt, except with short sleeves. And khaki pants. Like he's going to the office, not the dig, but he was like that. Formal. He wouldn't call Dr. Doll just Doll. I don't either. It's not respectful." Her nose wrinkled. "But Dr. Hardy's shirt looked white. I mean, bright white, no dirt or sweat or anything. I suppose it could've been the streetlights that made it look so white. Or maybe he went home to change first? That's usually what I do when I get back to the dorm. Take a shower and change. We're always gross after a day at the dig."

Seemed to Marek that he would want to unload the finds before he changed. But then, Marek didn't care if he walked around in sawdust or drywall dust. For some people, appearances were everything.

After they let a relieved Mariah go, Marek and Karen watched the figure on the mound, unmoving except for his clothes, his white shirt and khaki pants rippling in the stiff wind. Otherwise, he could've been a statue.

Karen sighed and got up. "If we're going to talk to him, ask him if he changed his clothes, we'll have to take a hike."

Marek thought about it. "I'd rather wait. If he's a suspect, we need a motive. And I can't see one right now."

With a sigh of relief, Karen headed toward the Sub. As she pointed it north back to Reunion, he made some calls. As for the profs and grad students, NAS or anthro, few were even in residence over the summer, and of those who were, none admitted to loaning out their keys.

"None of it makes any sense," Karen said when he told

her. "The students at the dig who had keys seem to be telling the truth. They're most likely in the clear. None of them had transportation, unless they got a ride from someone else back to the dig. Doll has no solid alibi other than room service receipts but also has no motive that I can see. Bork confirmed Richie's alibi. But someone with a key put that maul in the lithics carton sometime after Hardy left the lab."

Marek pointed out, "Unless it was Hardy himself, and he lied to us."

"Right. Again, what motive? Did he disagree with Hunter over the maul, like Richie did? I just don't see it—a man like Hardy being moved by someone else's opinion. You don't live in academia as long as Hardy has without getting into spats over theory. Heated, yes. But if Hardy was going to go after someone for that, I'd think he'd kill Richie. To all accounts, while Hardy disliked Hunter's research focus, he seemed to think Hunter was a good student."

Marek glanced at her. "Anyone would be, next to Richie Legrange."

The stretch of Sioux quartzite–chipped road stretched into the horizon. "Too true. Where do we go from here? I don't see how anything about the Spirit Society or a bundle figures into it. And we don't have enough to get a warrant to search Hardy's car and house. Judge Rudy would throw me out of the courthouse, much less the court."

As they pulled up to that said courthouse, Marek knew that was all too true. Fishing expeditions weren't allowed on Judge John Franklin Rudabaugh's watch. A man who was all work, no play. The judge practically lived in his chambers. He and Hardy were peas in a pod in that respect.

What, Marek wondered, would cause Judge Rudy to kill? Only something very, very fundamental to the core of his being. He would kill in defense of the law. What about Hardy?

When they walked into the office, they found Seoul chatting with Josephine. The young deputy was practically bursting as she did a little jig. "Me and Mom are going to Flandreau!"

Marek smiled at her. "You heard back."

Seoul raised her arms in victory. "We did! We're supposed to meet Chief Goodthunder tonight at the final wacipi. Umm..." She looked beseechingly at Karen. "If it's okay with you, I mean. I'll be here for my midnight shift, but... Chief Goodthunder told her there's a lot to the story, and he wants to meet her—and me—in person to tell it."

"Fine. Good. I hope it goes well." Karen smiled but looked dissatisfied. "Did Goodthunder tell her *anything*?"

Seoul shook her head, the liver color dancing in the fluorescent lights. "Only that he's looking forward to meeting her, that it means a lot to his family, and that we're all welcome anytime. I still don't know why Inyan was such a pill about it all."

Marek kept his mouth shut, but Karen apparently decided that was free game. "Martin Goodthunder is Two Fingers's stepfather."

Josephine let out a whistle. "Oh, my. That does throw a wrench in the works."

Seoul's face went through a number of quick emotions, from delight to shock to worry. "Does that make me and Inyan like step-relatives? Is it taboo or something?"

Marek hadn't opened Pandora's box precisely for this reason. Seoul and her mother would no doubt have many questions that only Goodthunder could answer.

"The idiot," Seoul said with deep feeling. "Why didn't he just say so?"

"Because it wasn't his story to tell," Marek said.

"Do he and his stepfather not get along?" Josephine asked. "Often happens."

"They get along fine so far as I can see," Karen reported. "A lot of respect both ways."

Seoul's face filled with relief. "That's good. I told my mom about him. Inyan, I mean. She thought his name was way cool. Weird that it's the first time I've ever heard it, but then heard it twice."

Marek, about to go to his desk, turned. "Twice?"

"Yeah, I mean, once other than Inyan himself. He told me I could use it. That was a day." She poofed her short bowl of hair. "I also heard it from one of the diggers. His name was Norton. While we were waiting for you to finish up with Dr. Hardy, he was telling me about the area and about Lewis and Clark, about when they came up the mouth of White Stone River. He told me in Lakota, that's Inyan Ska."

Marek felt his brain tingle. "Where is that river?"

"Oh, it isn't called that anymore. It's the Vermillion River."

Which still covered a great deal of land. But it was tantalizingly close to the dig. Miles, anyway.

"Except for a small creek," Seoul went on blithely. "The one at the base of Spirit Mound. It's called White Stone Creek. That's pretty cool. Inyan told me that he considers the mound sacred, and he's gone there during times that troubled him."

Karen looked at Marek. "Hunter circled that creek. With exclamation marks."

Suddenly, things were starting to fall into place. But they were missing a crucial connection. "We need to go talk to Two Fingers."

"What? Why?" Seoul tagged after them. "Can I come?"

"Might as well," Karen called back. "You just gave us a new lead."

"I did? How?"

But they were already getting into the Sub. Marek waited until they were on the way before he said, "Hunter was right, in more ways than one. Two Fingers is the key. We need to know what he told Hunter when he last saw him, the weekend before Hunter was killed."

"Personal stuff," Karen recalled. "He didn't want to talk about it."

The short drive ended at a small refurbished farmhouse on the outskirts of Reunion. Like their own bungalows on Okerlund Road, it sat on the bluff overlooking the Big Jammer. It must have reminded Two Fingers of his home overlooking the Big Sioux. Except the Big Jammer was far less placid and the birds far less vocal.

Before they could knock, the door opened. He glanced at them then at Seoul's squad. "What happened? Did you find the killer?" Then he stilled. "Or does this have to do with my stepfather?"

"We have a new lead," Marek told him. "We need to talk to you. It's personal."

Karen assured him, "We'll keep it out of the record if we can, but it's important."

Gaze hooded, Two Fingers looked at them for a long moment then at the awkwardly silent but hopeful Seoul, and opened the door. "Come in."

The first thing Marek saw in the small entryway—obviously placed there to be seen—was a high school graduation picture of Two Fingers and Hunter Redwing-Digges mugging for the camera. Perhaps it had been placed there only recently.

"You had braids," Seoul burst out, pretty much confirming that. She'd certainly been inside Two Fingers's house before, unlike Marek.

Marek took a harder look at the photo. Two smiling faces in graduation gear in purple and yellow. Both wore braids. None of the earlier pictures of Two Fingers Marek had seen at Delma's had shown long hair, though none as short as it was now.

"I cut off my braids at Dartmouth," Two Fingers explained. "People started talking to me after that. As if they were afraid of me before. Like I was either wild or a museum exhibit. Or maybe they expected me to utter wise sayings about Mother Earth and the environment and were disconcerted when I didn't say anything. I was just an eighteen-year-old kid far away from my family for the first time, just like many of them."

"Why not grow it back?" Seoul asked. "I like it."

Two Fingers rubbed his crew cut. "It wasn't allowed in the Air Force. As a police officer, it isn't good to give people another handle on you. Maybe one day when I'm old, if I make it, I'll wear it long again. Or not. Some do, some don't."

Two Fingers moved into the living room, and the rest followed, Marek at the rear. More pictures were revealed, some he recognized from Delma's wall of ancestors, along with paintings, some of which he recognized from walls of the Diggeses's home. In style, if not substance, at least.

Karen asked, almost sharply, "What's that?"

Marek turned and followed her long finger to an old fringed and beaded pouch tied closed with what looked like new thongs. On the outside, the pouch had loops that held a pipe.

Two Fingers took a long moment to answer. "A sacred bundle."

CHAPTER 30

Karen lowered her finger slowly. Was the Spirit Society bundle right here in her deputy's living room? Had Hunter just found out about it? Or had he found it and brought it here?

"Whose?" Marek asked gently.

"It's important," Karen underlined.

Two Fingers's dark eyes moved between Marek and Karen. "It belonged to my Mandan ancestor Two Fingers. He was said to be a great warrior. He died in the smallpox epidemic of 1837. Not all personal bundles are passed down. Only from those with great power."

He nodded toward the bundle. "This one, as was the tradition in the Mandan, was passed down on the maternal line for several generations. Then they started to adopt the Hidatsa tradition of sons, but my great-grandfather Christian Two Fingers, who was ill at the time, deferred that honor to his son."

Two Fingers paused as they recalled that that young man had killed himself. "So it was held for me to grow up, to become a man. Only after I spent some time at Fort Berthold during the summers and had returned from Afghanistan and went through inipi was I deemed fit to become its keeper." As he watched both deflate, Two Fingers tilted his head. "What did you expect?"

"Arikara," Marek answered. "But it may be a good thing it's not."

Karen turned on him. "Why?"

Instead, Marek, in one of his out-in-left-field questions, asked, "Why new thongs? Everything else is old."

"When it was entrusted to me, I was told the thongs would need to be replaced because when it was opened for the ceremony, two broke. I had to save up for a feast and giveaway and get time off."

Karen frowned. "All that for a couple broken thongs?"

Two Fingers spoke quietly and simply, as if to a young child. "It's sacred." Then thoughtfully, as if to himself, he said, "I still need to properly honor the old thongs."

Karen once again was reminded just how different her deputy's culture was from her own.

Seoul stirred beside her. "Do you know what's in it?"

"Yes, but I can't discuss that. I don't know what all of them mean. Some were interpreted for me. Some, I can guess. Some are a mystery."

Seoul seemed to accept that. "Do you have a bundle? Personal one?"

"Yes."

Karen opened her mouth then shut it.

Faint amusement played in the dark eyes, but Two Fingers nodded. "It has to do with my own journey. Things along my own path, no one else's. You do it, too. You just put them out for everyone to see. Little things like rocks and shells or a feather. Scrapbooks." He looked blandly at Karen. "Trophies."

She smiled at that. "They wouldn't fit in that bundle."

"No, I suppose not. But with you, it's two things, you separate your life journey and your spiritual journey. So you might pick up a special rock from a time when you went to the beach with a grandparent you loved and then wear a cross or get a fish tattoo or something. For us, it's all one."

Marek nodded toward the Two Fingers bundle. "When did you do that? Get the new thongs."

"On Greasy Grass Day this past June."

Seoul, quiet until now, asked before Karen could, "Greasy Grass?"

That flash of smile was welcome in the tense atmosphere. "Victory Day. June twenty-fifth. You might know it as Custer's Last Stand or the Battle of Little Bighorn."

Karen blinked. She'd been born and raised and spent most of her life outside of the military in South Dakota and had never heard of either Greasy Grass or Victory Day, at least not in that context. To her, Victory Day meant the end of World War II. She did know that Columbus Day had been changed to Native American Day in South Dakota back in the 1990s through the efforts of a Lakota journalist named Tim Giago, whose editorials often were published in the *Argus Leader* that she'd read for years as a Sioux Falls resident. So far as she knew, South Dakota was still the only state to have made that holiday name swap, though a number had created a different Indigenous Peoples Day.

"But why is it called Greasy Grass?" Seoul seemed endlessly curious. Karen got that. It was suddenly part of her deputy's heritage. "Was that a battle tactic or was the grass greasy with blood?"

Two Fingers's lips twitched. "It was the Crow name for the Little Bighorn River. The grass would get wet in the morning and soak the horses and warriors riding through so that they looked greasy. At least that's what I was told."

Marek continued to look at the bundle. "You said that you and Hunter, the weekend before he was killed and after you returned from Fort Berthold, talked of some personal things. Did you possibly talk about the Spirit Society of the Arikara?"

Please, please, yes. Karen held her breath.

Two Fingers shook his head. "No, I don't think so." He paused. "Not directly."

Though it killed her, Karen forced herself to keep quiet. He would either tell them what that meant, or he wouldn't. They could, once again, be on a wild-goose chase.

"Hunter and I weren't really speaking much when I was first entrusted with the bundle. Only more recently did we talk about it." Two Fingers hesitated. "Last weekend, Hunter asked me about my experiences in Fort Berthold, since he was on an Arikara dig. A lot of things happened when I was there, part of various ceremonies. Private things."

Karen thought that was all they would get. But then Two Fingers got a strange look on his face, as if he, too, started to see connections.

Finally, he said, "I dreamt of a woman in white who kept trying to wake me, but I was ill and unable to speak. After I spoke of my vision, an elder told me about a legend among the Arikara that one of their lost bundles was taken by the last child, a daughter, of the last keeper and member of the society. He died of smallpox in the first wave back in the 1780s. She put on a white dress and wandered away one day, and they say she entered the spirit land and was never seen again."

Karen barely breathed. "How did Hunter react to that?"

"Intrigued. Excited. He said the woman in the white dress was found in most of the Great Sioux Nation winter counts. It was one of the great mysteries. He showed me the pictograph from the winter count he was studying, but it didn't mean anything to me other than awe that I had been given such a vision. He was disappointed. I asked him if he'd ever shown the winter count to Unci, and he said no, that he was looking at a Lakota or Nakota origin, not Dakota."

Karen smiled at him. "And you told him to have another think."

Two Fingers nodded. "I told him Unci's mother was Nakota. But that she rarely spoke about them and hadn't been to the Yankton reservation since she was a child. Neither of us really expected anything to come of it. Obviously, it did, as Unci told us. The woman in white was my however-times great-grandmother." He searched their faces. "But what does that have to do with Hunter's death?"

"You may not have heard yet," Karen told him. "Hunter was killed with the Mound Builder–Arikara maul found at the site on Friday."

"I see." But it was obvious he didn't see.

"I didn't know that," Seoul said, looking put out.

"We haven't had time for an incident meeting. We went from W.H. Over to ARCHLAB to the crime lab in Sioux Falls. They confirmed blood on the maul. DNA will take time, but there's little doubt it's Hunter's."

Seoul grimaced. "I'll bet Hardy isn't a happy camper."

"That's putting it mildly." Marek's gaze went from the bundle to Two Fingers. "The woman in white wasn't the only pictograph your great-grandmother showed him that excited Hunter. There was another much later in time."

Two Fingers frowned then nodded. "Unci said her uncle said, 'Inyan Ska.' Twice. And Hunter laughed and said that I was the key to everything."

"What did the pictograph look like?" Seoul demanded.

Two Fingers answered. "A creek, a hill, with a bundle under it."

What Karen had seen as a pouch, he'd obviously seen immediately as a bundle. Cultural context. "Do you know the name of the creek at Spirit Mound?"

"I didn't know it had one," he replied.

Seoul burst out, "It's Inyan Ska. White Stone Creek."

"And Hunter circled the creek on the map in his car with exclamations points," Karen added.

Two Fingers's jaw dropped. Then he looked much as Hunter must have with Delma: as if the world had opened up in revelation. "The bundle was there. Right *there*." His dark eyes rose to the bundle of the first Two Fingers. "The lost bundle of the Spirit Society of the Arikara."

Seoul waited several beats. "Okay. That's great. That's

wonderful. One mystery solved. But... how does that get us any closer to finding out who killed Hunter?"

Still looking at her Native deputy, Karen hooked her thumbs into her belt. "What would Hunter do with that information?"

Now the wonder dimmed. "He'd rush off to tell someone who understood, who would be as excited as he would. And then..." His gaze went back to the bundle.

"He'd feel conflicted," Marek offered.

"Yes. Bundles aren't meant to be seen, to be studied. They're to be honored. Even venerated. He would know that, too, whatever his training. No, he wasn't raised as I was, as Stands By Him was, but he'd know. Not in his bones as we do, but in his heart, he'd know."

While some of it might have been about Tommy Knotts, Karen was pretty sure that all those long looks Hunter had given Stands By Him were instead about the bundle.

Karen searched each face in the room. Saw the knowledge there. Now all of them were on the same page, Native and wasicus. "We know who. We know why. But how can we prove it?" When there was only a thoughtful silence in reply, she said, "Okay, I'll contact Judge Rudy and see if I can get a warrant. And I'll call in the troops."

An hour later, she entered the office, holding up a warrant. "I did battle. I won. Barely."

Whoops rose. Two Fingers tilted his head. "You've still got your scalp."

Karen clawed her fingers through her hair. "I'm lucky it isn't hanging in Judge Rudy's cloakroom. He wasn't happy to be interrupted from his court-break reading of the latest opinion—including footnotes—of the latest Supreme Court case. You'd think I asked him for a lollipop, not a warrant, the glare he gave me. If looks could kill."

She looked at Marek. "You fill everybody in?"

He nodded from where he was idly scrolling through a website on his computer.

"Good." She turned back to the room. "We'll set up an interview. When that's in progress, Kurt, Bork, and Seoul, you execute the warrant. Anything you can find, anything at all, you text me. Got that?"

Kurt nodded, Bork mmm-ed, and Seoul saluted.

"Walrus, you're on call." His windsock mustache drooped, but he nodded. Law and order had to go on in Eda County regardless. "Two Fingers, you're in interview with me and Marek."

He blinked but nodded. Karen felt he deserved to be there. And he knew how to keep his mouth shut. "This is going to be really dicey. We have very little hard proof, but—"

"We do now," Marek said abruptly, looking up from his computer.

"What? Seriously?" Karen moved behind him to see the image on the screen, watched him right-click, and did a whoop herself.

CHAPTER 31

When Marek opened the door and ushered in their interviewee, Karen was sitting at the table with a lot of papers in front of her. Two Fingers stood awkwardly in the corner between file cabinets, holding a notepad and pen.

Karen looked up with a tired, drawn look. "Thank you for coming in."

"I'm here under protest." Dr. Alden Hardy sat heavily in the chair that Marek held out. He pulled out a bandana and wiped it across his brow. "I don't appreciate being constantly dragged away from the dig. I have important work to do and only a week left in the season."

Marek took the final seat. "Then let's get it done. I've got a soffit to finish."

Dr. Hardy stared at him. "A what?"

"Soffit. Has something to do with roof overhangs. Don't ask me." Karen shrugged at the professor. "He's a half-time detective, half-time carpenter. The latter is better paid, believe me."

When Hardy's brows furrowed and he looked at Two Fingers, Karen sighed. "Don't mind him. He's learning the ropes. A lot of young cops wash out after they figure out just how much tedious work is involved. It's not high-speed chases and gun battles most of the time. I'd rather they learn that sooner rather than later."

Hardy grunted. "I can identify. It's the same in archaeology. The Indiana Jones wannabes wash out sooner or later. Sooner is better."

Like Richie Legrange, unless his father was able to whip him into shape.

Karen folded her hands over the papers, looking very weary. "Okay, what we're doing here is refining the timeline and confirming and corroborating statements from last Friday. We would like to ask—"

"Shouldn't there be a Miranda warning?" Two Fingers asked. When Karen stared at him, he shifted on his feet, looking very unlike the deputy Marek knew. "Procedure."

Marek hid his smile. Talk about code-switching. And he did a bit of his own. Marek sighed heavily and pulled out his recorder. It wasn't hard to feign impatience, as Karen had given him many opportunities to see it in action. "All right. By the book." He rattled off the Miranda warning then waited for Hardy to agree—which he did after a pause during what must have been some inner conflict. Marek threw down his recorder and crossed his arms, the very picture of bored impatience with procedure. He had other fish to fry. "Done."

They'd used a cassette tape recorder when he'd first come to Reunion. Karen had explained that it was harder to tamper with than digital. But Larson had assured her that any digital tampering would be known by comparing the file to something called a checksum. The recorder's silence and small size often made it forgotten, as had happened with Hawks. For this interview and the previous ones for Hawks and Stands By Him, they also had a very rudimentary video camera that was hidden and very rarely spotted.

Karen took Hardy through the tedium, point by point, of his previous statement. "Now on Friday, you said you last saw Hunter after he'd loaded the cartons into the van, and you took off. Is that correct?"

"It is."

"Do you know what time that was?"

Dead Spirits

"Sorry. It was after dark. That's all I can tell you. I am not tied to my phone like so many today are, especially students, but sad to say, many professors as well."

Karen didn't look up. "And you drove directly to the ARCHLAB to drop off the finds."

For the first time, Hardy hesitated. "I... I believe that night I went home first to change before dropping off the finds."

Marek stirred from his arms-crossed position. "Why the hell would you do that? Those cartons had to have some dirt on them, too."

Hardy's nose flared. "My mother was a stickler for a clean appearance in public. I was pretty rank and dirty. I might have run into colleagues or students."

"Sounds like my mother." Karen wearily tapped her pen and shot Marek a cease-and-desist order by glare. "Cleanliness is next to godliness."

Hardy snorted but made no actual comment.

Karen cleared her throat. "Okay, so you changed at home then went to the ARCHLAB to drop off the finds. We're guessing sometime between ten and eleven p.m."

"Sounds about right."

Karen continued to tick down her written notes. "And you noted that the carton with the stone stuff—"

"Lithics."

"Yes, right. Lithics. That it was lighter than it should have been. But you didn't open the lid."

Testily, he said, "I didn't notice *at the time*. Only when you asked me about it later did I realize that it was indeed light. I am no slouch, but it should have been harder to put up on that high shelf than it was."

The pen continued to tap. "And at no time during the transfer did you open the carton or notice the maul was missing."

"Correct. Someone must have returned it later. I still think one of the NAS students must have snagged a key from the secretary or an adjunct. Perhaps in conjunction with one of the protesters."

Karen finally looked up. "Let's be very clear about this point. It is very important for the timeline. Did you see the maul at any point Friday night after you left the dig?"

His brows lowered, but his voice was firm. "I did not."

Marek didn't move a muscle, but inside, he was jumping for joy. Karen made a note on her list of notes and said, "I think that's all we—"

"Um, Sheriff?"

"What is it now, Deputy?"

Two Fingers cleared his throat. "I just want to follow all possible avenues of investigation, check them off, like you're doing."

Marek blew out a breath, but Karen sighed. "Go ahead, Deputy."

Two Fingers looked endearingly earnest. "When Hunter Redwing-Digges returned to the site earlier on Friday, one of the student diggers overheard him talking to Dr. Hardy about a sacred bundle."

Karen frowned but turned to Dr. Hardy. "Any comment?"

The professor had stilled. For a moment, Marek thought he would call for a lawyer. Or simply shrug and make no comment. Then he said, "It's possible we discussed bundles. Generally. Though the chances were remote, there was always the possibility of finding one on a dig."

Karen had made a new entry in her list of notes. "But you had no knowledge of any specific bundle that he may have been speaking about?"

Hardy hesitated. Then he shook his head. Karen lifted her head, waiting for the answer, as if she hadn't seen the shake of the head. She had excellent peripheral vision, Marek knew.

Marek spit out, "It's an easy answer. Yes or no."

"No," the professor said.

Marek did another flip in his mental gymnastics.

"That's curious." Karen frowned down at her notes. "One of my sources relayed that, on your office calendar, you wrote 'HRD Flandreau Spirit Bundle.'"

That source was Seoul, who'd texted Karen before the interview started. Two Fingers whistled then reddened and went back to his notepad.

Karen lifted her head. "That was on Friday of last week."

Hardy froze. Then he relaxed. By sheer dint of will, Marek guessed. "Okay, I remember now. Sorry. I have so many students, so many projects, that it's hard to keep track. That's why I must have written it down. It was just one more of Hunter's wild-goose chases based on that fake winter count he was obsessed with. I don't pay them any mind any longer. He asked for time off. I didn't want him to go with just one week left on the dig, but he was insistent, so I let him get it out of his system."

But the trip had been far more productive than either had bargained for. Marek had no doubt that Hunter had told Hardy about what Two Fingers told him about the visit to Fort Berthold. At least generally enough to get the time off from a notoriously time-parsimonious professor to pursue it.

Karen was looking a bit more interested now. "And Hunter found nothing about it in Flandreau?"

"Nothing relevant. That must be what the student overheard. Yes, yes, now I remember. He just said he hadn't found any new leads on the bundle—assuming it ever existed." Dr. Hardy waved a dismissive hand. "Typical when you go chasing legends. Archaeology is a science, not an adventure."

Marek thought Doll might disagree. She would likely say it was both—in balance.

Once again, Two Fingers cleared his throat. "Umm... the note said *Spirit* Bundle. Not just any bundle. I've got some Arikara. That's a big deal."

Dr. Hardy was growing more antsy. "It was just a wild

theory that Hunter had, that's all. It didn't pan out. Look, I need to get back to the dig. Any more serious questions?"

Karen shot Two Fingers a look that had him retreating back to his notepad. "We appreciate your time, Dr. Hardy. Just a few more things. As I told you at the dig earlier, we have identified the maul as the murder weapon." She pulled out a photo and put it in front of him. "Can you confirm that this is the maul under discussion, the one that was found on the dig on Friday?"

He glanced down. "Yes, yes. Is that all?"

She tapped the printout. "Do you recognize this picture?"

Clearly out of patience, he snapped, "I just told you, it's the Mound Builder–Arikara maul under discussion."

"I mean the picture itself."

"Oh. It's from my presentation last Saturday night." He started to rise. "Can I go now?"

Karen looked up from the printout. "To be clear, this is a picture you took, for your presentation?"

"Yes, of course, I always create my own PowerPoint presentations. I'm not a dinosaur. I may not have my eyes glued to my phone all the time, but I know my way around a computer."

Karen pushed another piece of paper in front of Hardy. "Care to explain that, then?"

Hardy stared down at it and fell heavily back into his seat.

The printout showed the creator, the date stamp, and even the location of where the photo had been taken. Which Marek had discovered as he'd right-clicked on the presentation that had been uploaded to Dr. Hardy's faculty page.

The picture of the maul had been taken with Hardy's phone camera at 10:47 p.m. on Friday. The GPS location matched the ARCHLAB. The maul had indeed been returned to the lab after the murder.

By Hardy himself. He must have cleaned it at the dig before taking it to the lab.

It was a nice judicial circle. The maul used to kill Hunter Redwing-Digges was the same maul that had tripped up his killer.

CHAPTER 32

Staring at the printout, Hardy ran his hands down his face, his hands trembling. "I... I was wrong. Now I remember. I found the maul there in the lab. On the table. It must have been put there when I went home to change. I figured Hunter left it there—that with the confrontation with Hawks, he just forgot to load it into the van. I took a quick picture and put the maul in the lithics carton. I just... forgot. I was tired. It was a long day."

The professor wasn't convincing himself, much less them, but Karen's phone pinged before she could poke holes. She took out the phone. The text was from Bork.

Let him explain this one. "Care to tell us, Dr. Hardy, how you got blood on your shoes, your car seat, and on clothes stashed in a container in your basement?"

Hardy's head fell into his hands.

Marek said gently, "You couldn't leave it there at the site. The maul."

His body slumping, Hardy mumbled, "It's evidence."

Yes, indeed, it was. Of murder. Karen felt more relief than satisfaction. Hawks had been a sheer pleasure. Taking down Hardy was more like hard work. Had to be done. This was a man who would not do well in prison. Hawks would land on his feet there. He was a chameleon with the eye on one thing: himself.

"Tell us what happened," Karen told him. "The truth this time."

Hardy closed his eyes. "I never meant it to happen. It was an accident." Misery etched his face as he opened his eyes. "The maul just slipped out of my hand. All I wanted was to get his attention, to shake it at him. I forget just how frail, how small, he was. I was horrified by what happened. I mean that."

That may or may not be true. But he'd been willing to let someone else take the fall, preferably one of the protesters. Native protesters. Two birds, one stone: Hunter and a protester.

"Let's go back to when Hunter returned from Flandreau," Marek said.

"All right." Hardy took a big breath and sat up straighter, as if a weight had been lifted. "I let him go to Flandreau because he strongly believed that he had a lead on the woman in white in the pictograph from the winter count. Not just that, but possibly the Spirit Society bundle." When he saw they understood, he sighed. "I see you have, despite appearances, been diligent in your search. In any event, I was highly dubious of any lead generated from a dream and a bunch of elders, but as that bundle would have potentially validated my own theories, I was willing to let him follow his latest lead. When Hunter returned, he pulled me aside and told me that he knew exactly where the bundle was. It was—"

As Two Fingers made a strangled sound, Karen held up a hand. "Anything on the record is theoretically available to the public, Dr. Hardy. I am not sure you want to broadcast that location, if indeed Hunter was correct. Archaeological site locations that are not actively being dug are usually kept secret, right?"

A faint light of respect lit his eyes. "Yes. Very well. The last thing I want is some treasure hunter digging it up. Hunter insisted he'd figured it all out and would tell me the whole story when the others had gone. When we finished digging and got rid of those feckless protesters, we went out to the finds tent where Hunter had left the maul as the last item to pack up. Hunter told me then that he'd changed his mind. That he wouldn't tell me where the bundle was. I couldn't believe what I was hearing. He said it had to go back to the MHA. Unopened. That it was powerful, spiritual, and they had the right to decide what to do with it."

Hardy snorted. "I told him he was listening to too much New Age crap. He said it didn't matter if it was true or not, but what the bundle symbolized to a people who'd lost so much. He refused to show me where it was. Or where he thought it was. I'm beginning to doubt that. I deal in science, not woo-woo."

It was exactly that woo-woo that had solved the mystery of where the bundle lay. If Hardy had worked with the MHA, rather than excluded them, a compromise might have been reached. Just what, Karen didn't know, but it at least would have been a possibility.

Outrage replaced the misery in the professor's craggy face. "That bundle needs to be found, to be studied. The bundle itself is no more powerful than a rock. Except in knowledge. Knowledge is power. What Hunter did, refusing to let an archaeological team uncover it with all the care and contextual knowledge necessary to properly assess it— giving it into the hands of the ignorant—is tantamount to professional malfeasance."

Hardy cupped his currently free hands. "Hunter had so much right there in the palm of his hand. And he threw it away. A path to academic tenure, a coup for his fellow Natives, everything. He had everything to gain, nothing to lose but the dubious gratitude of backward know-nothings."

Karen wasn't gullible enough to believe that Hardy's anger was all in the name of disinterested science. "You also had a stake, though, didn't you. You believed the lost Spirit

Society bundle would at last prove your theory connecting the priestly class at Cahokia to the Arikara."

"Yes, but it was knowledge to be *shared*. Not to be hoarded and buried. That's the crime."

"So in anger, you hit him with the maul."

"It slipped out of my hand," Hardy insisted. "I intended to shake it at him, to show him what was important, what solid evidence was, not the mumbo jumbo of religious zealots. He turned just as I picked it up, and I swear, it just flew out of my hand."

Hardy could go with that. He might even get a manslaughter with it. That depended on the forensic reconstruction. Anything was possible. And the defense lawyer would play a part, and she guessed the single-minded professor hadn't spent much money in his life. He could afford the best. Karen was cynical enough to believe that Hardy had a much better shot at manslaughter than Stands By Him would have if he'd been the killer with the same excuse.

Karen nodded at Marek, and he switched off the recorder. Mission accomplished. They had justice—or at least wowicake, the truth—for Hunter.

But she wasn't quite done with the professor. "FYI, Dr. Hardy. My deputy here is the friend of Hunter's who told him about the woman in white. And the great-grandson of Delma Two Fingers, whose uncle was the keeper of the winter count that you dismissed as fake."

Predictably, the professor didn't acknowledge Two Fingers's loss. Only the loss of the bundle. He rose to his feet and demanded, "Does she know where it is?"

"No," Two Fingers answered. Truthfully. "If Hunter knew, it wasn't because she told him where it was."

"It was at Spirit Mound," Dr. Hardy informed them. "Somewhere. All Hunter said when he first told me was 'It's here. Right *here.*' That's why I pushed the dig closer to the finds tent." His eyes burned below the heavy brows. "The dig at Spirit Mound must continue despite my temporary absence. Abigail will see to it. She's not as good as I am, but she's good enough, and she can report to me."

Karen thought there wouldn't be a chance in hell that Dr. Doll would sign on again for another season. Or to be his minion. But Karen, barely, held her tongue.

To her surprise, Two Fingers didn't. "If you'd done what Hunter, and the protesters, asked of you, you might have what you wanted, Dr. Hardy. It wouldn't have been a given that the MHA would have turned down your request."

That was greeted with scorn. "You think not? You haven't dealt with NAGPRA. I have. It's decimated our profession. Science depends on replicability. Taking the evidence away from comparison with new finds, new technologies to study? It's as good as buried."

There would be no peace pipe smoked here. Karen supposed that, to justify what he'd done, Hardy couldn't even contemplate the possibility that he'd been wrong. In his view, he had a right to the bundle, not to own it, but to extract knowledge from it, dead spirits be damned. "Deputy, please take Dr. Hardy down to the jail and book him."

Two Fingers hesitated, nodded at her, then led the professor out. Her deputy didn't look particularly happy, but he did look... relieved. The weight, the responsibility, was lifted.

After they left, Karen said, "Hardy doesn't see it. It was right under his nose. It was oral tradition that led Hunter to the location of the professor's holy grail."

Karen went to her desk and called Abigail Doll. The woman was shocked, but in the end, not terribly surprised. "His is a mind of singular focus. That often doesn't end well. A bundle might've been a coup, but it's not worth a life. Balance, I tell my students. And no, I have no desire to return to the dig. I suspect it will be shut down with the unwelcome media attention that will soon hit us. In fact, I may cut the dig short. None of the parents are going to feel comfortable until they have their kid home again. It may not make sense, since the killer is in jail, but I can guarantee you, that's what they'll feel."

By the time she hung up, Karen saw that Walrus had returned from the farm-accident callout he'd gone to. She filled him in.

"Geez, all that over some bundle of old stuff?"

Two Fingers heard that as he returned from the basement jail. "It's not just stuff."

"What, then? Gold?"

Their Native deputy turned Dakotan. And he was, more than any of them, Santee Dakotan and South Dakotan. "That's sacred, private."

Walrus threw up his hands. "Geez. You want us to learn to respect your ways. But then it's all secret. So if we ignore you guys, then that's bad and we aren't listening. If we try to learn your ways, then it's cultural appropriation, and that's bad. We can't win."

The dark eyes clouded. "Haven't you won enough?"

Walrus's sausage-fingered hands turned up. "Hey, just trying to understand. I still don't get the whole thing with Inyan Ska. I mean, yeah, it's your name... hey, do you have an Indian name, too?"

When Two Fingers looked at him, Walrus looked put-upon.

"Geez, that's secret, too?"

"It's not used lightly. And it can change as we change." His lips twitched. "My mother's name as a girl translates as Dancing Wind."

"Sounds cool to me," Karen said.

"A dancing wind, to us, is a tornado."

Oh. Appropriate. And not much changed. But apparently, it had. "So it changed?"

"Yes, it's changed, but that's for her to give to you or not. My family know mine, those at my naming ceremony know it, and when I die, it'll be in my obit. Perhaps it will be different then than it is now."

Walrus put his hands on his rotund belly. "Well, okay,

but don't die, okay? I'm not that curious. Anyway, I don't get the 'twice' thing. Karen said Inyan Ska was White Stone Creek. I get that but not why the uncle said it twice. Was he some kind of prophet, knowing Two Fingers here would be the key?"

Even Two Fingers looked doubtful, though not dismissive.

"It could just be to emphasize it," Marek suggested.

"Maybe, but still..." Walrus hit his head. "Geez. Duh. White stone, right? There's that big weathered boulder near the top of the mound. Came from Minnesota or something and was plopped there at the end of the ice age. It's pretty darn white. The uncle and that family, you said the Rockboys came from southeastern South Dakota. Think of their name, even. And they'd know Spirit Mound. They'd know that stone. What do you want to bet that's where that bundle was buried? Under a rock. Literally."

Two Fingers stiffened even as his eyes widened. He said nothing.

But it made sense. It made perfect sense. Willis Rockboy left the Spirit Society bundle under the biggest white rock near White Stone Creek at Spirit Mound before he'd been hauled off to the insane asylum by wasicus.

Karen liked to think that she'd learned a little over the last several days. She lowered her voice, but it was no less intense for all that. "None of that goes on record. Anywhere. Nor do the words *Inyan Ska*. That's not to be discussed with anyone. Not even Laura, Walter. Do you understand?"

Though her affable deputy seemed a bit baffled at first, he got a load of the dread on Two Fingers's face. "Yeah, sure. Lips sealed. Wouldn't want Hardy to get wind, anyway."

After getting an approving nod from Marek, Karen told Two Fingers, "We'll leave it in your hands. Tell your family, the MHA in Fort Berthold, whoever you need to, and decide what happens next. If anything. That's what Hunter wanted in the end. And I think that's what you want. If that means the bundle stays buried, so be it. It'll stay buried."

Two Fingers regained some of the weight he'd lost after Hardy's confession. Though it went against the grain of his upbringing, he looked all three of them in the eye with suspiciously bright ones of his own before saying simply, "*Wopida.* Thank you."

CHAPTER 33

After giving the media an update on the arrest of Dr. Hardy, Karen walked back into the welcome coolness of the office and glanced at the clock. Only five o'clock. Even Blake had been uncharacteristically restrained with his questions, which made her job easier.

Of course, they weren't the first to run with the story. She'd mended things with Nails Nelson by letting him break it first. No doubt he would ride that for a while.

Marek looked up from his desk, where he'd been recording his notes on the investigation for Josephine to type up. "We done?"

No doubt he wanted to get back home. Becca had been spending a lot of time with Karen's father while Marek was on the investigation. And heck, maybe Marek actually did have a soffit or something to finish.

Letting out a breath, Karen decided to let herself think of her own abandoned plans. She had plenty of sun, but she didn't have white sands. The Caribbean beckoned. Maybe she and Larson could salvage some of their honeymoon if they took the redeye tonight. They'd planned on returning Wednesday night, so that still gave them two full days. If Larson could disentangle himself from work, that is. She took out her phone to text him, and it rang in her hand. She held up a hand to keep Marek from leaving.

After she took the call, she looked at Marek. Talk about mixed emotions. "We're going to Flandreau."

His Okerlund pale-blue eyes lidded. "*We* are?"

If she was in, he was in. "We are. Special invitation from Delma. Final wacipi tonight. Apparently, Dr. Grant is going to bring the Rockboy winter count, and there's going to be some kind of repatriation ceremony."

Marek hesitated. "Okay if I bring Becca?" Nikki was too busy, he knew, with the new school year coming up to go with them.

Karen called back then nodded. "She's more than welcome. As is Larson."

Marek's brow quirked. "Who called? Two Fingers?"

She shook her head. "Winona. I couldn't turn her down. That would make us wasicus look bad with our screwy priorities."

Marek got to his feet and left the recorder in the locked dropbox on Josephine's desk. "Sounds like half the roster will be in Flandreau tonight."

Karen had given Two Fingers the go-ahead to take the night off to be there with Seoul and her mother. She wondered if that qualified as the official meeting of the parents. Though it wasn't about the couple, if indeed they were, but Seoul's mother.

Marek left while she squared away Walrus and Kurt as backups for Bork. Seoul had said she'd try to make her shift, but Adam said he'd just bring a puppet from the show to imitate her if needed. If anyone could pull it off, he could, and would likely bring the house down doing it. A bit of acting talent, or at least code-switching, was a bonus in police work.

Karen reached Larson just before he left Sioux Falls. She would meet him there and pick him up. Not exactly the honeymoon of her dreams, but it would have to do.

When Larson slid into the Sub half an hour later, he looked dubiously at the A/C. "That work?"

Gritting her teeth, Karen patted the dash. "Of course. And will for the entire trip."

"You know, cars are inanimate."

The Sub sputtered.

"I stand corrected."

On the drive north, Karen filled him in. Larson shook his head. "Hiding bloody clothes in the basement. Pretty stupid for a smart man."

"Smart, yes, but no heart. I don't think he ever imagined that we'd even look at him. Plenty of time to dispose of the evidence once he got the bundle."

"You think he'll get off light?"

"I don't want to think so. But... I'm Dakotan. I've seen some pretty lopsided sentences when the two parties involved were Indian and white. Not in the Indian's favor. But maybe times have changed."

Larson gave her a skeptical look. She agreed. What could she say? All she could do was make the case. Larson or his ilk would determine whether it was a slip or a slap of the maul.

When they arrived at the wacipi, they were waved through immediately. Apparently, word had gone out. Karen parked the Sub near the exit this time so they could get out if needed. Then they walked back as Larson watched everything with his bullet-gray eyes. She imagined that he felt even more alien in this environment than she had, coming as he had from the Chicago projects. She left him at one of the food vendors as he tried to decide between plain fry bread and taco fry bread.

"Karen!"

She turned at the gleeful sound of recognition and caught Becca on the fly. The girl had fry bread in one hand and a jingly bracelet around her wrist. Marek trailed her slowly, his head moving from side to side as he walked slowly through the crowd, looking like a buffalo who'd strayed among antelope.

"Contributing to the Indian economy, I see," Winona said as she walked up to them. Her eyes widened at the sight of Marek's dusky-skinned daughter with pale-blue Okerlund eyes. "This must be Becca. Hi, I'm Deputy Two Fingers's mother, Winona."

Though Becca tended to be shy around strangers, she smiled easily at Winona. "Hi, I'm Rebecca DeBaca Okerlund. You have a pretty dress. Dad said maybe I could have one that jingles when I'm older, but I got a bracelet instead." Her brow furrowed. "Does Two Fingers really eat dogs?"

Marek winced as Winona shot him a look. "I have no idea where she got that."

"Uncle Arne said so," Becca informed them. "I don't want anybody to eat Gunny."

Karen let out a breath. "Sorry. That would be my father."

Winona merely shook her head. "A long, long time ago, we did eat dog meat. So did Lewis but not Clark, when they crossed into our lands. During a special ceremony, we would eat dog meat to... take their spirit into ours."

Becca frowned. "Like eating Jesus?"

"Eating..." Winona laughed. "Oh, yes, the body and blood of Christ. Very like."

Becca tilted her head. "Do the dogs rise again?"

Karen bit her lip. The questions kids asked.

Winona managed to field it, though. "Ah... in the spirit world, I believe so, yes. But we no longer eat dog meat. Things change. Your Gunny is safe."

A girl in a beaded crown called out, "Hey, Becca, come look at this!"

Apparently, Becca had already made a friend in the crowd of brightly dressed girls. Karen let her down, and she ran off to join them.

Winona tracked her. "That's an old soul. Hispanic?"

Marek tracked her as well. "And Tewa."

Surprise had Winona turning back to look at him more closely. "Enrolled?"

"No. Under the blood quantum. And her grandfather was forced to choose between his Tewa life and his white wife. He chose the latter. I wasn't even aware of the Tewa connection until my wife died. I'm not sure what to do about it."

Winona watched Becca pointing to one of the ribbon shawls, obviously asking her new friends about it. "We lose so many. Does she know them, her Tewa family?"

"She's met them." Marek shifted on his Blunnies. "Once."

Karen had met them as well. Good people. But the culture, as here, was alien to her.

"Once is not enough," Winona told him sharply. Then she sighed. "But it will never be enough. I have no answers for you. My son was raised steeped in the Santee culture, even more so than I was, as Unci tried to correct her mistakes with me. Yet he's not enrolled. It hurts him. It hurts us. But for others…" Her gaze went to an approaching threesome.

Karen waited for them to arrive. She'd talked to the Diggeses immediately after Hardy's arrest, to let them know before it hit the press. They'd been thankful to her but not excited. Nothing would bring Hunter back to them.

With them was Anita Asplund, a Viking goddess even more out of place than Karen. She looked drawn and very, very pale.

Peggy Digges nodded at Winona then at Karen and Marek. "I see you also got Delma's invitation tonight. They are going to honor Hunter tonight."

That explained a lot. Delma had insisted they find Hunter's killer. They had. In Delma's world, that meant a ceremony. Karen could get behind that. She asked Anita, "Morning sickness?"

"Not just morning," Anita said with a weak smile. "But I am okay right now." When Peggy patted her arm, Karen lifted a brow. "I am going to give the baby to Trent and Peggy to raise and go back to Sweden as I planned."

An interesting choice. Karen had pretty much done the same, so she had no basis for criticizing that choice, though perhaps Anita took her silence as such. Winona seemed more resigned than anything.

"I will visit. I will not refuse to see the child. But my uncle would not understand. All he has is his research and, when he notices, me. A Native child would bewilder him. He would not be hostile, you understand. He just would not know what to do."

Marek asked, "What about the tribe, the family?"

Her hand went to her stomach. "The child will be under blood quantum. The Diggeses know how to raise him to know his heritage and will take him to Standing Rock to know his family there. It will not be what Hunter wanted for himself, but he had enough Indian blood to be enrolled. My child will not. I cannot change that."

Trent cleared his throat. "We want to give the child what Hunter wanted."

Peggy, her eyes bright, nodded. "We are very grateful. It helps."

More than justice. Karen got that. She was happy for them. And even for Anita. Though having given up a child for adoption, Karen knew that it would always be there—a what-if. Karen was lucky to have a second chance with Eyre. She would never be Eyre's mother. But they were settling in to something, more like an aunt–niece relationship, perhaps.

Marek asked, "What about Sphinx?"

Anita smiled a bit wryly. "Armon Ladeaux took him. He said they have an uneasy truce, just as Armon and Hunter had, and Sphinx reminds Armon to look at the other side."

The three moved off as the crowd started to filter toward the arena. Karen started the same way when she saw a familiar and very unexpected face. The woman caught her look and stopped abruptly, as if she'd been caught doing something illegal or at least unacceptable.

Marek had scooped up Becca. He pursed his lips as he saw the woman. "I'll save you a seat."

Leaving her to face the woman alone. Great. "Hi, Mary. I didn't expect to see you here. How is Al?"

"Fine, he's fine. Now that the Baytons have him back on the payroll. Many of my friends from the park are still struggling. I try to help out when I can."

Karen had first met Mary while she, Al, and a number of others had been homeless and living in Grove Park. Some of the homeless had been able, with the media attention, to find work and housing. Others had drifted away. Karen had always liked Mary, despite her blood connection to a truly evil man, and was glad she had finally found her footing.

And shifting from foot to foot, Mary said, "I bet you want to know what I'm doing here."

"I assume you're a tourist. But why are you looking like you're hiding from the law?"

"I just didn't want anyone who knows me to see me here," the woman confided. "No one in my family would forgive me if they got wind of it, not that we ever talk anyway, but I'm curious."

And that made Karen curious. "Why?"

Mary lowered her voice. "My ancestors were at New Ulm."

Karen didn't see the connection. Or even recognize the name. "Pardon?"

Mary's eyes widened, as if she'd never imagined the name wasn't common knowledge. Karen had run into that a lot lately. "My immigrant Johnson ancestor was killed at New Ulm in Minnesota, and his wife was raped and taken captive during the Sioux Uprising."

It took Karen a few seconds, but she realized Mary was talking about the Dakota War. Different names for different viewpoints?

Mary nodded as she saw Karen understood. "She was pregnant when she was let go at Camp Release in North Dakota. She married a widower who'd lost his wife and three children to the Indians. She told him the child was her husband's. After the boy was born with Indian in him, she tried to pass him off as part Italian, but everyone knew. Especially with a name like Johnson. He wasn't no Scandinavian, that's for sure. His stepfather beat him something fierce just for existing, and everybody shunned him. He ran away when he was twelve. A big-boned man, my grandfather said. He passed off as older and worked on the railroads. He hated Indians, even though he was half one, and maybe that's what drove him to drink. He married a white woman from back East who believed the Italian story and had a passel of kids. He abused them all, from what I hear, then shot himself one Christmas morning. The whole Indian thing was hushed up. But my brother Ed found out the truth from our grandfather when Grandpa wasn't able to hold his liquor or his mind together at the end. Maybe that's where all the anger, the violence, came from, what happened at New Ulm. I don't know. It's a cycle, isn't it? Generation after generation of abuse, of drink, of no-good men in my family."

Mary glanced around at the color, the arena, the dancing. "But this is part of me, too. I'm just curious. I wouldn't claim to be Indian. I've been taught to forgive by my church, but I'm not going to forget."

There was a haunted look in there, nonetheless. How long did it take to get out of that rut, that circle, if one ever could? What if her own Okerlund family had been decimated like the Johnsons? Justice was the Okerlund way. What was justice here?

Many wrongs, many wronged. Mary and Two Fingers were two sides of the same coin.

Then it hit her. Mary Johnson's brother Ed was Two Fingers's rapist father. He'd also raped Mary, his own sister. Not a man of honor by any stretch. And Two Fingers had had no desire to make any overtures to the Johnson family, which Karen understood. But what if knowing that he got Dakota blood from his biological father pushed him over the blood quantum?

Would that balance the wrongs, at least a little?

CHAPTER 34

Afterward, Karen couldn't recall all the details of the repatriation. A blur of color, music, and dancing, with the scent of herbs wafting in the wind, the ceremony was powerful and moving. And one part, she would never, ever forget. There wasn't a dry eye in the arena when a trembling Delma Two Fingers took into her well-worn hands, from the open hands of Dr. Osirus Grant, the winter count that had come down through centuries to her and her people.

Karen also found out that Indian time could, apparently, travel at lightspeed when it was important. A number of Rockboys had come from Yankton for the event, humble and grateful—and accepted. A reunion of a family fractured by its loss now had a bridge for peace.

Hunter's ceremony was also moving. Though he'd been a member of Standing Rock, not Flandreau, he'd spent most of his life here, and Karen saw that the entire contingent of the school, including Dana Todacheeny Ellis and Armon Ladeaux, were there.

When it was all done, the emcee said, "One last thing before we end the honoring ceremonies."

Winona and Delma had risen, both carrying something in bundles, and they walked slowly out to the middle of the grounds.

"Will Sheriff Karen Okerlund Mehaffey and Detective

Marek Okerlund of Eda County please step onto the sacred grounds?"

For a second, Karen froze. As before, she hadn't understood half of what the emcee had said, as it was either in Dakota or simply unfamiliar to her, but she understood that. What the heck? Larson nudged her with his elbow, as he was using both hands to eat his fry bread taco. She looked over at Marek, who hadn't moved a muscle.

Becca pushed at her father's back. "That's you! Go!"

That got some laughter from those nearby. Marek rose, glanced at Karen, and gestured for her to go first. Great. Nothing like having the eyes of a bazillion strangers on you while you walked their sacred grounds. She did recall someone saying that you should never walk across the grounds unbidden. Well, she'd been bidden.

Once Karen and Marek were facing Winona and Delma, the emcee said, "We wish to honor those who have brought truth and justice to Hunter Redwing-Digges. And who helped bring the Rockboy winter count home. Delma says that Hunter was another great-grandson to her. And that she told these two to find Hunter's killer. And guess what, folks. These wasicus did just that! Give them a hand."

A hearty round of applause erupted. Very, very different from their initial reception. But it all still made Karen itch to get out of the limelight. She'd spent years under those lights as a basketball player, without undue anxiety or misstep. But she didn't know how to conduct herself here. She might unknowingly give offense.

Winona took one of the bundles and moved behind them. Great. Were they going to throw something on them? Some kind of cleansing or un-wasicu ceremony?

"You'll have to kneel down," Winona said behind Marek, who didn't look back, but did drop to one knee. And Karen saw what he couldn't. Yet. Winona unfolded a stunningly beautiful quilt in all the colors of the wacipi, bright and almost dancing in the glancing sun as Winona placed it around Marek's shoulders.

A star quilt. The words—and the awe—must've escaped her, because Delma's face wrinkled with a smile. "I made them. I just didn't know who for at the time."

As the star quilt was draped over her own shoulders, Karen felt the tears flow. And despite the heat, she didn't have any desire to shrug the quilt off. She knew what an honor it was to receive a star quilt from Native hands.

Maybe if her people had taken the tradition of giving rather than taking everything in sight, their country would have been better off.

What could she say? So she said simply, "Wopida."

Surprise slackened some of the wrinkles in Delma's long-suffering and long-suffered face. "You have learned to hear. *And* when not to speak." That was accompanied by a significant look that was also more than a bit shiny. "Wopida."

Karen understood then that this wasn't just because of Hunter. Delma knew the whole story of the winter count and the bundle now. Only a handful of them did. And they would take it to the grave, if that was the decision.

After the wacipi was over, Larson tangled his fingers with hers as the eagle shadow flew its last flight over the medicine wheel and the moon shone down on the placid Big Sioux. At its banks, he said, "Better than the Caribbean."

"And we don't have to fly red-eye."

But their night was not yet done.

Seoul came up with Marek and Becca. "I'd like you to go with us to Martin's house. He said he would tell us there about my grandfather. He wants to show us things."

"Sure," Karen said. It would also, she hoped, give her a chance to tell Two Fingers about Mary Johnson. "Thanks. I'll admit I've been curious."

"Understatement of the year," Seoul echoed. "Mom's tied in knots."

If she was, she didn't look it. Mrs. Durr glowed in the moonlight. Karen hadn't met her before, only Seoul's father, Sheriff Kent Durr, and he hadn't been particularly happy with Karen at the time. Though they'd parted on good terms. She didn't wonder where he was tonight. It was hard for a sheriff to get away. That she'd managed it that night without being called back was a minor miracle.

By the time Karen pulled the Sub into one of the gravel slots at the Goodthunder–Two Fingers homestead, she was yawning.

"Not sure I'm invited," Larson said.

But as Marek walked into the Goodthunder house with Becca in his arms, she said, "Looks to me like 'and guest' applies here." On the way up, she'd already told him of the tangled relationships between Seoul, her mother, and Martin. Not to mention Two Fingers. "Might as well get this mystery solved, then we can head home and hit the sack."

When they were directed into the living room, Karen had to marvel at just how different this house was from Delma's. The decor was decidedly Native Nouveau. Or modern. Lots of abstracts or semi-abstract art of feathers, dancing, drums, and flutes that she suspected came via Peggy Digges's gallery. Interspersed were framed band posters showing the evolution of Winona and her band from angry punk to mature Native rocker.

Becca, in her father's arms, had been sleepy when he carried her in, but was now wide-eyed, studying each and every bit of art in the room.

One large painting hung as a focal point over the fireplace. Karen suspected from its impressionistic style the painting was another JoAnne Bird. Instead of a Grand Entry, though, this one was of four white horses with ambiguous riders. Were the four horses an echo of the four horses of the Apocalypse? All the horses had red circles for eyes and forelocks with four lines of red. The background was a dark, intense multi-hued blue. Each figure looked to be throwing something, perhaps a spear, into the dark angry sky.

"*Return of the Thunder Beings*," Martin said.

Rather than ask what they were, she said, "Appropriate." The thunder part, at least.

Winona brought out a tray. She offered first dibs to Seoul's mother. "Dani, isn't it?"

"Dan-Bi," corrected the tiny woman, who was even shorter than her five-foot-nothing daughter. She took something from the tray that looked like shortbread.

Taking one, Karen found out that's exactly what it was.

"What does your name mean?" Winona asked. "If anything."

"Sweet rain," Seoul replied.

Martin blinked, looked at the painting above the hearth, and nodded. "Appropriate."

Once everyone had been served, all eyes fell on Martin. Seoul's hand snuck out to grasp her mother's. "Who was my grandfather?"

Martin seemed to be gathering his thoughts as to how best to answer that simple question. Karen understood. How did you describe a life?

"I am sorry I didn't respond until Detective Okerlund prompted me to look at my matches. We are wary of those claiming to be our kin." Martin shifted in the recliner, sitting straighter. "Your grandfather's name was Alexander Goodthunder. Everyone called him Sandy."

An "ah" escaped Dan-Bi. Santa, Santee, Sandy. All very similar-sounding names to someone who didn't know the language. "We thought his name was Santa," Dan-Bi explained.

"He was a generous man," Martin said with a sad smile. "He was my half-uncle. My father's eldest brother. His mother died on birthing him."

A sound of distress came from Dan-Bi. Karen wasn't sure if it was the mother's death or that the man was also clearly

Dead Spirits

dead. Or both. But the tiny woman remained silent, just put her other hand over the one clasped with her daughter's.

"My grandmother raised him as her own," Martin assured her. "And since she was a younger cousin of his mother, that was easy to do. My uncle never lacked for love." As if hearing his words, he went on hurriedly, "From his parents. He had girlfriends but no one serious. After high school at the Flandreau Indian School, he joined the Army."

Score one for her side, Karen thought.

"And he was sent to Korea," Seoul finished.

"Eventually, yes. He was stateside first. When he'd come home, he'd toss me in the air and give me sweets and tell me I'd be a great warrior one day. I loved him. Everybody did. He was a good man. Not without flaws. Too easy-going in some ways. And he hated to harm anything or anyone. A gentle man. That made the Army a challenge. He was going to get out when he returned from Korea, despite my grandfather's disapproval, and work the land." Goodthunder took a deep breath. "But the transport plane back to the States hit bad weather and went down in the Pacific. They never recovered the bodies. It nearly killed my grandfather. He was never the same after."

Karen saw the tears streak down Dan-Bi's face. "He didn't abandon my mother."

"Or you," Martin said gently. "I knew him well enough to know he meant what he said about returning for you both. To have some part of him back, it will be good, for my family. And, I hope, for yours." He got up and got a framed photo off a side table. "Here is your father. Corporal Alexander Magazu Suta Goodthunder."

Although she didn't have as good a look at it as Dan-Bi, Karen could see the photo well enough. Obviously, it was an Army official photo, with the American flag in the background. His face was wider than Goodthunder's, with good humor in his warm brown eyes and a hint of fun and laughter in his wide smile under a buzz haircut and prominent cheekbones.

"Magazu Suta?" Seoul asked.

Once again, Martin looked at the painting. "Hard rain. Many tears were shed the night he was born. We believe that the Thunder Beings bring the rains from the west each spring. He was born on April the first."

Seoul leaned forward, her eyes bright with curiosity as her mother's trembling finger traced the lines of a face that held the outline of hers, in miniature. "Do you do rain dances?"

That got an actual laugh from Martin and a snort from Winona. "No. No, we don't. Sorry."

Seoul, her eyes studiously away from Two Fingers, asked, "What was his blood quantum?"

"Full. He was, like I am, fully Santee Dakota. You are a quarter. Your mother is half. Both of you are eligible to become enrolled members. That is your birthright."

Winona looked torn but kept her mouth shut. Two Fingers hadn't said a word the entire time but took Seoul's free hand when she offered it.

"But perhaps not our right," Dan-Bi said, looking at her daughter and Two Fingers.

"Whatever you decide, you will always be welcome here," Goodthunder said. "There are many more of my family who want to meet you, but we decided I should tell you first, since you contacted me. We didn't want to overwhelm you. We are a large family."

"Tell me about it," Winona said. "I married into a clan. It was a shock, let me tell you, going from just me and Unci and Inyan. Martin is one of twelve. He says he became a policeman so he could tell the others to shut up. He was the youngest."

"Do you have other pictures?" Seoul asked. "I'd love to hear more about him. Mom looks so much like him, it's uncanny. A mini-Sandy."

Looking pleased, Goodthunder opened his mouth.

Karen cleared her throat. She rose to her feet with Larson just a millisecond behind her. Marek took another second but rose as well.

"We should get going," Karen told Goodthunder and Winona. "It's been a pleasure, all around, and an honor."

Seoul's face fell. "Perhaps we should also..."

Winona shook her head. "Martin has so much more to show you, to tell you. You will stay with us tonight."

Seoul beamed but turned to Karen. "Sheriff? What about my shift?"

"Go ahead and stay. It's not every day that a woman gets a new grandfather." Karen glanced at Dan-Bi, who seemed transfixed by the photo in her lap. "Or father. I'll cover if need be." She smiled at Seoul. "I'm happy that you've found family you can claim with an open heart." Which wasn't the case with her Native deputy. "Two Fingers, can I talk to you?"

Correctly interpreting that meant alone, Two Fingers released Seoul's hand and got to his feet. He followed them out. Marek searched her face, his brow quirked, but he took his once-again sleepy daughter to his Silverado without comment. Larson went to the Sub to wait.

Karen walked over to the darkened cabin where Delma must be sleeping off the excitement of the day. Karen stood at the edge of the hill overlooking the Big Sioux. The moon cast diamonds on ripples from a single boulder in the placid river. Not a bad spot to spend the remains of one's days. She wouldn't mind the same from her own bluff view.

Karen didn't hear Two Fingers step up beside her, but she felt him in the darkness. Had he practiced that silent step as a boy? Or did it come naturally through the genes? He was a hunter, a warrior who had chosen a different path than his people. But some of that had been forced on him. What would he do if a new path opened up to him?

"I ran into Mary Johnson at the wacipi." When that got no response, she said, "Ed Johnson's sister." Karen would never make the mistake of calling him Two Fingers's father. "She didn't ask to see you. She never has. I am not sure she is even aware of your existence, at least the blood connection, only that her brother raped a number of women, herself included."

A breath of a sigh stirred the air. "I didn't know that."

"I'm not here to stage a reunion. That's your business. She and Al Bayton landed on their feet. She seemed to be doing well and looking out for the others as best she could."

The air stirred again. "She's of a different cut."

"Apparently. She's had a hard life. As did her Johnson ancestors."

And without any embellishment, she told him the story. When he remained silent, so silent she couldn't hear his breathing, she said, "Just thought you might want to know. It could push you over the blood quantum limits."

He finally moved forward into the moonlight where she could see him. Hope flared in his moon-reflected eyes. Briefly. Then it died. And deep in those dark eyes, something sad and haunted lived again. The moonlight made his gaze almost ghost-like. Or spirit-like. And so deep that it seemed to seep from the man into the land in a way Karen had no words for.

She shivered in the warm air.

Finally, Two Fingers said, "The boy wouldn't have been enrolled or on the tribal census. It's possible that he was recorded on the regular census as an Indian, but that's a long shot. Most likely, there's little hope that it can be documented. Just stories." His lips twisted. "Oral tradition. Not to be trusted."

Karen blinked. "You don't believe Mary's story?"

"I do. I was thinking of Hardy's stance on tradition. It gives me no pleasure, to know that one rape long ago led to another down the same road. Circles. Our cultures defined us. He grew up white and was rejected by his people. I grew up Indian and was rejected by my people. At least by the tribe. Those who matter to me consider me Indian." He looked over at the silent, moonlit cabin. "Unci had a lot to do with that. She's a remarkable woman. My rock."

Well, Karen had done what she could to balance things. He would pursue the lead that might lead to enrollment, or not, as would Seoul and Dan-Bi. At least it gave them options. Bury it or no. If Seoul and Two Fingers did make a couple, and if they had kids, they would equal a quarter if Two Fingers was able to convince the council—or if they changed their rules.

Hopefully, some of the scales of justice, for both sides of this enigmatic man, would one day balance in his favor. He deserved it.

But she thought of Hunter. He'd deserved better. Life didn't always balance. Death canceled all cultures in the end. Except, perhaps, for the remains.

And the remains of her day were gone. Time to go home.

CHAPTER 35

THE NEXT SATURDAY MORNING, DEPUTY Inyan Ska Two Fingers slid into his car and looked back at the mound he'd just come from, framed by a dusky rose and baby-blue sky. Any evidence of the ceremony he'd just held at the summit had been whisked off by the stiff wind. That wind came from the east, designated by the color yellow on the medicine wheel and the direction of the rising sun, a new day.

But the scent of sweetgrass still clung to his clothes.

To his relief, he'd been alone for the whole time, which wasn't always the case. But today, he'd been the lone man on the landscape. Appropriate enough, as he'd honored the old thongs that had held his Mandan ancestor Two Fingers's sacred bundle. His MHA kin had, among many other things, taught him of Lone Man, who had walked with First Creator before the earth was created.

Two Fingers had been told that the old thongs must be left to the elements in a sacred place. He'd originally intended to return to Fort Berthold, to the hill where he'd dreamt of the woman in white. But knowing where the Spirit Society bundle now resided, knowing how all his family had combined to bring him to this place, he believed it fitting.

He'd called the MHA Tribal Historic Preservation Office and talked to the director. She was a distant cousin, as were just about all who remained of the MHA. She'd been almost speechless with joy. She knew what it would mean to the remnants of the Arikara tribe to have one of their most prized sacred bundles returned to them, especially after all they'd lost, from smallpox to Pick-Sloan. The sense of renewal, of hope, was there in her voice.

But she also understood the bureaucracy, the sensitivity, and the outright difficulty of dealing with wasicus with their thirst for knowledge versus the tribe's veneration of the sacred. That the mound was part of a county park, and that Two Fingers had connections in Eda who were sympathetic, would help greatly. He'd left it in her hands.

She'd called back a few days later with the decision of the elders.

The bundle would, for now, remain buried. But there was a young woman who was finishing her degree in anthropology at North Dakota State who wanted to be an archaeologist. Her Indian name translated as White Dress. From a young age, the elders had recognized in her a pure spirit. She'd sat at their feet, learning their stories. She was also a descendant of the original Two Fingers and had been at the Two Fingers bundle ceremony.

Wearing a white dress.

Two Fingers had felt no surprise. Nor had he felt any impatience at the delay. Indian time. He smiled faintly as he remembered Unci scolding his boss. To her credit, Sheriff Mehaffey had learned. And he would be forever grateful to her for bringing the winter count back to Unci and the Rockboy clan.

In some academic journal somewhere, Dr. Osirus Grant would no doubt write up the discovery of a recently corroborated winter count, the Yankton Rockboy Winter Count. And all of the contextual information from Unci would be out there, except a few words.

Inyan Ska. Inyan Ska.

Two Fingers hoped that Hunter would be given credit in the article, and from what Marek had told him of Dr. Grant, that likely would happen. His friend's tireless pursuit had led to it all. And it hurt that he would never see the delight on his friend's face again. Hunter had survived neglect and his own devils, only to fall victim to wasicu greed. It was an old story. If the greed was for knowledge, not gold, that was just another form.

He took one last look around. At the mound and the surrounding cornfields. Maize. Mother Corn. Some things never changed. The diggers were gone, their tents dismantled, the scar on the earth filled with rich dirt from the bottomlands. The dig would not be renewed per the university, which was dealing with its own blowback over the arrest of one of its own.

But it was a new day. A new dawn. Natives were finally finding their voice. Not one voice, but many, and that was all to the good. Old and new joined hands.

Two Fingers pursed his lips, put his hands on the wheel... then sat there, thinking of the Two Fingers bundle. Talk about hands. He took his off the wheel, looked at them, and touched his thumbs to his pinkies. Thank goodness he didn't have to give up a few digits to prove his manhood. That would make typing up reports difficult.

He glanced up again as the sun rose fully off the bluffs to brush the hill of little devils where a sacred bundle of the Arikara was buried. A red-winged blackbird dove from the mound and arrowed toward him. It flew straight at his car like a heat-seeking missile then veered up and over his windshield. But not before Two Fingers saw what it held in its beak: a thong.

Two Fingers closed his eyes. Grandfather Two Fingers. Hunter Redwing-Digges. Old and new. Dead they may be, but their spirits still lived.

Wopida, Wakan Tanka.

Then Two Fingers turned his car to the north—the direction of white and wasicu—and home. For now. To fulfill his name as best he could.

He Who Seeks Truth.

AUTHOR'S NOTE

BORN AND BRED ON THE Great Plains, I am tied to this land that Native Americans lived, died, and were buried on. Knowingly and unknowingly, they have impacted my life. I walk on their bones. I watch the sun rise and set on a landscape that, while vastly changed from the hunting grounds full of bison to farmland full of corn and beans, still has many of the features that Zitkala-Sa wrote of. As she did as a child, I wandered the wild river bluffs and floodplains of the Missouri River, and when I first read her short essay "The Great Spirit," I felt an immediate kinship.

In middle school, my younger brother and I took Lakota lessons. Not, I will admit, for any higher purpose, but to speak a language our older brother didn't know! Alas, it didn't stick, but I can still count to ten in Lakota, though the pronunciation is no doubt wanting. I do remember our Lakota teacher's vast patience with our fumbling wasicu tongues.

My first love in art was a painting that once hung in Slagle Hall at the University of South Dakota. It was *The Woodgatherer* (elderly grandmother carrying kindling on her back during a snowstorm) by Oscar Howe, who was still living when I was a child. I went in awe of him. After he passed away and I was a poor college student, I scraped together enough to buy a signed print of *The Woodgatherer*. Though the print colors are sadly faded compared to the deep blues of the original, I have dragged it along with me at every stop along my journey. Years later, I discovered JoAnne Bird, a Santee Dakota artist, and she and Howe form the core of the art hanging on my walls. Not by plan, but by love.

After reading Kent Nerburn's *Neither Wolf Nor Dog* with the Lakota elder repulsed by the babbling of whites who wrote about Native Americans, I almost didn't write this book. But when I created the team of deputies for my mystery series, I deliberately added Two Fingers. I felt at the time, and still do today, that having a white-bread team to reflect East River Dakota didn't reflect the heritage of my native land. I'd deliberately picked Scandinavian, German, Slavic, and English. To ignore the significant Lakota, Dakota, and Nakota (Sioux Nation) presence seemed like a writerly slight. They'd already been wiped off much of the Great Plains. Why would I wipe them off my fictional geography? So in this book, I took the point of view of my bumbling wasicus and only in the very last chapter do I dip momentarily into the mind of Deputy Two Fingers, who has always been a man—and a culture—apart in my mind.

As for the book itself, the Spirit Society of the Arikara and its sacred bundle are entirely fictional, though loosely based on the Ghost Society. The woman in a white dress is an actual pictograph from various Great Plains winter counts and whose origin is unknown.

Spirit Mound is a real place in Clay County—north of Vermillion on Highway 19—that I summarily co-opted into my fictional landscape. It is actually a state park, not county, but I placed it in Eda County so that my investigators would have jurisdiction. Spirit Mound is one of the few specific places on Lewis and Clark's journey that is known without a doubt. Like Karen in the story, I visited Spirit Mound as a child when it was still a cattle farm and was vastly disappointed. When it became a state park, my family would often make the short trek up to the top and it has become one of my sacred sites. I visit almost every time I am in the area. Before writing this book, I made another trek. On my return from the mound, a red-winged blackbird zoomed past me, dipping a bit, and arrowed toward the summit. I took it as a sign—and the opening and ending of my book.

PRONUNCIATION GUIDE

Arikara: uh-rick-uh-rah

Brule: brool

Caddoan: cad-doh-ahn

Dan-Bi: dan-bee

Diné: din-neh

Flandreau: flan-droo

Halmeoni: hal-mo-nee

Hidatsa: huh-dat-suh

Inipi: ee-nee-pee

Inyan Hoksila: ee-yahn hoke-shee-lah

Inyan Ska: ee-yahn skah

Iyeska: ee-yay-shkah

Magazu Suta: ma-gh-ah-zoo soo-dah

Mandan: man-dan

Mdewakanton: mid-ah-wah-kah-ton

Nadouessioux: nah-doo-wee-zhoo

Nambé: nahm-bay

Ojibwe: oh-jib-way

Okipa: oh-keep-ah

Sicangu: see-chahn-ghue

Tewa: tey-wuh

Tiospaye: tee-oh-spay

Tipi: tee-pee

Unci: uhn-chee

Wacipi: wah-chee-pee

Wakan Tanka: wah-kahn tahn-kah

Wamanus a: wah-mah-noos ah

Wasicu: wah-shee-choo

Wopida: woe-pee-dah

Wowicake: woe-wee-chah-kay

Wowicake sni: woe-wee-chah-kay shnee

Zitkala-Sa: zit-kah-la-shah

CAST OF CHARACTERS

Asplund, Anita. Music teacher at the Flandreau Indian School. Swedish.

Bakke, Jessica. Works under Dirk Larson at the South Dakota Division of Criminal Investigation (DCI) in Sioux Falls. Has a scar on her face from a violent assault.

Bayton, Mary Johnson. Wife of Al Bayton. Sister of Ed Johnson.

Bechtold, Kurt. Senior deputy in the Eda County Sheriff's Office. Unmarried. Lives with his unmarried sister, Eva, who bakes goodies to stave off her many phobias.

Bjorkland, Travis "Bork." Swing-shift deputy in the Eda County Sheriff's Office. Unmarried. A native of Minnesota.

Digges, Peggy. Adopted mother of Hunter Redwing-Digges and wife of Trent Digges. Gallery owner.

Digges, Trent. Adopted father of Hunter Redwing-Digges and husband of Peggy Digges. Flandreau City Council Member.

Doll, Dr. Abigail. Codirector of the archaeological dig at Spirit Mound. Professor at the University of Colorado at Boulder.

Durr, Seoul. Night-shift deputy from Onawa near the Loess

Hills in Iowa. Recent graduate of Briar Cliff in Sioux City with a double major in criminal justice and music. Daughter of Sheriff Kent Durr and his wife Dan-Bi.

Ellis, Dana Todacheeny. Superintendent of the Flandreau Indian School. Navajo.

Goodthunder, Winona Two Fingers. Granddaughter of Delma Two Fingers, mother of Deputy Two Fingers, wife of Martin Goodthunder, and mother of Jaydyn and Shania. Rock musician.

Goodthunder, Martin. Chief of Police at Flandreau Reservation. Husband of Winona Two Fingers and father of Jaydyn and Shania. Stepfather of Deputy Two Fingers.

Grant, Dr. Osirus. Curator at the W.H. Over Museum in Vermillion. African American and Native American.

Grigsby-Clark, Ann. Retired teacher from Virginia and related to the explorer William Clark. Following the Lewis and Clark Trail.

Halvorsen, Blake. Son of Sig and Lynn Halvorsen and fraternal twin of Lance. A mass communications major at the University of South Dakota. Works as a summer intern at a Sioux Falls TV station.

Hardy, Dr. Alden. Codirector of the archaeological dig at Spirit Mound. Professor at the University of South Dakota.

Hawks, Tonto. Protestor at the archaeological dig at Spirit Mound. Claims to be Native American but has a murky past.

Johnson, Ed. Rapist of Winona Two Fingers and biological father of Deputy Two Fingers.

Johnson, Eyre. Pronounced "Air" and named for fictional character Jane Eyre. Archivist for the privately funded Eda County Archives housed in the old Carnegie Library in

Reunion. Biological daughter of Karen Okerlund Mehaffey. Adopted by Karen's old basketball coach, Darrin Johnson, and his (now ex-) wife Professor Anne Leggett in Vermillion. After a fire destroyed her apartment, Eyre now lives with Karen at 22 Okerlund Road.

Ladeaux, Armon. Native American teacher at the Flandreau Indian School.

Larson, Dirk. Agent with the South Dakota Division of Criminal Investigation (DCI) in Sioux Falls. Divorced. Father of Maddie and Brandon Larson. Formerly a homicide detective in Chicago, Illinois. Once a professional basketball prospect. Recently moved from Sioux Falls to Reunion and married Sheriff Karen Okerlund Mehaffey.

Legrange, Richard "Richie" Anderson, Junior. Graduate student at the University of Colorado at Boulder, where his father is head of the anthropology and archaeology department. Part of the archeological dig at Spirit Mound.

Martin, Ed. Eda County state's attorney (county prosecutor).

Mehaffey, Karen Okerlund. Acting sheriff of Eda County. Widow of Patrick Mehaffey, a Bosnian War casualty who lingered in a coma for many years. Daughter of former sheriff, Arne Okerlund, and half-niece of Detective Marek Okerlund, who is four years her junior. Biological mother of Eyre Johnson. Was an outstanding basketball player at the University of South Dakota in Vermillion. Former Army officer in Bosnia and police dispatcher in Sioux Falls. Took over as acting sheriff after her father's stroke. Lives at 22 Okerlund Road in the bungalow where she grew up. Recently married to DCI Agent Dirk Larson.

Mehaffey, Patrick. Deceased husband of Karen Okerlund Mehaffey. An Army medic, he drove over a landmine in Bosnia and was in a coma for many years before his death.

Mettis, Mariah. Undergraduate student at the archeological dig at Spirit Mound.

Nelson, Rusty "Nails." Disabled Vietnam veteran who lives above the old Carnegie Library in Reunion that now houses the county archives. Operates the low-power FM radio station YRUN and reports news from Eda County. Native of Bandit Ridge in Eda County.

Okerlund, Arne. Former sheriff of Eda County, son of Sheriff Leif Okerlund, father of Karen Okerlund Mehaffey, and half-brother of Marek Okerlund. First married to Hannah Mock and second to Clara Gullick, the widow of his childhood friend. A stroke ended his career as sheriff. He and Clara adopted Clara's grandson and babysit Marek's daughter, Becca. Lived at 22 Okerlund Road until his second marriage. Now lives on Okerlund Road in the old Stan Forsgren house.

Okerlund, Clara Gullick. Widow of Vern Gullick and mother of Deputy Rick Gullick (deceased). Grandmother of Joseph Jaramillo Okerlund. Married to Arne Okerlund after the deaths of her husband and son. Lives on Okerlund Road at the old Stan Forsgren house.

Okerlund, Hannah Mock. Deceased. First wife of Arne Okerlund and mother of Karen Okerlund Mehaffey. Died of ovarian cancer when Karen was in the Army. Raised among the Eder Brethren, she fled as a young woman.

Okerlund, Leif. Deceased. Former sheriff of Eda County and father of Arne Okerlund by first wife, Kari Halvorsen, and father of Marek Okerlund by second wife, Janina Marek. Grandfather of Karen Okerlund Mehaffey. World War II veteran. His second marriage caused a rift between himself and his elder son (Arne).

Okerlund, (Leif) Marek. Always called by his middle name. Part-time detective for Eda County. Part-time carpenter.

Dyslexic. Son of Sheriff Leif Okerlund and second wife, Janina Marek. Half-brother of Arne Okerlund and half-uncle of Karen Okerlund Mehaffey, who is four years his elder. Moved from Reunion to Valeska in Eda County with his mother after his father's death. Left Eda County after high school and ended up in Albuquerque, New Mexico, where he was first a carpenter and then a cop, eventually rising to the rank of homicide detective. Lost his wife, Valencia De Baca, to a drunk driver. Their daughter, Becca, was in the car and survived. Lives at 21 Okerlund Road in the bungalow he spent his childhood in. In a relationship with Nikki Forsgren Solberg.

Okerlund, Rebecca "Becca" De Baca. Young daughter of Marek Okerlund and Valencia De Baca. A precocious artist, she was mute after losing her mother and unborn brother to a drunk driver but gradually recovered after the move to South Dakota.

Okerlund, Valencia "Val" De Baca. Deceased. Wife of Marek Okerlund. Daughter of Joseph De Baca and New York artist Adrienne Fiat. Killed with her unborn son by a drunk driver in Albuquerque.

Redwing-Digges, Hunter. Adopted Native American son of Trent and Peggy Digges. Enrolled at the Standing Rock Reservation. Social studies teacher at Flandreau Indian School. Graduate student at the University of South Dakota and part of the archaeological dig at Spirit Mound.

Rudibaugh, Judge John Franklin. Also known as "Judge Rudy." Presiding judge at the Eda County courthouse.

Russell, Laura Connor. Childhood friend, basketball teammate, and college roommate of Karen Okerlund Mehaffey. She is the wife of Deputy Walter Russell and mother of three boys. Works as an elementary-school teacher in Reunion.

Russell, Walter "Walrus." Day-shift deputy in the Eda County Sheriff's Office. Originally from Aleford in Eda County and married to Laura Connor. Father of three boys. Pheasant hunter and gun enthusiast.

Sininen, Arvo "Blue." Works under Dirk Larson at the South Dakota Division of Criminal Investigation (DCI) in Sioux Falls. Finnish from the Black Hills.

Solberg, Annika "Nikki" Forsgren. Adopted daughter of Elmer Forsgren, a distant cousin of Karen and Marek. Biological daughter of the Eder Brethren. Made up her surname on leaving for California after high school. Artist and English school teacher in Reunion. Lives off Okerlund Road in a former one-room schoolhouse. Tutors Becca Okerlund in art. In a relationship with Marek Okerlund.

Stands By Him, Jerome. Protester at the archaeological dig at Spirit Mound. Graduate student in Native American Studies at the University of South Dakota.

Tisher, Norm "Tish." The Eda County coroner. He has no medical training other than that gleaned as a local mortician. A native of North Dakota.

Two Fingers, Delma. Widow of Christian Two Fingers, grandmother of Winona Two Fingers Goodthunder, great-grandmother of Deputy Two Fingers and Jaydyn and Shania Goodthunder. Elder of the Santee Dakota at Flandreau Reservation. Mother was a Rockboy from the Yankton Reservation.

Two Fingers, Inyan Ska. First and middle name pronounced *ee-yahn skah*. Swing-shift deputy with the Eda County Sheriff's Office. Mixed maternal heritage of Dakota (Santee), Nakota (Yankton), Mandan, and Arikara. His biological father Ed Johnson (Caucasian) was his mother's rapist. Mother enrolled at Flandreau Reservation in South Dakota but Two

Fingers does not meet the blood quantum requirement. Dartmouth graduate and former Air Force pilot.

Van Eck, Adam. Reserve deputy on the night shift for the Eda County Sheriff's Office. Former Broadway actor who continues his passion in Sioux Falls.

White, Dr. Oscar Micheaux. Forensic pathologist and native of Sioux Falls. Named for African-American filmmaker Oscar Micheaux, who homesteaded in South Dakota.

ACKNOWLEDGEMENTS

To all the Native Americans I have encountered over the years, I thank you for showing me your dignity and your resiliency. To the Flandreau Reservation, for allowing wasicus to attend your wacipi. To Chad, for the history lesson on the Major Crimes Act. To Ryan, for telling me about his experiences on the Lower Brule Reservation. To Greg Olson, author of numerous books and articles on the Ioway tribe in Missouri, for reading the manuscript to make sure I hadn't inadvertently caused grave offense. To Carlton Gayton, whose dreamcatcher hangs over my bed, and to JoAnne Bird, whose *The Dreamcatcher* hangs at the foot, much thanks for giving beauty to my dreams. And as always, my deep thanks go to my editor, Stefanie Spangler Buswell, proofreader, Kim Husband, and beta readers, Kelli Cotter, Sheila Molony, and Cherie Weible.

ABOUT THE AUTHOR

M.K. Coker grew up on a river bluff in southeastern South Dakota. Part of the Dakota diaspora, the author has lived in half a dozen states, but returns to the prairie at every opportunity. Website: www.mkcoker.com

Made in the USA
Middletown, DE
30 August 2024